CARTEL PUBLICATIONS
PRESENTS

QUITA'S
DAY SCARE
CENTER

IF YOU THINK THE KIDS ARE BAD,
WAIT 'TIL YOU GET A LOAD OF THEIR MOTHERS

A NOVEL BY
GINA
WEST

Library of Congress Control Number: 2011939843
ISBN 10: 0984303014
ISBN 13: 978-0984303014
Cover Design: Davida Baldwin www.oddballldsgn.com
Editor: Advanced Editorial Services
Graphics: Davida Baldwin
www.thecartelpublications.com
First Edition

Printed in the United States of America

What's Poppin' Fam!!

Wow...Feels like we are on the go so much these days, that I actually look forward to sitting down and prepping this letter to you. It gives me the opportunity to be still and reflect on our blessings and our supporters. The Cartel Publications, Cartel Café' & Books & Cartel Urban Cinema has been showing off this year. We have great books (23 titles to date), great movie/documentary projects and a great bookstore that continues to gain momentum. We cannot wait to bring all of our hard work and passion into your worlds with, "Pitbulls in A Skirt" – The Movie and our newest documentary project, coming soon. Things are continuously in the works for The Cartel and we owe it all to your love and overwhelming support! From our hearts to yours, thank you!

Aight Fam, in keeping with tradition, with every novel we drop, we shine the spotlight on an author who is either a vet or a new comer makin' their way in the literary world. In this novel, we recognize:

"*Eyone Williams*"

Eyone Williams has penned novels such as, "The Fast Lane"; "The Cross"; his latest novel, "Lorton Legends" and The Cartel Publications titles, "Hell Razor Honeys 1 & 2". This man is non-stop with the hits and grinds to the fullest, always! We at The Cartel Publications appreciate and truly respect his literary journey and hustle.

On that note Fam, I'ma let ya'll get to it! Remember, life is a blessing! Live it and love it to the fullest!

Be easy!

Charisse "C. Wash" Washington
VP, The Cartel Publications

www.thecartelpublications.com
www.twitter.com/cartelbooks
www.facebook.com/publishercharissewashington
www.myspace.com/thecartelpublications
www.facebook.com/cartelcafeandbooksstore

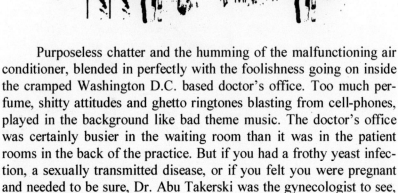

OFFICE ANTICS

Purposeless chatter and the humming of the malfunctioning air conditioner, blended in perfectly with the foolishness going on inside the cramped Washington D.C. based doctor's office. Too much perfume, shitty attitudes and ghetto ringtones blasting from cell-phones, played in the background like bad theme music. The doctor's office was certainly busier in the waiting room than it was in the patient rooms in the back of the practice. But if you had a frothy yeast infection, a sexually transmitted disease, or if you felt you were pregnant and needed to be sure, Dr. Abu Takerski was the gynecologist to see, because he never took an appointment he didn't keep. He was certainly about getting his money.

Eighteen-year-old Evanka, crossed her legs every other minute, as she sat next to her boyfriend Doo-Man from southeast DC. She was nervous because she was looking for one person in particular, Quita Miles, who was nowhere in sight. "You look scared, shawty" Doo-Man said, tugging at his baseball cap. He stroked his fine black goatee and rubbed her knee. Doo-Man was a looker and he knew it, which made him arrogant to some and irritating to others. "If you pregnant I got you. My peoples already said you can stay up my crib, I told you that. Just relax."

She smiled and said, "Thank you, baby. I know it's a lot but I prefer to be with you than at home while I have our child. The daycare center at my house is too crazy to raise a kid. I ain't trying to put you out and stuff."

"I keep telling you it ain't a problem." It was obvious that although he said one thing, he felt another. Part of him, the part belonging to his mother, knew she was making this baby shit up. But he wanted a child so badly, that he was willing to entertain her, unless he found out today she wasn't telling the truth. "You got my kid," he rubbed her flat lower stomach, "so you got me, unless I find out differently." Doo-Man proceeded to text his cousin Brooke, who was coming home from college in Florida.

Evanka swallowed air, and grabbed a magazine off of the chipped wooden table. She thumbed through it until she realized it was about technology and didn't hold her interest. When she glanced across the room, she saw a woman reading the Vibe magazine, while stashing the Source and the "O" under her thick thigh, so no one else could have access to them. Loving an opportunity to start shit she asked, "Can I read the Source please?" Evanka pointed at her jean-clad leg. "Since you not looking at it now."

Karen Delray lifted her thigh, read the title on the mag she wanted and put her thigh down. "No you can't," she grinned. "I'm looking at all three of them." She stared at the floor. "Pick one of them joints up over there."

Evanka was about to charge toward her until Doo-Man gripped her arm and said, "Not going through this shit with you today." He let her go. "So be sure that's what you want, cause I'ma bounce if you do." Evanka looked at him, then back at the girl, and slammed her body back into the uncomfortable metal seat. *Quita better hurry the fuck up before I go off in here. How the fuck you gonna take all the magazines when you not reading them?* She thought.

Although on the surface it would appear as if the staff had over-booked appointments, which in some cases was true, the office was *still* run better ever since Quita Miles had taken over. Prior to her leadership, the previous office manager, Debra Walker, allowed her personnel to run the show. She was so young and eager to fit in, that she neglected her responsibilities and as a result, her patients suffered. The final straw was when Dr. Takerski was faced with a malpractice suit, due to her negligence by interchanging a patient's records with another, resulting in the woman receiving a full hysterectomy. Now that she was gone, things were run differently.

Quita wasn't the official office manager yet, but everyone knew that Dr. Takerski was making an announcement early next week, and that they had better fall in line. Some feared that if Quita got the position, they wouldn't be able to come back late from breaks, talk to the patients any kind of way, and blast patient confidential information about the floor, like they were on a talk show…and they were right.

"Can you sign off on this," Kimi Dale asked, Valencia the go to girl when Quita wasn't there. "It's for a delivery." Valencia took the board and signed Erica Kane. "Girl, you signed the wrong name again!"

"Oh snap!" she giggled. Valencia had about fifteen aliases, and would often sign the wrong name, because she got confused. She scratched it out and signed her real name, Valencia Malone. When she was done with that the phone rang and she quickly answered, hoping it was her ex-boyfriend Tech. "Thank you for calling Dr. Takerski's office what you need?" Valencia asked, in a ghetto tone, while popping her gum. The call interrupted her conversation about how big Luke from Southwest's dick was, and how her ex-boyfriend Tech would be begging to be back in her life, any day now, so irritation was expressed in her voice "Are you there or what?"

A soft-spoken woman said, "Uh…yes…I'd like to make an appointment please."

"*Well,*" she proceeded rolling her eyes, to get a few laughs from her co-workers. "What you want to see the doctor for?"

"Excuse me?" The patient asked, to be sure she heard her correctly. "I don't understand the question or your reason for asking. Besides, I never had to say all that before." Her condition was sensitive and she didn't feel comfortable telling someone she didn't know.

"Let me repeat myself for the retards who don't understand english," Valencia started in a condescending tone, "What…do…you…want…to…see…the…doctor… for?"

"Oh…ummm," she paused. "It's kinda private. I'd rather tell Dr. Takerski instead of saying it over the phone."

"Well when it becomes *UN*private, give us a call back!"

CLICK!

One of the medical assistants balled over in laughter, while the other rolled her eyes, and proceeded to file the charts in her hands. "Girl, you wild as a mothafucka," Terry Christopher, said. "That shit was mad funny, but if Quita find out, you know she goin' off right?! So you better be ready for that shit. That girl is serious about her patients."

"And what you think she gonna do to me?" Valencia responded placing her hands on her hips. "She ain't my mothafuckin' mama. She better lose some weight, before she keels over from all that fast food she be stuffing in her face. That's what she need to tend to, instead of worrying 'bout how I handle business."

"Yeah okay," Terry laughed. "You can pretend you ain't trippin' now if you want to, but I know you gonna be singin' a whole new song the moment she gets back from lunch. You know how she be acting when they say we did them wrong." She looked at Evanka who was staring dead in her direction. "She acts like they her cousins or something." Terry rolled her eyes at Evanka and focused back on the bag of chips in her lap. Evanka lived up the street from Valencia, and ran a ghetto day care center with her mother. She stayed in everybody's business, but got mad when people got into hers.

"I'm tryin' to figure out something?" Valencia responded, as she looked up into the air and back at Terry. "What makes you think I really give a fuck about Quita? Ya'll be around here running like chickens with your heads cut off, because you think Quita is God. But I don't. I been knowing that bitch for years, and she not all that just because she gonna get a promotion that belongs to me. She's just another girl who trying to be me that I have to add to the list of fakers. So remember that shit the next time you try to throw her name in my face."

"I thought Quita was your friend?" Kimi added, as she placed the last patient's chart in the file cabinet and slammed it shut. "Why you talkin' behind her back now? That shit burns me up 'bout you. So fucking two-faced."

Valencia gasped at how hard she came at her. "Shut up, Kimi! You and Terry can both ride her dick together if you want to!" She paused. "You just mad because you pretty much a nobody."

"Fuck is that supposed to mean?"

"Exactly what I said!" She pointed a finger in her face. "You don't go nowhere, you don't hang out with nobody but me, Quita and maybe Terry, so nobody knows you…A nobody." She repeated again. "Get it? So you need to mind your business, before I start delivering your ass, too."

"You so fucking disgusting. No wonder why you don't have a man no more." Kimi walked up to her and stood in her face. "Oh wait a minute…I remember now why no niggas wanna fuck with you, including your little on again off again boyfriend Tech." She laughed and placed her hands on her hips, when she saw she hit a nerve. "Oh yes, I might not know too many people because I'm not a freak in these streets, but I know enough to shut shit down."

Valencia didn't want to walk into the trap by asking what she was talking about, but she opened the door first. There were so many rumors swirling around Valencia, that Kimi was liable to say anything, so she had to be careful. "And what do you think you know about me, bitch? People love saying Valencia's name out they mouth because it tastes so sweet."

Kimi laughed. "To hear you tell it I don't know a lot…just that the real reason why Luke from southwest stopped fucking with you was because when he licked your belly button, while fucking, he said it smelled like shit." Terry and Kimi laughed so hard, they forgot they were at work. "And that Tech be embarrassed to be around you, that's why he called off the marriage and ended the relationship."

"I broke up with Tech! And he gonna be calling here pressing me out like he usually do."

"We'll see about that, girly girl." She paused, sat down in her chair and clicked at her keyboard. "I heard Brooke coming back in town…I wonder how he'll act then."

Terry giggled, and tried to cover her mouth.

"Fuck you, bitch!" She pointed at Kimi. "Fuck both of you!"

As they were laughing Quita walked into the office five minutes early from lunch carrying orders for everybody who placed one. The hoop gold earrings dangling from her ears, were too big for her face, and made the two massive French braids hanging down her shoulders look super ghetto. She wiggled up to the counter, and the sack of rolls in her cheap jeans, made her look like Mrs. Tire. Quita was cute in the face, but because she didn't wear her clothes correctly all the time, people rarely noticed her beauty.

When Karen saw her, she stood up and said, "Quita, can you tell me when I'm gonna be seen? I been here all day."

Quita and Karen had history, and they both couldn't stand each other. It was just a matter of time before things between them jumped off. The only thing was, they grew up in the same hood, favored each other, and had similar traits. By all accounts, they should've been friends. "Whenever I ask them bitches, they say the doctor isn't here yet."

As professionally as possible she said, "Then I guess he isn't here. You're gonna have to wait, Mrs. Delray." She stated, as if she didn't know her first name.

Karen sat down and said, "You swear you so fucking better now that you got your little job. But I hope you remember, I know more about you than these people around here do. Remember that shit."

"Whatever, Karen," Quita walked away. She knew she was trying to get her into trouble on her job and she refused to give her the satisfaction. "I'll get to you when I can."

Upon seeing everybody laughing at the counter, and figuring it was about her, she walked behind the counter and placed the bag down. "What's so funny? Ya'll look like you're about to pass out from all the laughter."

"Nothing," Valencia responded, looking at the other assistants, daring them to repeat the story about her funky ass navel. "We were just remembering something that happened earlier that's all."

"It sure don't seem like nothing," Quita replied, sensing they were purposely trying to exclude her. That's the only part about being the future boss, people stopped letting her in on inside jokes. But since she was about the money, it was an isolation she was willing to accept. "I hope ya'll working, too."

"Well it *was* nothing," Valencia spoke for them all. "Like I said, it was just an old joke."

"*Okay*," Quita responded, boring with her already.

"Did you get my food?" Kimi interjected. "I'm starving over here."

Kimi, Quita's closest friend, was different from Valencia. Unlike Valencia, she was proud of Quita and her accomplishments. She felt out of everyone, Quita was deserving and because of it, she had no problems taking orders from a friend. But Valencia felt she should've been next up for the position because she had more seniority than Quita. Feeling herself one afternoon, she was bold enough to take her concern to the boss. At first she asked what inspired his decision to groom Quita for the Office Manager position, and when he explained how dependable she was, Valencia offered her boss a little pussy. Dr. Takerski was so embarrassed, that he pretended as if he didn't hear her. Later that day, she slid him her resignation, which he gladly accepted, before wishing her well on her job search. Unemployed and stupid, she snatched the letter back before he logged it in, and she decided she'd better take a few calls. She'd been there, angry and bitter ever since.

While she was removing the food from the Friday's restaurant bag, the phone rang. "Can you take the food out of the bag for me, Terry?" Quita asked. "I wanna get this phone." Valencia was at the printer adding some sheets to a file, when she attempted to jump in front of Quita to snatch the phone from her hand. It was funny seeing a 5'4 inch Valencia, wearing teddy bear scrubs dive for her, like she was trying to slide into home plate. She damn near knocked everything off the counter in the process. "I have it, Valencia," Quita laughed, snatching the phone out of her hand. "Finish what you were doing."

"I got it, girl! You just got back from lunch and you still have a few minutes left." Valencia said, reaching for the phone. "I think it's for me anyway. Enjoy your lunch and take the rest of your break."

"This is the office line," she laughed holding the receiver. "Everybody knows you get your calls on the other line...now beat it! Tech ain't callin' you yet," she continued giggling. Valencia reluctantly returned to her original duties, turning her head periodically, to see if the flack from how she treated the customer would come back to bite her. "Thank you for calling Dr. Takerski's office how may I help you?" Quita said in a professional tone.

"Ummmmm, uh...ummm," the patient on the other line was crying hysterically and this startled Quita. "I...I...want to..."

"Hello?" Quita moved a few spaces away from everyone. "Are you okay? Do you need us to send an ambulance?"

"No," the patient responded between sniffling. "I'm calling to make an appointment. Can you help me?"

"Sure," she nodded, sliding into her seat to pull up her information on the computer. "It's no problem at all. What's your name?"

"It's Velma Carter."

"Oh, Mrs. Carter!" Quita was relieved that she knew who the distraught patient was. "It's Quita! I didn't know it was you at first...you had me worried for a sec."

"I'm sorry, it's just that...well...I'm having a bad day that's all."

"I understand. How can I help make things easier for you to-day?"

"I have vaginal itching and it's gotten worse." Quita frowned because of TMI (TOO MUCH INFORMATION). "So I need an appointment."

"Oh," she paused, due to being embarrassed at hearing such sensitive information. "I see. You know you don't have to tell me *exactly* what's wrong don't you?"

There was a brief moment of silence. "Actually I wasn't sure. I just called, and was unwilling to tell someone what was wrong, and the person hung up on me." Quita looked at the assistants, as the phone remained suctioned to her ear. "That's why I'm sort of upset. I feel uncomfortable enough as it is and now this," she continued taking a deep breath. "I just hope my husband doesn't get whatever I have. I just want this all resolved."

Quita didn't have the heart to tell her that if she was burning, Mr. Carter probably gave it to her. She knew he was a whore to more than ten of their patients, including the woman in the waiting room with two mags stashed under her thigh. "Don't worry about anything, Mrs. Carter. Whoever disrespected you will be hearing from me," she looked at the members of her staff, who hugged the background of the office, outfitted in colorful scrubs speckled with various cartoon characters. "I apologize for anything you experienced when I was out of the office. Just know that whenever you call, you're only required to give the basics. But let me get your appointment set up for you now…everything will be alright."

"I hope so," she laughed.

"It will." When she finished with the appointment she asked, "Who took Mrs. Carter's call?" Suddenly work was the most important thing in their lives, but it was Valencia's awful hard-working employee routine, which answered Quita's question. "Why you talk to that woman like that, Valencia? And before you lie, please know that I don't believe shit you gonna say in advance anyway."

"What are you talking about?" she never looked up from the chart, which was upside down in her hands. "I barely answered the phone all day."

"You know what I'm talking about," Quita replied, taking the chart out of her hand, turning it right side up, before handing it back. "Just tell me why you treated Mrs. Carter like that."

"*Because*," she responded as if Quita was boring her. "They're supposed to tell us the nature of their visit and she didn't!" she yelled, smacking the chart onto the counter. She didn't feel like playing her fake routine any longer, especially after she'd just told Terry that she wasn't afraid of Quita. "And I don't appreciate you talking to me like I'm a child on the floor either. All I know is, whenever they call in, they're supposed to tell us what the appointment is about. And she wouldn't, so she got hung up on. It's as simple as that."

"No they're not, V! They're supposed to give us general info and you aren't supposed to be hanging up on patients either. That shit ain't right!"

"Now look who's being unprofessional. Cussing and shit," Valencia retorted, placing her hands on her hips. "I wonder how many of the patients out there heard you." Quita looked around the front office, and her eyes rested on Evanka's. She quickly averted them back to Valencia, unwilling to deal with her yet. They had business off record that needed her attention and time. "Just so you know, you're not the boss yet, Quita." When she saw the audience increasing into the waiting room she prepared herself to really perform. "Are you in need of some dick or something? 'Cause you acting extra uptight!"

There was a brief uproar of Ooooh's and Ahhhh's before Dr. Takerski walked into the office. "We'll finish this later." Quita pointed, her long pink nail in her face. "Count on it."

Valencia rolled her eyes and focused on the boss. Everybody but Quita presented their best fake personality, as if he didn't know they were full of shit. He would've fired them a long time ago, but learned awhile back that the best way to run an office in the hood, was to employ people of the like.

"Where you going tonight?" Kimi asked, the doctor. "You got a date or something?"

"Yeah, Dr. Takerski," Valencia added. "Those shoes real fly!"

"Fly?" He blushed, looked down at them and moved his feet. "What is this fly?" He continued in his Pakistan accent.

"Fly," Valencia repeated, due to his ignorance in ghetto slang. "It mean's you're looking really good," she playfully nudged him. "You been around us too long not to know how we talk by now."

"I'm still learning."

"Right...all them degrees on your wall from Harvard and stuff, you should know all of our lingo by now." Terry laughed, saying the same shit Valencia said, just in a different way.

"Right." Valencia responded. "But he does look good enough to get whatever he wants tonight." The doctor felt uncomfortable because of their previous run in. "Mrs. Takerski better watch out...somebody might snag you. And soon too, with your fine ass."

"Oh come on...stop it now," he laughed. "I'm not trying to do any of the things you speak of. I love my wife."

"I can't wait to see how you dress at the company party," Valencia said. "You bringing wifey?"

Dr. Takerski's office was just one in twenty, he and his business partners owned in and around the metropolitan DC area. Every year they would throw a company appreciation event, and usually nobody brought their wives. The staff members loved the functions, because they could see how the doctors really were, after having a few drinks and dancing on the dance floor. Secrets would fly out that they would often forget in the morning.

"Oh...I don't know, if I'm bringing the wife." He responded. "She doesn't like to party too much." Everyone laughed.

"I suggest you leave her at home," Valencia said, pressing the issue. "It'll be more fun without her."

Their fakeness was making Quita's stomach churn. She usually tuned their shenanigans out, but she was still angry with Valencia. Her terrible acting job was the reason Evanka stepped to the counter. She was irritated that they were having so much fun, yet she was still waiting. "Quita, can I talk to you?" She looked at the group crowding around the doctor, as if he were prey. "In private?"

Quita ushered her to the side, away from her co-workers and said, "I know what this is about, but you can't talk around them." Quita was trying to avoid someone from over hearing their conversation. "Let me put you in the room so we can get everything started."

Quita grabbed her wrist and tried to direct her next movements but Evanka snatched her arm away and said, "Do you have that for me? What I paid you for?"

"I said, yes." Quita whispered in a harsh tone, before looking at her co-workers who were still entertaining the good doctor. "What you trying to do, get me late or something? If I said I was going to do it, that means I'm gonna do it. So stop pressing me out."

"I'm not trying to cause problems." She held her head down and looked at Doo-Man, who was looking at the Source magazine, the hater let him use, which she denied Evanka earlier. "I just really need you to do this for me that's all. I'm gonna lose him if you don't. He's my everything, girl!"

Quita wondered what she was going to do, when he found out she wasn't pregnant months later.

"You'll get what you need. Now let me get back to work."

Quita ushered her to the room, pulled the knob to close the door, and slammed the chart in the shelf on the door. She walked back to the front desk. At first she was going to talk to Valencia about the dick comment earlier, but she decided to deal with her later, outside of the job. Instead she signed the chart for the diagnostic deliveryman who dropped off a few lab results. She was hoping it came that day because she had several patients in the waiting room looking for their outcome. When she reviewed the lab work on one of the patient's, Quita was devastated. Throwing herself back into her chair, she felt beads of perspiration form on her forehead. *How could this happen to somebody who didn't deserve it?* She read it over and over but the name on the results were the same. Charlene White had contracted HIV, as a result of being raped some time back.

Quita glanced over at Charlene who just walked in, and sat in the seat next to the patient hogging the magazines. Very rarely, she'd bring her son Cordon, but after Quita convinced the doctor to ban children because of their unruly behavior, it stopped altogether. Charlene's husband Flex, loved her to death. He didn't fit the mold of the average womanizing drug dealer. Flex would do anything for her and had done anything for her. The moment he laid eyes on her, he knew she would bare his kids because of the innocence in her eyes and the way she loved fully from the heart. With the birth of his first child, Cordon, their bond was solidified.

Things were going great in their marriage until a few months ago, Flex's father Leroy, raped his wife when she dropped off his grandchild. Charlene never told her husband, for fear that he would kill his father, bring him back to life and murder him again. She knew he deserved nothing short of death, but she couldn't bare the weight of the crime over her mind and heart. She loved her family, and wanted to move about the business of taking care of them. First, she needed to get the results. Quita knew Charlene personally, and knew that if ever there was a person who didn't deserve this fate, she was it.

After Valencia witnessed Quita's mood change, she knew something was wrong so she decided to pry. "Are you okay, Quita?" Valencia asked, stroking her shoulder softly. Quita shot daggers in her direction, remembering their conversation earlier. "You still not mad at me are you? We get into it all the time, but at the end of the day, we're still friends."

Quita shook her head and said, "Naw. I'm done fighting with your ass, for today anyway," suddenly beefing with Valencia seemed ridiculous. "I got something else on my mind right now. I'm trying to figure out how to deal with it."

"Well what's wrong? If you ain't mad at me, you should let me know."

"Do you really care, Valencia? Or are you just patronizing me again?"

"Now why would I do that?" she laughed. "You're probably the only one who can see right through my bullshit. I fucks with you, girl. You know that shit." She paused. "I'm not gonna let this little job fuck up what we have. I mean even though you took my position, we still cool."

Quita looked at her seriously and said, "I didn't take anything. You ruined your own chances of being boss…not me. You too busy looking to have fun instead of looking to do work."

"I'm just fucking with you." She said although she was deathly serious.

"I don't know about all of that," Quita responded, cutting the first smile since before she read the results. "And Kimi does a good job of reading through your shit too. She knows your ass too good."

"Naw, big baby," Valencia responded in a condescending tone, "Let me make a correction...Kimi *thinks* she knows me, but for real all she knows is that vibrator she uses in her locker on her lunch break." She giggled to herself. "She think we don't see how her legs be shaking under the stall while she on the toilet jerking off."

"If I were you, I wouldn't tell nobody else that shit again." Quita pulled her shirt down to hide her muffin top. "Looking under stalls in the bathroom makes you look crazy. Not the other way around."

"Whatever," she tried to laugh her humiliation away. "Now tell me what's wrong with you, or do I have to beat it out of you first? Cause I hope you're not thinking about that Bricks person, no one has ever met, again."

"No I'm not thinking about *Bricks*! You act like he was the only person I ever dealt with."

"Then what is it?!" Valencia responded as she slammed her right foot down on the floor, as if she was on the verge of a temper tantrum.

Quita was trying to determine if she should tell her about Charlene because she and the other girls on the job loved kicking patients' business around the office. For instance, they had a patient called Queenie, who had one abortion after another for the past couple of years. No matter how many times Dr. Takerski plead with her to take birth control, she refused, saying that it was the last time she'd be in his office for that situation anyway. She stayed with a fresh case of Pelvic Inflammatory Disease. Truth was, she wasn't responsible enough to take the pills, and relied on abortions as her birth control method. And as a result, she was the laughing stock of the office, whenever she came in for an appointment. Her business was broadcast so much, that Valencia told someone on the outside about Queenie's sexual escapades. The news eventually reached her husband, who divorced her immediately, and subpoenaed the doctor's records for the trial.

"I don't know if I should tell you, V. You ain't too good with keeping secrets."

"You're right. I'm not good with keeping secrets," she paused, "I'm great with keeping secrets! Now you can't hold nothing from me, especially when I tell you everything."

"Valencia, this ain't about me this time so it's different."

"Well who is it about?!" Valencia jumped up and down. She was so nosey she was acting like a child. "If it's about a patient I'm gonna find out anyway. I do work here too you know? Unmotivated to say a word, Quita didn't part her lips. "Come on...the suspense is killing me!"

Just then Karen walked up to the counter to inquire about the status of her appointment. An irritated Valencia responded by saying, "Mrs. Delray, PLEASE! We'll call you when we're ready and not a minute sooner. Now go sit down somewhere and hog up a few more mags!" The patient stormed away, shaking her head in disgust.

"You see what I'm saying," Quita said. "Look how you just treated her. Damn, V, that shit don't make no sense. You *are* at work!"

"Girl, please. You know that bitch is impatient and you know you don't fuck with her." Quita didn't want to confirm what was true. "Some people deserve the business. It ain't like I do it to everybody. Just because you be coddling these patients, don't mean I should too."

Without saying anything else, because she would be wasting her breath, she slid Charlene's chart over to her. When Valencia read the results, she placed her hand over her mouth and gasped. Her eyes quickly looked over at Charlene, making it apparent to everyone present, that they were talking about her. She would have shared the information with Kimi, because she didn't know her, but Valencia slid up to her first. "Stop staring, V! Damn! She gonna know something's up now."

"She gonna know something's up anyway after she gets these results."

"Do you have to be so insensitive *every* second of the day?" Quita stood up and walked to the file cabinet. "Ignorance at its finest, I swear before God!"

"I'm not trying to be insensitive," Valencia responded walking behind her. "I just can't believe this shit, Quita! How the fuck this happen?"

"A long story...but now I have to go tell her."

"Wait...I thought you had a half of day today." She asked in a quizzical stare. "Now if you don't want it, I can take it. I wanted to hang out with Tech anyway."

"I thought you broke up with him?"

"I did."

"Girl you're a hot ass mess!"

"You taking your time off or not?"

Her words sounded like music to Quita's ears. Quita forgot all about the half of day she took and the reason. Originally she was going to pop up over her long-term crush Bricks' house, but he was too busy with his girlfriend Yvonna to give her the time of day. Now, however, the half day schedule came in handy. "I do have a half of day! Oh my God...I forgot all about that shit."

"Luckily for you and bad for somebody else." Valencia shook her head.

"Who? Charlene?"

"No," she frowned. "Me." Quita shook her head. "Anyway, why she got the nerve to be pregnant, too." Quita's eyes widened. "Wait...you didn't see that part on the results?"

Quita removed the chart, looked at the results and leaned into the wall. "No...I didn't." There was a brief moment of silence. Quita felt for Charlene's situation, but she didn't want anything to do with it anymore. It was too stressful and too emotional.

"Wait until Flex finds out." Valencia said.

Quita stormed up toward her and used her weight to pin Valencia into the file cabinet. It rocked a little. "Listen, bitch, you better not tell her husband shit. Do you hear me?" She never talked to Valencia this way but she was serious.

"What are you talking about?"

"I know how that mouth of yours flaps, and I will kill you if I find out you did her like that."

"Okay...," she turned her head to prevent from smelling Quita's breath. "Now get out of my face, you smashing me!"

Quita stepped away from her and said, "Good...now can you set her chart up for the doc for me? I got to get out of here."

"Don't worry about it, Quita," she reassured her. "I'm gonna take care of everything here, just like how I use to before I got you the job." She paused, still believing putting in a word for Quita was her single greatest mistake. "You still hanging out later right?"

"Yeah...I gotta find something to wear first," she grabbed her purse, food and keys. "But I'm not driving, so you got to pick me up. I drove last time remember?"

"Alright, big baby," Valencia replied. All she wanted was for her to leave because the environment was always lax when she wasn't around. "I'll see you later...now get out of here and do you! We gonna be fine!"

"Oh...you should wear the orange dress you bought. It looks good on you." Quita offered, as she walked toward the door. Charlene stood up and moved toward her to catch her before she left.

"Hey, Quita!" She smiled. "I wanted to speak but you were busy over there. I hope you not letting her get on your nerves again." She giggled. "I know how crazy V can be sometimes."

"Girl, she can't bother me. I don't pay her ass half the attention she thinks I am most times," she paused clearing her throat. She couldn't look into her eyes.

"You're leaving already?"

"Yep," she replied *still* unable to look at her. "I have a few things to take care of at home."

"Oh...Well, I'll see you later. Take care."

"You too," Quita said as she opened the door to bolt out of the office. "Before I go," Charlene held the door open to hear what she had to say, "I wanted to tell you, whatever happens...I know you'll be okay. Remember that."

Charlene stood in the doorway, as the door slammed against the side of her body.

17

CAN'T DRIVE AWAY RAIN

Valencia left work and the people around her, who made her forget about the problems in her personal life. Now that she was alone, she had time to focus on how suddenly things appeared to take a turn for the worse. She turned on her cell phone, hoping that Tech would reach out to her first, since their break-up a week earlier, even though she demanded that he never call her again. With Bitch after bitch who entered their lives, Valencia was positive that she could never be enough for him. But whenever she ended the relationship, she realized her anger made the decisions her heart couldn't.

Normally Tech would call the first day of the break up, despite her hanging up on him repeatedly. He'd beg, pop up over the house they once shared together, but this time, there wasn't any of that. There were no calls, no pop up visits at her job and most importantly, there were no cries and pleas of apologies. She couldn't help but wonder if he was actually able to move on with his life. And now, as she drove in her car, she wondered if she would be able to move on too.

Valencia was one of those girls in high school, who always had "*It*". She excelled in everything she did with an emphasis on boys. If she was in a crowd of the prettiest girls in the room, every boy present would choose her. But now at 26, she learned that what most men wanted was between her legs and not on her face. Times had changed drastically since high school for Valencia because now she was in competition with the majority, not just a couple of her friends. They wanted a woman with good conversation, goals and not just someone who'd look cute on their arms or felt warm in their beds. Her 5'4 inch height, tiny waist and natural black shoulder length hair made her more attractive than some females but she was still *average*.

While listening to Anthony Hamilton's CD, the rain began to beat heavily on her black Honda Accord. With the phone still open in the passenger seat, she'd glance at it periodically hoping Tech's heart ached so much, that he would die before he went another minute without hearing her voice. *Die Tech. Die because you can't talk to me. Die because you can't live without me! Call me please!* When the phone finally rang, she was shocked into submission. Looking at his name across the cell phone screen, she picked it up and pressed it so closely to her ear, the back of her earring stabbed into her skin.

"Where are you, Tech? I miss you so much! Let's meet up to-day!"

"Tech? This is your mother, silly girl."

Valencia removed the phone and looked at the number. It was her mother; her mind had played tricks on her. "Hi, mama." She sighed.

"You don't sound like you're too happy to hear from me now." She laughed. "Anyway, is this my daughter the nurse?!" Vivica asked, while Angela Bofil's music mixed with multiple voices, screamed from the background. "Is this my baby who will soon be a doctor? Who will make her mother so proud!"

"Yes it is, mama," Valencia lied, knowing full well she was a medical office assistant, with no aspirations to go back to school for nursing, and certainly not for medicine. "What are you doing? It sounds like there's a party going on over there."

"You know how your mother is," Vivica responded, her voice full of joy and happiness. Vivica had every reason to be happy. She was the top Plastic Surgeon at John Hopkins hospital in Baltimore, and she recently purchased and renovated a beautiful brownstone next to the Baltimore Harbor. "I'm over here entertaining my friends. Your aunt Dezie is over too. She wants to know why you haven't returned her calls. She says she misses you."

"I've just been so busy, mamma, you know with the doctor's office and all. I have to stay on my game."

"Are you okay, baby?" Vivica asked, detecting something sad-dening in her daughter's voice. "You don't sound like yourself." She moved into her bedroom to hear her clearly. "Are you and Tech having problems again?"

Valencia smiled because her mother's love never failed. She always knew when something was bothering her because she truly cared. She could hide from some, but not from her mother. "Everything's fine mamma. But I gotta go now. I love you...bye...bye." She hit end on the phone before her mother had a reason for a rebuttal.

Valencia noticed a bright orange Psychic sign off of Kenilworth Ave and decided to pull over. After ending the call, she sat in her car staring at the sign, which was blurred a little from the rain falling heavily on the window. She had always been taught that messing with psychics was wrong...religiously. But for the first time ever, she was running out of resources and she decided to give it a try. Curiosity was getting the best of her.

When she walked inside, she was surprised to see that the office was more contemporary than she thought it would be. The sleek black leather sofas and the upscale furniture made her believe that whoever owned it, wasn't that different from her after all. Staring at the 32-inch Plasma screen TV on the wall, she smiled when she saw it was on the movie, "*Ray*", one of her favorites. There was something about Jamie Foxx that just did it for Valencia, and for a moment, it numbed her broken heart. She signed the paperwork the receptionist gave her, paid the fee and the woman walked it to the back.

After the last few people were seen and gone, Valencia was having second thoughts. *This is sick! I can't be in here. What if somebody sees my car outside? I would never hear the last of it.* She thought. She picked up her purse and shook the rain off her umbrella on the floor, when a beautiful black older woman appeared from the back. "Are you Quita?" She asked reading her application.

"Uh...yeah...I'm Quita." Valencia didn't know the entire reason she put down her friend's name, as opposed to her own name or one of her many aliases, she just did. Part of the reason was that she hated herself more than she realized. So much so, that if she was going to get her palm read, maybe Quita's good aura would rub off on her and make her life look better.

"Well I'm ready for you now," she smiled. "Come on back."

As Valencia walked in the back and entered through a door, the room's cozy atmosphere put her immediately at ease. The fireplace crackled and the soft comfy eggshell love seat, embraced her body like a warm hug. The psychic sat in a matching love seat while the cherry wood round table sat in between them. "Can I get you some coffee...Donuts, or a bagel?"

"No," Valencia responded trying not to look into her eyes. "I'm fine."

"Well I'm Bula, and I'll be answering any questions you may have regarding your life. So don't be afraid, this won't hurt a bit."

"I don't really believe in this you know?" Valencia assured her. "I'm just here to get out of the rain. I couldn't really see out there, and I was afraid I would get into an accident. So I decided to pull over. I'm not one of them people who believe in all that psychic mumbo jumbo. So you can't really mess with my mind. I'm a Christian."

"Well if you came here, there must have been a reason. Rain or not." She smiled harder. "You see, Quita, I believe that there is a reason for everything, whether we know it or not."

"There isn't a reason!" Valencia was upset that Bula continued to imply that she wanted to be there. But most importantly, she was upset because she didn't want to buy her reason that everything happen for a purpose. If it were true, how could she explain Tech fucking with her mind and heart? "So, please, stop saying that. You don't know anything about me."

"We'll agree to disagree," Bula smiled. "You happen to believe that because of the rain, you ended up here. But I happen to believe that you're here because the rain has been pouring into your life, and you're coming to me to get answers. Here I am."

"Humph, whatever you say." She shrugged.

"May I have your hands please?" Bula remained professional, despite Valencia giving her a hard time. "It's time for me to read your palms." Valencia didn't. "Humor me...your hands please."

Valencia reluctantly obeyed and gave the thirty-something year old woman her hands. As Bula looked into her palms, Valencia looked into her eyes and noticed how warm they appeared. She couldn't help but wonder how she managed to get into a lifestyle, which in her opinion was nothing more than a hoax. Bula's soft brown hair fell flawlessly over her shoulders, while the Chinese cut bangs introduced her beautiful hazel eyes perfectly. Valencia even peeped the BeBe one-piece dress she was wearing, and the Louis Vuitton bag, which sat across the room on a chair. Her hands were as soft as the leather sofas in the waiting area.

"You lead a heavy life," Bula started, as she observed the lines in her hands as if she were reading a book. "Very heavy. You have to learn to slow down and watch the things you say and do, to the people in your life." Valencia remained silent. Although the psychic was right so far, she didn't want to tell her anything that could help her out. As far as she was concerned, most people who wondered into psychic establishments led heavy lives anyway. She had no intentions of paying her for obvious information and would demand a refund quick. If she wanted to keep her cash, she had to work harder. "You see these four lines? Well, this is your heart line, this is your head line, this is your life line and this is your fate line, which not a lot of people have." She continued, going over each line with her index finger. "Now I see danger for you, Quita. Eminent danger. Be careful and be sure to treat people like you want to be treated. If you do, then your life will take a turn for the better, if not, may God have mercy on your soul."

"What do you mean danger?" Valencia asked, snatching her hands away and ignoring the treat people kindly statement. Her eyebrows rose. "I don't like people wishing bad shit on me."

"I mean, if you don't change the way you're living," Bula responded as she gently pulled her hands back. "It will eventually catch up with you." She pointed into her palm. "Right there."

Valencia was scared. Although the accounts Bula gave her were *still* very general, she realized that there was some validity to her statements. And most of all, there were some things that she wanted to change but she didn't know how. "This is crazy!" Valencia yelled as she grabbed her purse off the floor. "I can't believe I gave that woman twenty dollars out there, to come in here and meet you! I want my damn money back! And I'll tell you something else too," Valencia continued as she walked toward the door. "I'm going to call the Better Business Bureau to have this place shut down. You ain't nothin' but a fake who steals people's money, and tries to get into they heads! You ain't even no real psychic!"

Under the sounds of thunder booming outside from the storm, Bula softly said, "I'm not a fake...but you are. And unless you stop lying to everyone in your life, including those who are closest to you, you'll lose everything and everybody you love." Valencia was stunned silent. "And Quita is a good friend to you, be careful of how you treat her. If you don't one day what you put out will pay off in the worst way. "Have a good evening, Valencia."

Valencia ran out the door and fell onto the concrete, scratching her knees before finally making it to her car. Once inside, her heart pumped so hard, that she feared it would pop out of her chest. All types of thoughts entered her mind and she wondered how Bula knew she was a liar. She wondered how she knew that Quita was a friend and most importantly, she wondered how she knew her real name.

BRING YOUR THINGS

It was quiet when Quita walked into the doctor's office and she had a splitting headache. Valencia and Kimi kept her out all night, even though all she wanted was some rest. Nobody ever hit on her in the club anyway, so the nights out with them were usually for their benefit and not hers. When she sat her purse on the counter, the patients appeared to know something she didn't. *What the fuck is going on today?* She thought. It was highly likely for the patients to know certain things, because the assistants didn't understand the meaning of speaking on the low, while at work. To the patients, the window leading to the area the assistants worked in, was nothing more than a movie screen.

"Good morning," Quita said, as she sat in her chair in front of her computer. "Where is Kimi and Valencia?" Normally they were there, already at work, so their absence was odd.

"I don't know." Terry shrugged. She seemed out of it, like she wanted to ignore her. "They were just here."

"Why is everybody acting so funny?"

"Girl, I don't know," Terry said, obviously attempting to avoid eye contact with her. "People just tired I guess." She shrugged, as she stood up to file her charts.

"I know you lying," Quita said. "So what happen? You might as well be real with me because I'm gonna find out later."

When the phone rang, Terry rushed to answer it without even acknowledging her question. A minute later, Dr. Takerski walked into the receptionist area. "Quita...I'd like to see you in private for a minute," he said with his accent. "Follow me please."

"Uh...sure," she responded as she placed her purse in her drawer and locked it up.

THE CARTEL PUBLICATIONS PRESENTS

He stopped, and turned back around to face her. "And Quita."

"Yes sir," she said preparing to follow him. "Bring your things. All of them."

"Oh...okay," she responded inquisitively as she unlocked the drawer and removed her purse and keys. She didn't know why but her heart told her something was terribly wrong. If she wasn't sure, she would've sworn she was about to be fired. *What's going on? I know I didn't do anything to get me terminated! I'm always on time. I work really hard, and I love my job. What the fuck is all this about?*

Once inside the office, Dr. Takerski took two deep breaths, rubbed his sweaty hands on his brown pants and removed his glasses. "This is very hard for me," he started. "You wouldn't believe how hard this is, and it kept me up all night." He swallowed. "Unfortunately, I'm going to have to terminate your employment, and it's the hardest thing I've ever had to do."

"What...what? Why?!" Quita leaned in to hear and see him clearly. "You can't be serious. I work so hard for you. Whenever you need me, I'm here. Whenever you ask, I stay late. I'm here more hours in a day than I'm at home. Don't do this to me, Dr. Takerski! I need this job...it's my chance at a new life."

She was hoping that he'd say, he was just joking and that the new forty five thousand dollar position that he promised her would began today. But instead he said, "I am serious. And this is effective immediately."

"Sir," she said slowly. "What happened when I left? I'm totally confused." She tried to prevent the tears from streaming down her face but they wouldn't stop. She knew in her heart that she didn't deserve this type of treatment. She did a few things on the side, but so did the good doctor. She was aware of the bonuses he received by offering patients new medicines, not fully tested. Nobody said anything to him because he always greased their palms. Even the doctored record that she was going to give Evanka, to lie that she was pregnant, wasn't needed. After taking the pregnancy test yesterday, she learned that she was having Doo-Man's baby after all. So if she had done something wrong, she would've muscled up to it, accepted her fate, and walked out of the door with her head held high, but that wasn't the case. In her mind, she was an exemplarily employee.

"Yesterday, before you left you were supposed to get my charts together for my next patients."

"And I did, sir."

"No, you didn't. When I met with Mrs. Delray about her test results, they were all wrong."

"Sir, I made sure all of your appointment charts were in order before I left out of here." She lied; wondering how asking Valencia for a favor, could result in her dismissal. "You must be mistaken."

"No...you didn't. Mrs. Delray wanted the results from her lab work and based on what you had in her charts, I advised her that she was HIV positive and pregnant."

"WHAT?!" Quita screamed, scooted in closer to his desk. "That's outrageous! Those results were for Charlene!"

"I know, but they were in Mrs. Delray's chart, with her name on them and everything. And to prevent her from filing suit, she asked that the person responsible be fired. I've had this practice for fifteen years and can't take another hit like this. So," he continued taking a deep breath. "I have to let you go, otherwise I'll risk yet another malpractice suit. I'll be ruined, Quita. I really hope you understand."

"Sir," she sobbed. "You can't do this to me. I care for my mother on my own. She's sickly. If you fire me, what am I gonna do? She needs me. I'm all she has!"

"I'm sorry, Quita. I really am. But there isn't anything I can do for you now, I've already begun your termination proceedings. Mrs. Delray was so distraught about her results that she had to be taken out in an ambulance last night. And when she was retested in the hospital with a mouth swab, they were able to confirm that she was not positive, but negative."

"How is that possible? HIV tests take days!"

"Not if you have the proper technology. And most hospitals do."

"Dr. Takerski...please...let me explain." She leaned in closer. "I can do this. I can make this right!"

"I'm sorry, Quita, but I have to let you go. There really isn't anything left to say. I'll send your last check to you in the mail. Good luck."

Good luck! Good luck?! How in the fuck can he tell me good luck when he's firing me? What kind of luck can I possibly have now? With her face wet with tears, she got up and looked down at him. "You know, this job changed my life. You don't wanna know the kind of woman I was before you gave me a chance. All I wanted to do, was right by you and your practice, but you fucked that up for me didn't you? You can't stand to see a black woman successful! You're just like the rest! You better hope I don't start knocking folks over, in my pursuit to take care of myself and my family!"

He looked up at her and said, "I'm sorry you feel that way," he looked down at his clasped hands again, "Now please get out of my office."

She grabbed her purse, keys and lunch. Then she took the walk of shame down the hall and past her co-workers who were staring in her direction. She wished she could've been teleported from his office to her car but she realized it wasn't humanly possible. Instead, she held her head high and passed those who she was sure already knew her fate.

What am I going to do about my mother?! Who's going to take care of her? Out of everyone in the office, Kimi and Terry were the only ones, who bothered running behind her and asking if there was anything they could do. But they were too late because she was gone.

ONE FAKE BITCH

"So how did it go today, Quita? With the job search?" Valencia asked, as they sat in Dave N Buster's at Arundel Mills mall, in Maryland. Kimi and Terry decided to take Quita out to cheer her up, and Valencia jumped on the bandwagon so she wouldn't look bad. "You had to have found something by now."

"Not good." Quita hung her head down. She was beyond depressed. "Can you please tell me how the charts got missed up, Valencia? I need to know what happened after I asked you to do me that favor. Maybe if I can clear up the misunderstanding, I'll be able to get my job back."

"Girl, he already hired somebody else." She said flatly. "Don't even worry yourself about all that. You can do better anyway."

"What? Who he hire? I just got fired the other day!" She wanted to cry all over again but she was tired. "It doesn't make any sense."

"Not sure yet, but it may be me." Kimi and Terry rolled their eyes at her. "Anyway I thought we made a promise to never discuss work when we're not there?"

"Wait a minute, you brought up my job search. Not me."

"Your job search, not your old job." Everybody shook their head at her antics.

"Well that rule should change since I don't have a job there anymore."

"But we do," Valencia looked at Kimi and Terry. "Right ya'll? We wanna have fun when we all go out." They remained silent. "You being too heavy for me with all of this shit. Relax."

"I'm sorry," she said as she tried to swallow her soup. "But I've been thinking about this shit for the past couple of days. I don't understand what went wrong."

"Look, let's just enjoy ourselves tonight and worry about that shit later," Valencia continued as she devoured her soup and crackers. "Because thinking about it now ain't gonna do nothing but ruin our night. You bringing me down already." She sighed. "Now, back to me, do you guys believe in psychics?" Valencia continued totally off topic. "I think it's weird but that's just me. I don't really knock no-body else."

"No," Kimi laughed as she nibbled on her chicken strips. "Why you ask that? You calling them 1-900 numbers? I always thought you could be a little weird, Valencia. Are you about to prove me right?"

"Kimi, don't do that." Quita interjected, wiping the corners of her mouth with a napkin. "I hate when ya'll go at each other like that."

Kimi rolled her eyes. "It's okay, Quita. She just jealous like the rest." Taking a sip of her drink she said, "Anyway…somebody else I know went to one," Valencia sipped her drink. "I told her she was stupid but she didn't believe me."

"You sure it wasn't' you?" Kimi continued, looking into her eyes. She was the one person who knew when Valencia was full of shit. She realized that whenever Valencia talked about a friend of hers, that friend usually was herself. "You can keep it straight if you are. We not gonna laugh too much."

"No it wasn't me! What the fuck I look like going to a psych-ic?" Valencia yelled.

"Calm down, girl," Kimi looked at Quita through the corners of her eyes. "I'm just asking that's all. Personally I think the shit is weird. Real weird, and if I were you, I would tell your friend, to keep that shit to herself."

While Valencia was running her mouth non-stop, they all spot-ted a six foot two inch, light skin dude, with a low haircut and waves, staring in their direction. He was so attractive, he stood out from the crowd. "I mean got damn," Valencia said as if she was irritated. "He's been staring at *me* all night. I hate that kind of shit."

"Who?" Kimi asked. "His fine ass?" She pointed. "What the fuck can you hate about him?"

"Yes…and stop pointing!" Valencia said hitting her finger.

"What I want to know is, how you know he's looking at you?" Kimi inquired. "How you know he ain't looking at me, or Quita?"

"Or me." Terry said.

"You not the only bitch over here," Kimi said.

Valencia looked at all of them. "Yeah right," She giggled. "You wish you could be sitting at a table with me, and have someone pick you over me," Kimi frowned. "The only time that shit is possible is in your dreams, but then you'll eventually wake up. Trust me."

"Whatever! Valencia," Kimi added. "You not the hot shit you think you are. Get over your fucking self."

Just then he walked over and extended his hands to all of the women for a friendly shake. When he approached them, he looked edible in his Gucci jeans, and dark green Star Wars t-shirt. His sense of style was innovative and refreshing. "I came over to introduce myself instead of staring at you all-night." He smiled at everyone, but looked at no one in particular. "I don't want ya'll to think I'm crazy or nothing, I just like what I see."

"It's cool," Valencia blushed. Her friends looked at each other and shook their heads. "I get it all the time. I'm just glad you made your way over."

He looked at her strangely and said, "Anyway, I'm Demetrius."

"Hi Demetrius," they said unanimously.

"You're all some very beautiful women." Valencia gave them the look like, *I told you so.* You would've thought he was talking about *her* personally. "The best looking women in here, in fact."

"Yes we are beautiful," Valencia said. "And I'm happy you decided to come over and finally make yourself known. Instead of staring over there looking all creepy." He frowned. "Besides, we don't bite."

He smiled and said, "I hope you don't bite, ma," he winked causing Valencia to further think he chose her. "And you're right…I'd be a fool not to come over here and open my mouth." His eyes rolled over all of them. "So let me get down to it, I'd hate to break up the group, but I was wondering if I could steal one of you for a drink at the bar. If you don't mind."

Quita and Kimi were silent. They needed more than that before making any moves, and following him to the table. While Valencia couldn't help but smile, thinking that someone as fine as him, could be exactly what was needed to get over Tech. She had plans to fuck him on the first night and everything if he proved himself. When it was quiet for a little while longer, Valencia said, "I don't think my friends would mind if I'm gone for a few minutes. Ya'll gonna be good right?"

"Whoa," he said with his hands up. "I shoulda been more specific. I'm actually coming over here to kick it with you," he continued directing his attention to Quita. "I like my women a certain way, and she is stunning all the way around."

"Me?" she pointed to herself. She shook her head. "Stop playing games with me. I'm not in the mood. I just lost my job and I don't have time for it."

"Well let me get you there, in the mood that is." He was no longer smiling. He extended his hand. "Please…come join me for a drink."

He was serious and she wanted to jump up so fast, but she was afraid her weight would roll him over. Unlike her he was fit and in shape. "If you're sure, I guess I will get that drink with you." She accepted his hand and he helped her out of the booth. "I'll be back in a second." Kimi was so happy for her she couldn't contain herself. Not only was he fine, but Valencia was getting exactly what she deserved. Her face was tight as she watched them walk away.

Valencia had never been more embarrassed in all of her life. She hadn't even considered the possibility that someone who looked like him, would vie for her friends' attention, instead of her own. He was certainly her type of man and she usually got first pickings. But Quita although thick, was beautiful and looked especially cute that night, wearing a red dress by H&M and black open toe sandals. She favored Jennifer Hudson, in her heavier days.

When they walked off, he respectfully placed his hand in the small of her back to lead the way to the area he'd chosen. Once at the bar, he pulled out the stool and helped her get on top of it. Needless to say, he was a perfect gentleman. "I hope I didn't cause any problems for you and your friends. Your girl seemed to be upset with me, and that wasn't my intent."

"She'll get over it," she replied shooting him a smile. He was what she needed to put her in a better mood as she thought of what to do for employment. But she couldn't even look into his eyes because he was so attractive. "She has a man anyway, and is use to men who look like you, coming over to her. I guess you hurt her feelings. But, don't worry about her."

"Good for him." He winked, not liking Valencia's attitude. He hated bitches who thought they were so cute. "Can I get you something to drink?"

"Yeah, I'll take a strawberry Daiquiri with whipped cream."

"You got it," he winked. He walked off toward the end of the bar to get the bartenders attention. His absence gave her some time to adjust her dress, straighten her hair and apply more lip-gloss. The sound of people talking and having a good time played in the background like portraits on a wall and she felt alone. "You're shy aren't you?" He continued after returning with the drinks. "I can tell because of the way you look around and tug at your clothes when you think no one's looking." She remained silent.

"Am I right?"

"No...I mean, I don't think so."

"It's in your eyes and the way you avoid looking at me."

"I'm sorry," she cleared her throat. "But have you seen yourself?" She nursed her drink by stirring her straw. "Guys like you normally don't go for me."

"Listen," he said as he gently took the drink from her and turned her around. "I don't know who has gotten to you to make you think otherwise, but you *are* beautiful. Plenty of dudes would be busting their ass to be over here with you." She didn't believe him, her weight had her insecure. "So stop thinking like that. Now I don't want you to get all conceded on me either," he rubbed her knee. Something about him told her he was off, but she gave her intuitions a kick in the butt. "I want you to be confident when we are together. Besides, I love a whole lot of woman, and you look so good I want to eat you. You thick ma, just the way I love 'em!"

Although he was right, Quita was the girl in school who was known as "The Other One". Whenever a dude wanted one of her pretty friends in high school, and they were taken, they'd say, *I guess I'll holla at the other one then*, meaning Quita. But over the years she didn't care as much as she moved into womanhood. Her biggest problem was that she was often deceitful and surrounded herself around the wrong people. When she was in high school, her mother, who she provided for, told her to be weary of Valencia but she ignored her. Now she wished she had her mother's sound mind to listen to. Her mother suffered from dementia of the worst kind, and was living in a nursing home. It was for both of their own good.

Bertha Miles used to share Quita's two-bedroom apartment in Hyattsville Maryland, but when she came home one night after work, to find her mother in the middle of Bladensburg Road, she knew she had to place her somewhere she'd be safe, and would have full time care. So against her will, she put her in a very expensive nursery home. But now without a job, she would need to place her some place else, or care for her herself, which she couldn't afford to do with needing a job.

Quita enjoyed Demetrius' attention for five more minutes before she felt guilty and excused herself to return to her friends. She felt bad enough as it was because she came to Dave N Busters to be with them, but was gone for over thirty minutes. The moment she returned, Valencia went in with her shenanigans. Her jealousy was so heavy it was uncomfortable. "I want to say something but I don't want you to get mad," she started the moment Quita sat down. "I know you all sensitive and stuff."

Kimi just looked at Quita and shook her head. She knew Valencia was going to try to get her to cosign on some bullshit, because since they had been sitting at the table alone, she attempted to brainwash her into thinking that *she* was the one he really wanted. And that he was just talking to Quita for charity purposes, because she treated him rudely when he first approached the table. To let her tell it, he was being so generous, that he could have written Quita off on his taxes. "Okay," Quita responded not wanting to ruin her mood. "If you think I'm gonna be mad, don't tell me then. I'm having a good time and it's overdue."

She hadn't met anybody she liked since she lost her man six months earlier, and that was also Valencia's fault. She didn't want tonight ruined by one of her campaigns.

⟵———————————————————⟶

⟨SIX MONTHS EARLIER⟩

Valencia managed to convince Quita into believing that *all* men cheated, including her long-term beau Frank. On a mission to prove her point, she was able to walk Quita through the process of finding out for sure, which ultimately meant going through his personal shit. Not to mention, that before Valencia butted her nose into their business, Quita never had a reason to doubt him or his faithfulness.

Quita was told that the Valencia's, *Check-A-Cheat-Find-A-Cheat* plan, was fool proof and even if he were being faithful, she would never get caught. So she checked his cell phone, then his car when he was at her house sleep, and lastly she rummaged through his coat pockets. After invading his privacy for weeks at a time, she finally discovered a number with pink lipstick smeared on the edge, in one of his jackets hanging in her closet. He brought it over as an option to wear for the next day, when he took her out for dinner. She didn't realize that he hadn't worn that jacket in over three years, which exceeded the one-year time they'd been together...nor did she care. Valencia was right, all men cheated and she held the proof in her possession, so she thought.

Approaching him while he slept on her couch, she balled the number up and threw it in his face. The edge of it cut his skin, and blood dripped down his cheek. At first he didn't know what was happening, because she never spoke to him so coldly. He loved Quita, more than any man could love another woman, and he could never cheat on her. Why would he? She was thick like he liked, could cook her ass off, and catered to him from head to toe. In his book she gave him everything he needed and there was no reason to roam.

Frank was a good brother, who worked forty hours a week, and sometimes sixty, so he could put them up in a new home. But love or not, he would not tolerate her behavior. So when he finally understood what she was saying, he decided he couldn't be with someone who would betray his trust. Without denying his infidelity, he walked out of the door, and cut her out of his life forever. Little did she know, the next day, he had plans to ask her to be his wife. That's why he pulled out his good jacket.

The news of him considering her as his wife came as a surprise, because prior to that point, she never felt worthy of marriage. She ran into his mother one day while at the grocers, who expressed her dismay that their relationship was over, and that the prospect of having grandchildren in the near future was gone too. She explained to Quita that the number she found, was from a coat he hadn't worn in years, and that she destroyed her son's heart. Quita tried everything in her power to get him back, but Frank wasn't that type of dude. If he made a decision he stuck to it, believing second-guessing could lead to worse. It wasn't until she met Bricks, while walking to her car one day, that she even looked at another man after Frank, but he was unattainable also. She just couldn't catch a break when it came to relationships because good men were truly hard to find.

<hr />

"I'm gonna tell you anyway because you're one of my closest friends." Valencia said. "I know you're not use to guys approaching you like that so I'ma be real with you. And before I say anything, if you don't believe me, Kimi and Terry saw it too."

"No I didn't see shit! Do you, but don't put my name in it." Kimi interjected, waving her off with her hand. "You making up shit over there as you go along."

"I don't know what you talking about either." Terry added.

"Yes ya'll did see it," Valencia said, cutting her eyes at Kimi. "Anyway, Quita...he was looking over here the entire time ya'll were together."

"Well, how come he never seemed to take his eyes off me?" She paused, and looked over at him again. He was not with his friends. "It don't sound right."

"That's what they do," Valencia advised. "They make you think they ain't looking at your friends, when they really are. All men do that dog ass shit, so just be careful, girl." Kimi looked at Terry and shook her head. She was working her nerves to no end.

"I don't understand...if he wanted you...why didn't he come over and meet you?" Quita questioned. "You were talking directly to him when he came over. It would've been a perfect time to invite *you* to the bar."

"Or invited us all over for drinks." Kimi added. "It didn't make any sense to invite Quita over to the bar and leave the rest of us, if based on what you say, he wanted us all."

"I didn't say he wanted us all," she rolled her eyes, "I said he wanted me." She pointed to herself. Looking back at Quita she said, "I'm only telling you because I'm a true friend and if you get serious with him, I want you to know first hand. Anyway, any man that *fyne* usually got some other shit with him, that's why I didn't want him." As Quita thought about Valencia's statement, she thought of what her mother use to say before she lost her memory. If someone has to tell you they're a *true* friend, chances are they're not.

HOW THINGS ARE GONNA BE

(3 MONTHS LATER)

Everything had gone downhill for Quita, quick. She committed herself to additional expenses prior to getting fired and now she could no longer afford her new royal blue Honda Accord and other bills. While she was visiting her mother it was repossessed, and she still didn't have a job. It was just a matter of time before she couldn't afford the nursing home, so she gave up her apartment instead. If it wasn't for Valencia, she wouldn't have a place to rest her head. Quita was extremely grateful and jumped at the opportunity to live with her, until she could find another job earning the same money she did at the doctor's office.

Valencia's only request was that Quita care for her two children, Stone and Jenson who were four. Quita didn't mind because she was living with her rent free, and it seemed like a good enough idea at first. She soon found out that what she actually signed up for was a live in nanny/slave. Anything that Valencia didn't feel like doing, Quita did. And since Quita wasn't the kind of person who said no when she was being helped, the list of responsibilities grew by the hour. If Quita allowed things to remain the way that they were, she'd never be able to find a job, or have a life, because as Valencia's slave, she didn't have the time. She was tired most days, and worked harder than she ever had in her life.

Quita was on the phone with Demetrius, ever since they met, they were on the phone non-stop. She was really feeling him but didn't allow herself to care too much because she was afraid and fragile. Not having a job, and having a broken heart, was too much to ask at this point in her life. For the moment she tried her best to be perfect for him, whatever that meant. Her insecurity hindered her actions, and that gave him the impression she didn't want to be bothered.

"Baby, Valencia is here, be on your way to come get me," she said hanging up the phone. "Hey, Valencia!" Quita grabbed her purse and slipped on her shoes. She couldn't wait for her to come in so she could roll out. "Stone and Jenson are asleep, and they've already eaten dinner. If they wake up, I packed up their snacks and they're in little baggies on the top shelf of the fridge. Now, Stone only has half a piece of cake, because he ate some of his earlier. You know he gonna be slick and try to eat his sister's, but Jenson has an entire slice left, so don't let him fool you." The way she was running things off, you would have thought they were her kids and not Valencia's. "They already had baths too. I'm on my way out to meet D, so I'ma see you later. Bye, girl."

Her hand was on the knob when Valencia said, "Oh…you going out?" She sat her purse down, and kicked off her shoes. "I didn't know you were seeing him tonight." She seemed disappointed as she flopped on the couch. "I had a long day at work, and kinda wanted to hang out. But I hope you enjoy yourself, because I probably won't."

Quita turned around and said, "I didn't know you had plans. Why didn't you call me? I would've let Demetrius know." She threw the house keys down and plopped on the sofa next to Valencia. Her evening was over before it started.

"I'm sorry, girl. It's just that, I've been so stressed with my new position as Office Manager, at the doctor's office, that I really wanted to have a good time. It seems like all I do is work, come home and take care of you guys, and go back to work again. It's hard, Quita…So fucking hard." She sighed. "Anyway, do you, I'll watch a movie or something."

After that song and dance, there was no way Quita could hang out. "Well you go ahead," Quita smiled. "I can see Demetrius another time, I guess. You're right, you work hard and I don't have a job right now, so how ever I can help you, I want to do it. I can just chill here, eat my dinner and relax. I been dodging him for three months, so one more day won't hurt. Go ahead and have a nice time…I'll look after Stone and Jenson."

"Thanks, girl!" Before Quita could take it back, Valencia dipped downstairs to her bathroom that she called the Smoke House. She didn't like smoking upstairs and around the twins, so she used the bathroom in the basement to get her weed on. It was her sanctuary, and the place she spent at least three hours out of a day, just to clear her mind. She kept her weed there and often smoked so much, she appeared to move in slow motion when she would come back upstairs. Inside of the Smoke House was a tub, sink and a TV mounted on the wall. She also had it outfitted in plush pink carpets, a soft pink toilet bowl seat and expensive pink hand towels by Polo. She loved that room, more than she did her bedroom and it was truly her favorite place in the house.

After getting high, she jumped in the shower. Valencia loved their current living arrangement because with Quita in the house, she could do whatever she wanted, whenever she wanted. Before Quita started watching her kids, she had to pay a girl down the street one hundred fifty dollars a week, for each of her kids for daycare, and now she could greedily stuff her pockets with the extra cash. Despite the late nights out, and being gone for weeks at a time, Valencia managed to convince Quita that her being there, was putting her out, because the money she spent eating, was taking from her kids.

Valencia loved the arrangement so much, that she had plans to make it permanent, while Quita on the other hand was desperately trying to find a job. Whenever she mentioned going on an interview, Valencia would miraculously find something else concerning the kids for her to do. This went on every time, and never stopped. Stone and Jensen had never been healthier in all their lives with her living there. From physicals, to dental appointments, they were the epitome of children in good health. Prior to Quita living there, the only time the kids would go to the doctor was when they were sick.

Disappointed, Quita reluctantly picked up the phone and called Demetrius. He had been so patient with her, that she was afraid he'd lose interest. But to her surprise, he shocked her again. "D...it's Quita. I'm not going to be able to go tonight. I really wanted to so please don't be mad at me."

"Are you okay?" He asked in a concerned tone. "You sound upset."

"I'm okay, but I have to watch the kids again. I know you're on your way, but you can turn back around. Maybe we can hook up later next week. It'll be my treat." She continued, as if she had any money. "I'll call you later."

"She couldn't get another sitter?" He knew what kind of person Valencia was but would never tell Quita because he realized how much she cared about the bitch. "I really wanted to take you out, babes. I'm feeling you and I want a chance to show you."

"She couldn't get a babysitter and I'm so sorry." She sighed. "And with her letting me live here until I can get up on my feet, I got to show her my appreciation. I can't let her down. I really hope you understand."

"Fuck all that, I'm not gonna let you get away from me again tonight. If you can't go on the date, I'll bring our date to you."

She couldn't help but smile after witnessing how thoughtful he was, so she ran upstairs to get dressed. When she was as cute as she could be, she straightened up the house. Valencia's home, in a small hood in Maryland called Palmer Park, was huge. She had a finished basement, that she didn't use, and four large bedrooms. The living room was laced with all the finest electronics cash could buy, courtesy of Quita and the money she no longer had to spend on daycare expenses.

When Valencia was dressed, she was shocked to see Quita in her bedroom, singing to her Mary J. Blige CD. She wondered what she had to be happy for since she burst her bubble and ruined her plans earlier. "And why are you so happy?" Valencia walked into Quita's room, to give herself a once over in the door mirror. She looked sexy and she knew it because she was looking for sponsors, men to fuck her and help pay bills. "You'd think you were the one hanging out tonight."

"No reason," she smiled. "Unless you consider Demetrius coming over a good reason."

"Oh," Valencia was disappointed. She didn't understand why as hard as she tried to keep Quita down, somebody was always willing to lift her up. "Are you sure you'll be able to hear the twins with you having company and all? Because I'm gonna be mad if you're not."

She frowned. "I'm very overprotective of them, girl. You know how I am about my kids. They all I got outside of my mama."

"I know," Quita smiled, moving the hangers back and forth in her closet. "I'll go back and forth upstairs while he's here." She felt she needed to say something else to convince her that things would be cool. "And I'll keep the cordless phone next to me in case you call."

"Humph, well make sure he don't go in my room or nothin'. I don't like having too many people in my house." In Quita's opinion her last comment was strange, because in the past month that she'd been living there, Valencia had six different dudes in the house, including her ex-boyfriend Tech. Not to mention Valencia knew most of them only by their nicknames.

To avoid an argument, because it wasn't her house, she said, "Don't worry. He won't be anywhere near your room. I'll keep him plenty of company." She grinned, looking under her bed for her shoes.

"So what time is he coming over?" Valencia leaned up against the dresser, and witnessed Quita's disgusting happiness. "Because you sure did get changed up quick. I mean…you were already dressed, did you have to put something different on? Don't let that man run you around trying to look slim for him."

Quita ignored her rude comment, because she said that type of shit all the time. "He should be here in five minutes! Girl he is so like that! I can't believe how sweet he is. I haven't had a nigga treat me like this since," she swallowed and looked at her shoes, "Frank. I still miss him." Quita walked into her closet, to break up the mood she was in, and when she came out, she caught a jealous look on Valencia's face. "Are you okay? You seem like you have an attitude with me or something. I don't have to invite him over if you don't want me to. Just keep it real with me."

"Girl, please! Why shouldn't I be happy, I'm the one with a job and a place to stay? You living with me, even though I don't feel you're grateful enough."

"I am grateful. I really am, and if I don't tell you enough let me tell you now. I don't know what I would've done without your help. I don't care about giving up my apartment, but not being able to take care of my mother was gonna be hard for me. You couldn't begin to understand the sleepless nights I had, just thinking about it." Quita walked up to her. "So thank you, girl. For real." Valencia still wore a frown on her face. "You sure you not mad at me for something else?"

"No…I'm happy for you. If Demetrius wants to date you despite you not having a job or a place of your own that says a lot about his character I guess." She shrugged. "Not too many dudes would deal with a woman who don't have their own."

"Well…so far so good. Plus I don't plan on staying down long. I'll have a place of my own before no time." She smiled. "I'm just happy he's the kind of person he is."

"Did you tell him that you're still in love with Frank? Or that you checking for the nigga Bricks? That nobody but you have seen."

"Why you ask that?" Quita asked turning around to face her.

"No reason really," Valencia adjusted the jewelry and perfume on Quita's dresser. "I just wondered if he knew that's all."

"I'm not still in love with Frank. I think about him sometimes but that's the extent of it." She paused. "He told me he didn't want me, and I can't force him. And as far as Bricks, he's not my man to worry about. That's the crazy bitch Yvonna's problem."

While Quita was talking Valencia glanced down at her arm and noticed Demetrius should be there shortly. She decided to show him what he was missing by choosing Quita over her. She had the perfect outfit on to exhibit her curves and sexual features. So when the doorbell rang, she said, "Girl, brush your hair and bump the edges they look a mess. You not in Africa…I'll get the door."

"Thanks, girl! Tell him I'll be down when I'm finished."

Valencia wasn't paying her any mind. She was downstairs and at the door before she even remembered Quita was in the house. You would've thought he was coming to see her. Before opening the door right away, she let him ring the doorbell three more times. When she was sure he was ready to bare witness to her body, she flung the door open and said, "How are you? I hope I didn't keep you waiting too long. I came to the door as quickly as I could."

"You didn't keep me waiting because I'm here to see Quita," he responded with a slight attitude. "Is she home?" He looked into the house from the outside. "We got a date."

"Of course she's home. Well, she's in *my* house, she doesn't have a home of her own," she winked. He was getting angrier at every word she spoke. Truthfully he wished she'd just shut the fuck up. "She'll be down in a second. Come on in." She opened the door wider and he strolled inside smelling of the richest cologne. "She's upstairs." She closed the door.

"That's cool." He looked at his watch. "But I thought you were leaving," He sat a picnic basket, comforters and roses on the couch. "You're usually gone by now. I figured you'd be on a date or something."

"I am. I was actually just leaving when I heard the door ring." She paused. "Before you say anything, you don't have to say thank you for helping Quita. I would want somebody to do the same for me if I were in her position. We been knowing each other for a minute so it was my duty. Feel me?"

"Yeah. I do. But you know what, Quita is an extraordinary woman. I knew the minute I *CHOSE HER*. She'll come out on top no matter what situation she's in. She's just that type of person. So whatever ya'll got going on here, with me in her corner, won't last long. She'll be on her feet in no time."

Valencia didn't know what made her hate him more, the fact that he was truly feeling Quita, or the fact that when she was in the room, he acted as if she weren't even alive. Taking her queue to bounce she said, "Well...have fun if you can. Hopefully I'll see you around more often." she grabbed her keys and purse.

"As long as Quita's here, you can count on it."

Valencia grinned, walked up to him and kissed him on the lips. She snaked her tongued into his mouth, and when they separated a string of spit connected their lips. He wiped his mouth and spit on the floor. He was overly disgusted. "Talk that shit a few months from now. Later." She opened the door and left.

"Valencia gone already?" Quita asked as she came down the steps.

"Huh?" He wiped his lips again and wiped the spit away on the floor with his foot. "I didn't do anything."

Quita giggled. "Boy, I know you didn't do anything. I was asking if she left." She paused. "What's wrong with you?"

He walked over to her and they embraced in a warm hug. He wasn't going to tell her about Valencia because of the position she was in at the moment. "She's gone, baby. But let's worry about us."

The smell of his cologne and the feel of his muscular arms wrapped around her body made her feel tiny. She could feel he liked her, even if she wasn't sure why. Strangely enough, he was the first adult she talked to outside of Kimi and Terry, since she moved in. "Wow...that's an introduction I can get use to." She told him.

"Good, that's what I want." He stood back and looked at her outfit. "Well look at you," he replied stepping back to look her up and down. "You're gorgeous! And I don't say things I don't mean. Oh!" he paused moving to the couch. "These are for you," he handed her the bouquet of roses. Quita never received roses from a man and that included Frank. The look on her face was all he needed to continue his seduction. He spread a Ralph Lauren comforter in the middle of the floor and placed the picnic basket on top of it. When things were organized, he pulled out a cheese spread, crackers and the sandwiches. When he finished organizing the picnic, he pulled out a bottle of wine and a can of whip cream.

"Now what do you plan on doing with that?" She pointed to the cream. "You ain't getting freaky already are you? We haven't even started our first date yet." She giggled. "I have my eyes on you."

"You'll see what I have planned." He winked again.

She was just about to enjoy his company when her cell phone rang. She stood up and said, "Excuse me, baby. This may be Valencia." He nodded hoping she wasn't blocking his flow already. He couldn't stand that sneaky bitch. Quita answered the phone and said, "Hello."

"Quita, it's Kimi, I'm calling from my house phone, so you probably don't recognize the number."

"Well what's up?"

"I got to talk to you about Valencia. You got a few minutes so I can rap to you right quick?"

MONEY MAKING FLOW

While Valencia floated around the house, from the couch, Quita's eyes remained locked on her as if she were her prey. The twins, Stone and Jensen, sat by her feet and preoccupied themselves with toy blocks. "You okay, girl?" Valencia asked, placing her watch on, fastening the clutch. "You seem like you zoned out. What's on your mind?"

Stone placed a block on her lap and she said, "I'm fine. Working on being better."

"Good for you." She sat on the loveseat and adjusted her shoes. "One should always aspire to be better. Make that your goal in life. At least you don't have to worry about going to work anymore."

"Yeah…What a blessing." Quita responded in a sarcastic tone. "I guess I should be singing praises that I no longer have a job."

Valencia was so clueless and out of touch with other peoples' feelings, that she could not see that something was different with her friend. After all those years, Quita finally realized that the person she thought Valencia was, was a lie. Days earlier, Kimi kicked everything to Quita about why she was terminated, which she found out from Terry. First, she learned that Dr. Takerski was lying when he said that Karen's results were mixed with Charlene's. Not only did Charlene get the news that she was pregnant, and had HIV, but she also learned that Karen was not taken to the hospital. Quita's only thing was why did Dr. Takerski lie? He was the boss and all he had to do was give the word and let her go.

As Kimi continued with the revelation, she eventually found out that the reason the doctor lied was to appease Valencia. After a lot of work, he eventually took Valencia up on her sexual proposal and she taped their encounter, without his knowing. With the blackmail tape in Valencia's possession, she was able to get him to tell a lie of her choosing. Had she not run into Karen yesterday, Quita still would've been a little doubtful that Valencia could do her so coldly. But when she apologized to Karen for what happened at the doctor's office, and she told her she had no idea what she was talking about, she knew everything Kimi said was true. What Valencia did changed the course of everything. Quita was done with being a pushover, and she decided to get money by any means necessary.

"Alright I'm off to work!" Valencia announced, standing up and smoothing her scrubs out with her hands. "Take care of my babies and I'll see you later on tonight. I put the chicken in the sink in case you want to make dinner. It'll really help me out." Although she asked on the sly, Valencia was basically telling her how it was going to be. Slaves didn't have rights, and neither did Quita in Valencia's opinion.

When she walked out, Quita jumped up and looked out the window. She waited for her to pull off before calling Kimi. She had an idea on how to get that money but she needed help. The moment Kimi answered Quita said, "Let's open a daycare!" Quita yelled on the other end.

"Okay…who is this and what have you done to my friend?" She paused. "Because this can't be Quita Miles…who been missing in action for days. The one who I call and she never answers the phone."

"Yes it is and I'm serious," she paused, due to her excitement. "Let's open a daycare center! We will make so much fucking money! I can see it now!"

"Awww…you cursed," Stone pointed.

Jensen's eyes widened. "Mama, said not to curse, Ms. Quita."

"Mind your little businesses," Quita walked into the kitchen and leaned up against the wall so she could still keep an eye on the kids. Focusing back on the call she said, "Kimi, we can do this. I know you not making a whole lot of money at the doctor's office. So let's do this together."

"Quittttaaaa," she said stretching out her name. "Where this is all coming from? You should be finding another job instead of being bothered with a day care. Get out of that girl's house while you still can, she's not trustworthy. And you didn't even call to see how I was doing! I been calling you ever since I told you about that bitch but you didn't answer the phone. I was going through it and needed a friend. All you give a fuck about is Valencia, and she could care less about you. I'm not even going to work today because I'm stressed the fuck out."

"That's not true, I care about you too! And I didn't call you because I've been out of it. I've been trying to find out what I'm gonna do about my situation," Quita said, as she considered how selfish she was being. "I'm sorry Kimi. I got so excited about the daycare center idea that I didn't stop to think about your feelings. I can get the kids dressed and catch a cab to come over there if you want. You want me to come through? Just give the word."

"I'm good now. I needed you more back then…sometimes I feel like I'm on the verge of a mental breakdown. Just pray for me." She sighed.

"You got that, Kimi. You'll be on my prayer list everyday," she replied, as if she truly had one. "What's up with this money?"

"Tell me about this thing. How did this idea come about?"

"Well…I was thinking…since Valencia's doing me a favor by letting me live here rent free…"

"Rent free?" Kimi interjected, in an attempt to set things straight. "You watching my bad ass God kids! That ain't lightweight. Not to mention she was the one who got you fired. You doing her a favor that can never be paid back. You practically them kids' mother."

"Kimi, do you want me to kill this bitch?" She paused. "Because if you keep telling me that, I'm gonna go down to ya'lls job, and shoot her in the forehead. You know my record and you know how I can be."

"Let me be quiet…"

"I think that's best." She said looking at the twins again. "Anyway, I watch her kids and I'm home anyway. I figure I might as well get paid for it. I was thinking at first maybe we could watch 2 or 3 kids not including hers, until we get more comfortable."

"Two or three kids plus my god kids?" Kimi interrupted. "That's five kids! Girl, are you losing your mind over there? I know you haven't been around too many adults since you moved in, but who wants to deal with just anybody's kids."

"I'm not losing my mind! I want to get paid! And I'm thinking if we get about two or three kids, like I said, we can charge them lower prices until we have a legal operation. Or charge them more and take the worst kids ever. I don't know, Kimi! All I know is I want to get paid and I need your help."

"Oh...I get it." She laughed, sarcastically. "Now I see why you called me. You need something from me you can't do for yourself."

"I'm sorry, but they won't license me if they find out I have a record for attempted robbery. I need you to get licensed and I'll do the rest of the work. You won't even have to leave your job if you don't want to. I can run the shit myself and I'll give you a cut whether you help me or not. Although I need your help at first."

"Whoa..whoa...whoa!" Kimi laughed. "So you saying you want me to lie to the government? And basically tell them I'm running a daycare center I'm not involved in? What if something happens to those kids? I can't have that type of shit on my conscious. I'm not trying to be no felon, Quita."

"I know that. And I'm not asking you to either. I'm gonna make sure the kids are good. If I'm asking you to lend your name I'm gonna respect that shit and make sure shit go smooth."

"Why do you have to be legal? Why can't you just watch kids?"

"Because people don't like they kids being watched by people who are not licensed."

"But you got a record, Quita. What if the people find out you not licensed? Niggas snap if they think they kids are not being watched properly. And they sneaky. Mothers are very vengeful."

"I'm gonna be careful." She continued. "You know I would never have had that felony on my record if that other shit didn't happen."

"That's what you say. A lot of people say something different."

"So you do think I would've put a gun to that pastor's head had I known? Them niggas from the YBM lied to me! I was set up!"

"I hope not."

"Listen, if you are truly my friend than I'm calling on you. I need your help. Please." Quita was on the verge of tears. "I wouldn't ask you if this wasn't my last resort. The only reason I got that job at the doctor's office was because Valencia trashed my record and replaced it with hers before the doctor could see it. If I don't go into business for myself, this will be it for me." When she heard Kimi sighing louder she said, "Please! I need you!"

There was a brief moment of uncomfortable silence as Quita reflected on her current unemployment status. "Sorry, but I can't be around kids, Quita. I really want you to do well though."

"Aight, well...that's on you. I'm gonna put my plan into action anyway. And if you ever want to work with me once it takes off...because it will take off, my doors are always open."

THE WRONG MAN ALL THE TIME

The call with Quita made Kimi, more stressed than ever. She really wished Quita could be there for her, like she was there for Valencia. No matter how much she rooted her on, or marched in her corner, Quita would still find a way to bring up Valencia's name and sing her praises. And now she was coming to her for a daycare center idea, when she hadn't spoken to Kimi in days. To make matters worse, Terry said she saw them out at lunch yesterday, like everything was cool. Like she didn't stab her in the back, and get her fired. She felt she was playing herself soft, because she could never have carried shit like that, if Valencia did her that wrong. She was five seconds from saying '*fuck her*'.

When she hung up the phone, Kimi got out of bed and walked to the bathroom. Her entire body felt as if someone had poured a bucket of water over her. Once inside, she splashed cold water on her face. *Swoosh! Swoosh!* Before Quita called, she was a participant in the same nightmare that haunted her almost every night. *How much longer am I going to keep doing this to myself?* She thought. After the water dried on her skin, she looked at her reflection and saw the same person she hated. There she was…the mother who just seven years earlier, abandoned her baby boy.

To even think that it was a good idea at the time, caused her extreme nausea, especially considering Thomas, her son's father, said he didn't want her if she kept their only child. She believed in her heart that giving up her flesh and blood meant a long life with Thomas, but she quickly found out that she was wrong.

←——————————————————————→

⸺(SEVEN YEARS EARLIER)

The movie theater was filled to capacity, as Kimi sat in the back with her long-term boyfriend Thomas. Softly nudging him on the arm she whispered, "Hey, baby. I'm going to the bathroom. I'll be right back. You want something?" She felt like she had to take a serious dump, that couldn't wait until she got home.

"Huh?" He whispered, never taking his eyes off of the scream. It was on the best part. "Why you talking in the theater. You know how much I hate that shit."

"I'm sorry. I just..." she stopped before completing her sentence because she realized he probably wouldn't care anyway. "Never mind."

"When you come back bring me a small popcorn...extra butter." He said as he continued watching the movie screen. "And a soda too."

"Where's the money?"

"Girl, get out of my face and go get my shit."

"Yeah whatever, Thomas." As she made her way carefully down the steps in the theater, she focused on the exit. Her pregnant belly affecting her equilibrium in more ways than one, she found it difficult to walk. Ever since she discovered she was pregnant, Thomas rejected and neglected her. He made it clear that he didn't want the baby, and although her pregnancy came as a result of both of their actions, he didn't hesitate to lay the blame on her shoulders.

Easing past the movie watchers, she excused herself and ran down the steps leading out of the theater. She couldn't believe how her stomach ached and she was sure if she didn't hurry, she was on the verge of soiling her pants with her own feces. With each step she took, the pain grew more intense, so she darted down the hall, praying she'd make it to the restroom in time.

Flinging the door open, she ran into an empty stall and sat on a toilet, without placing a seat cover on it. Normally she would have, but the sensation to release her bowels was becoming unbearable. Sitting on a toilet, wet with the urine of strangers, she placed her hands on the sides of the stall walls and pushed with all her might. She cried out in agony because she never experienced so much pain in all her life. When she felt her flesh tearing between her legs, she screamed out, "Help me! Please! Somebody help me!"

"Are you alright in there?" Someone asked outside of her stall. "Can I do something for you?"

"Yes, please get me some help and tell my boyfriend I'm in here!" Kimi cried. "I think I'm about to have my baby."

"Okay...uh...what's his name? And what theater is he in?" She sounded concerned and Kimi was hopeful she'd help her out. "I'll go get him now."

"His name is Thomas and he's in the movie theater number 4. Please! Go now!"

The woman scurried away and five minutes later, came in with her boyfriend. He didn't care if it was a woman's bathroom or not, he wanted to know what was going on. For a second he was preparing to pull out his gat, thinking somebody was setting him up, until he saw the blood streaming under the door and heard Kimi wincing in pain. It was then that he knew exactly what was up. She was going into labor in a public place. At that time the plan changed, because all Thomas cared about was getting her out of the ladies room, before people started asking questions.

"I'm coming in, baby," he said softly. "Everything will be alright. Open the door for me." She unlocked the latch and he eased inside. He closed the door and said, "Get up...we got to get out of here." He hoisted her off of the toilet, pulled her panties up, followed by her pants. Blood was over everything...her clothing...his shoes, and his hands. He was focused and on a mission and there was nothing anybody could do to stop him. "She'll be alright, I'm taking her to the hospital." He told concerned by-standers. He didn't take a breath, until they were outside and moving toward his truck. "We almost there. Hold on, baby."

She heard him but didn't understand why they couldn't wait for the ambulance. The baby wanted out and it wanted out now. But Thomas wouldn't rest until he had her hidden inside of his Nissan truck. He placed her on the backseat, and she lay out, gripping the bottom of her stomach. "You think you can make it to my apartment, Kimi? I'ma drive fast as shit, so don't worry about that. I just don't want you to push it out while we driving."

THE CARTEL PUBLICATIONS PRESENTS

She raised her head and said, "Your apartment? I need to go to the fuckin' hospital, Thomas! What are you talking about? I'm in pain and am about to have this baby! It can't wait."

"No! That's not how it's going down." He yelled, placing the car in drive, while looking in the rear view mirror at her frightened face. "If we go there it'll be harder to leave and I can't risk that."

"It'll be harder to leave? Wha...What...What are you talking about?" She asked as the pain continued to rip through her body. She never imagined having a baby would hurt so badly. "I don't want to leave the hospital, I want help."

"We can't keep this baby. I told you that. We agreed on what we were goin' to do remember? So don't back out on me now, Kimi. It's time for you to step up and prove how much you love me. Just as much as I love you."

It's funny how he only told her he loved her when he wanted her to get rid of the baby. "But...it's our baby! I can't do this!" She shook her head. "I can't give our child up! I love him already."

Thomas began to drive erratically and Kimi was thrown around in the truck. He didn't say anything to her until he convinced her that there were now only two choices. Commit to have the baby and die right now, or give it up like they discussed. Slowing his pace he said, "It's either me or it. You can't have both of us."

"But why, Thomas?" she cried. "I love my baby already. Don't you? You haven't even seen him yet."

"If you have this baby to spite me, you'll be caring for it alone." She couldn't respond because the baby continued to push its way out of her body. So she rose up, removed her jeans, followed by her panties. She opened her legs and pushed every time she felt contractions. The back of his truck looked like a crime scene with blood and bodily fluids everywhere. When Thomas realized what was happening, and that she was going to have the baby now, he pulled the truck behind a row of stores and parked. They were surrounded by the night sky and since the stores were closed, it was very private. He got out of the truck and walked to the back. He could see the baby's head crown, and all he could think about was getting it over with. "You almost done. Just push for me."

Kimi bit down on her bottom lip so hard, it bled. She placed her hands on each of her knees and screamed out in pain, as the baby slid from her body. She pulled him out, and the amniotic sac rested on her stomach. Since he wouldn't cry, she stuck her finger in his mouth to clear his passageway, and hit his bottom. A smile spread across her face when he cried and looked into her eyes. He saw her. She knew it.

She laughed at that moment, and looked at Thomas hoping he could love him now, but the look in his eyes told her he was disconnected from the situation. Thomas took some dirty scissors out of the glove compartment and snipped the umbilical cord. Removing the baby from her arms, he wrapped him in one of the old jackets in the back of his truck. With the baby still crying, he carefully placed him in the passenger seat next to him.

Although she was in pain she rose up and said, "What you gonna do with him? What you gonna do with my baby?"

"Don't worry about that." He knew that he would have to drop her off first, before he handled his business. "Just lay back and get some rest."

"Thomas, please. Don't do this to me."

He looked at her sternly and said, "Don't make me tell you again, Kimi. I don't wanna hear shit from you, or I'll kill you and this mothafucka! You acting like you didn't know we couldn't keep a kid. Sit the fuck back...and shut the fuck up!"

She lay down and covered her mouth with both of her bloody hands to silence her cries. She couldn't understand how he wasn't even man enough, to consider the baby's safety. He was acting coldly and she couldn't understand how she loved him for so long. Now she knew why he didn't want her to go to the hospital. He knew the moment she breastfed him, she would never give him up.

Days after the incident, she wondered where her baby was and she watched TV religiously for news of his death. She received the news three days later, when Thomas brought her a newspaper article showing that a baby had been found dead in an abandoned car not too far from where she gave birth. Two days after that...Thomas ended the relationship for good. To think that she gave her baby up, only to be dumped by him, made it difficult for her to live. She had never been the same and she never saw him again.

←――――――――――――――――――――――――――――――→

After splashing her face with more water, she walked into the living room and called her new boyfriend Cash again. It was her sixth call and he still hadn't answered the phone. She figured just like the rest, he was tired of her, and decided to move on. Kimi was too clingy and too depressing for anybody to take seriously for too long. Since Thomas left her, she had ten boyfriends within a 7-year period. And there was one question that always seemed to help them to the door, *'Can we have a baby? I always wanted a child.'* Although some of them were willing to do the act necessary to get her pregnant, not one wanted the responsibility.

Kimi decided to call her boyfriend once more and surprisingly he answered. "Hello? Cash? Why you didn't answer the phone when I called? I been hitting you up nonstop. What…you trying to dodge me or something?"

"Yeah, what up? You got me on the phone now."

"What up?" She repeated. "*What up* is that yo ass still ain't here! Where are you?"

"Come on, man," he said as he blew air into the phone. "I am where I am. I got a mother already. I don't need two."

"What's up with you, Cash? Are we together or not, because lately you been tripping?"

"We together but I don't like when you try to clock me." He paused. "You worse than my mother."

She wanted some dick so she couldn't unleash on him. "Look…are you coming over or not?"

"I'll be there when I get there," he whaled, ending the call.

"I can't stand his ass!" She screamed, throwing the phone up against the wall. "He ain't good for nothing but nut, and even that needs work. I gotta find me another nigga!" Deadbeat men were all she knew and truthfully, they were all she was attracted to. The mean-er, the grimier, the better in her opinion although seeking them out, was never her intentions.

Throwing herself over the edge of the bed, she opened her dresser drawer and did what she normally did, poked tiny holes in the center of the condom with a safety pin. This way, when she had sex with him, she would increase her chances of getting pregnant. After damaging all of the condoms, she opened the next drawer and removed "Thicky" from the box she kept him in. As long as she had Thicky, she could always satisfy her needs. In her opinion the only thing she *really* needed a man for was procreation. Thicky was nice to her. Thicky did what he was told and Thicky never stopped working until she was satisfied, as long as she had batteries.

Sliding her panties down past her thick shapely thighs to her ankles, she slowly spread her legs to let Thicky invade her wetness. When he was as far in her as she could manage, she flipped the little button to set Thicky off. Once she did, the vibrations coupled with the constant motions of her hand pushing and pulling the dildo in and out of her pussy, caused her legs to quiver in pleasure.

Ummmmm. Shit! That was the beauty of living by herself. She could masturbate, play with her clit, and bust a nut anywhere she chose in her apartment. Although sometimes, she got it in at work too. Slowing her motions down, she felt herself on the urge of cumming but she wanted to prolong the satisfaction as long as possible, so she could cum harder.

With the left hand controlling Thicky, she used the right to fondle her breasts before sucking her nipples. The way she was fucking herself, an orgasm was eminent and in the near future. She was tired of making herself wait, and was just about to cum, when suddenly, Thicky stopped moving. "Oh no! Oh no! You can't be serious!" She slapped the dildo into her hand like a teacher would do a ruler. "Please don't do this shit to me." It wouldn't move. "I can't believe this is happening!"

Rustling through her drawer, she looked desperately for a pack of double 'A' batteries. When her search ended in vain, she flung herself face up on the bed and looked up at the ceiling. She was frustrated and pissed the hell off. When she heard a knock at the door, she tucked Thicky away, put on her pajama pants to find out who it was. She was caught off guard when Cash smacked her in the face, knocking her to the floor. "What...the...fuck?" She responded, trying to get her balance together. She saw colorful spots where his face should be and her nose stung. "Why did you just hit me? What the fuck did I do?"

"Why did I just hit you?" He said closing the door before bending over her body. "I hit you because you talk a lot of shit on the phone. And my mans told me I need to put you in your mothafuckin' place when you act like that. And you know what, bitch?" He yelled as he approached her, while biting down on his bottom lip. "He's right! You talk too recklessly, and I don't play that 'you not supposed to put your hands on a girl' shit!"

"Cash, don't do this shit," she pleaded, as tears fell from her eyes. "I was just wondering where you were because I missed you. I didn't mean to be disrespectful." The fear she felt in that moment was unexplainable. Its one thing when you know your man is abusive, it's a whole different thing to find out like this. "Whatever I did, I promise it won't happen again."

"I know," he responded giving off a bloodcurdling laugh. "Because I'ma see to it that you fall in line from here on out." he continued yanking a hunk of her hair, and pulling her face to his. Their lips mashed together and her tongue slid over the surface of his gritty teeth. "Now get in that room and take off yo shit! I'ma give you what you been asking for."

Once in the room, he raped her viciously and without regard for her 5'7 inch frame body. Now she felt like it wasn't a good idea to poke holes in the condom. After all, who wanted a baby by a crazed maniac? When he was done with Kimi, her once light complexion was now painted in red and blue marks over her thighs, arms and legs. He put his penis in every place he could think of on her body, just to bust a nut. When he was done, he pushed off of her, and left her alone on the bed.

MONEY MAKING QUITA

Two months later, Quita's daycare center, which she called *Teach Them To Grow*, was up and running. Quita dropped over three thousand dollars on the daycare, which included training classes, orientation sessions, furnishings and licensing. The center was divided into three different sections in the basement. There was the Kiddie Club, where all the children would learn or play together. The Cot Room, where they took their naps. And the Silent Corner, where the kids were put when they acted up. Although the plan was originally to keep five kids, in the end she would keep as many as twenty at any given time. Her requirements? Money…money…money.

Getting kids for her center was easy, because of her niche. She accepted the worst kids known to man, in exchange for the most money possible. The only kids she wasn't getting paid to watch was Stone and Jensen, who she was growing to care about anyway. Loving them was easy. They were both helpful with the other kids, and because they enjoyed being around other children, the twins looked at the daycare as their very own play world. They were so respectful and easy to get along with, people often forgot that Valencia gave birth to them.

"The Kiddie Club area is ready. I set out the lessons for the day and everything," Kimi said, after walking up the stairs from the basement. Quita was making peanut butter and jelly sandwiches that she would give to them as snacks in the evening, after they ate the lunch that their parents were required to provide. "Who we got coming today?" She washed her hands to help out and dried them on a paper towel. Lately Kimi seemed out of touch with reality and Quita never bothered to ask why for fear it would have something to do with not wanting to help with the center.

Quita looked up and in a low voice said, "We got the usual five." She cut the edges off the five sandwiches, and then cut them into fours. "We'll be alright though."

Kimi finished drying her hands on the paper towel and said, "The usual five? Please don't tell me that shit. I got a headache right now, Quita. For real, I don't have time for them all together at once. We said it was a onetime deal. Why you getting amnesia now?"

"Well what you want me to do? Turn them away?" She paused, placing the sandwiches in the Tupperware containers for later. "You agreed after you got the license for me to help me for at least three months before you went back to work. So keep your agreement and stop tripping."

"And I'm glad I'm here because this shit is in my name! You liable to do anything." She paused. "I might can deal with the rest of them, as long as Lil Goose's bad ass don't come. Remember there was a limit for him anyway. It was a one time situation…that's it."

"Well he coming too." She opened the refrigerator. "But the day will go by quick, like it never started to begin with. Just relax…I got this." She was getting on her fucking nerves. She figured if she had her way, they wouldn't watch any kids.

"Oh my, God! Quita, what are you thinking? Lil Goose is the devil come to life! And you know how terrible his mother Xtisha is! She didn't pick him up on time the last time. She left him here so long, you had to take him the school the next day." She stood in the middle of the kitchen floor with her arms folded over her chest. "Shit been going too far around here and I might have to put a stop to some of this madness."

"Kimi, your name is on this license but this is my center," she pointed her long nail in her face. "Ain't nobody can put a stop to this but me, and I'm just getting started. Please believe." She placed the sandwiches in the refrigerator. "You getting all built up because you don't want him to come, when you forgetting the main thing…and that's the fact that we getting paid."

"I know it's your center! But the Office of Child Care services says it's mine, and I take that shit very seriously."

"As well you should." Quita shot back. "Ain't nobody taking that from you."

"Good, because I need you to hear this and hear this good." She continued. "I was only approved to have eight people here at a time! And that was because my cousin Pooh was approved to help me out. What if they do a visit? We would be fucked."

"I don't want Pooh helping right now. She's too fucking grown."

"And I respect that...I'm just reminding you about our agreement, because it's obvious you've forgotten." She paused. "You have anybody over here you want, just as long as they drop a check off with their kids. What type shit is that?"

Quita was getting tired of her mouth, especially since Kimi was the one who begged to help her out after she went out on sick leave, because she wasn't getting her entire weekly check from FMLA (Family Medical Leave Act). Although Kimi never told anybody that Cash raped her, she did know being at work, and around Valencia, was the last place she wanted to be. She was with Quita everyday at the center and would be out before Valencia came home. It was the perfect plan, for the moment anyway.

After Kimi was licensed and ready to go, Quita felt confident that she had the daycare thing on lock. She didn't understand why people said running a daycare was so hard, when the money flowed so easily. In her opinion the only thing she could do without, was the process it took to get licensed. For instance, no one with a felony record was allowed to operate the daycare, and that included Quita. Then there was having to childproof the house, which irritated Valencia beyond belief because every socket had to be covered and baby gates had to be hoisted at the top of each stairway, even though they weren't allowed to go upstairs. But if she wanted to get that money, the home had to meet regulations. Valencia would huff and puff about the requirements, but as long as Quita was still watching her kids, she bit her tongue.

"Xtisha pays us $300.00 a week to watch Lil Goose's ass, Kimi! You can't be serious about not wanting him here. That's some good ass money. It's the reason we let him stay that one time to begin with!" Quita walked over to the fridge and grabbed an eraser off the top of it to wipe the whiteboard taped to the front. When she was done, she placed it back and wrote the names of the kids due that day, starting with Joshua.

"And he's coming too?" She leaned in closer. "I can't believe this shit! What is wrong with you?"

"I said the usual five, Kimi. So stop being melodramatic."

"Melodramatic?" She laughed sarcastically. "The kid shits on himself! I don't think he's ever used a toilet since he's been here. How is that melodramatic?"

"So we should turn him away because of that? We keep the ones no one wants remember? That's why we get the big bucks!"

"That's not what I'm saying, Quita. I know he has a problem. At least Joshua listens. Lil Goose is another story. If we aren't careful, he's gonna hurt somebody." She said seriously. "If you want me to continue to help you out, and let you use my name for this center, then you gotta make your decision. Me or the Goose."

"You just acting like that because for whatever reason, you hate kids! That shit don't have nothing to do with me, or what we doing here. I love kids and I love money more." Quita yelled. "That's probably why you can't have none! You too fucking hateful!"

Her words stung, even though she knew Quita had no idea about her life, and the fact that she abandoned a baby who later died. "That was wrong, but I'ma let that shit go because I know you being greedy right now. I told you how I feel about Lil Goose, the rest is up to you."

When Xtisha's white BMW truck pulled up in front of the house, Quita said, "If you want him gone, you tell her yourself. I'm not about to get into it with this chick."

Xtisha Daye and Barry aka Lil Goose, hopped out of the truck and strolled up to the house. Her long lanky body appeared to float, as if she was a ghost, up to the doorway. Her fingernails were so long and curly, that when she opened the screen door, she had to use her knuckles. They were painted in the colors of the rainbow, and matched her belt perfectly. She didn't leave the house a day without some splash of rainbow, although she claimed she wasn't gay.

"Hey, Quita!" Xtisha yelled, as the screen door slammed after they walked in. "I know I'm early but Lil Goose got kicked out of school again today. Girl, I wish they leave him alone! He just don't be interested in all that shit they be talking about in class. They need to make the activities more interesting, so he will pay attention, if you know what I mean." She knuckle scratched her head, which was littered in short tiny braids with no direction or purpose.

Quita looked at Kimi who was already shaking her head. They knew Xtisha's bullshit was coming there way in heavy dosages, so they buckled up. Lil Goose, a short fat kid who always wore a red baseball cap, over his eyes busied himself with the iTouch in his hands. He never left the house without it, along with the head buds that were stuffed in his ears. Quita made a mistake of taking them away from him last time, and he screamed so loud, her eardrum popped. The thing about him was, he had the innocent eyes of an angel. However, when you got to know him better, you'd soon realize he was as close to Satan as Damien from the movie, *"The Omen"*.

"We gotta talk," Quita said. She looked back at Kimi, "Well actually, Kimi has something to say to you. It's about Lil Goose. Go 'head...tell her."

Xtisha thought they were about to kick him out like every other daycare so she said, "Before you say anything I know I'm early." She popped the gum in her mouth loudly. "But the school be throwing him out over stupid ass shit, ya'll. That's why I'm really glad ya'll here now, because Evanka, and the rest of them dyke bitches down the street, be hating and don't want him to come back. If I don't have no day care, I'ma lose my job at the suicide prevention hotline. I need this work...I'm about to get a promotion and everything."

Quita looked at Kimi not believing she was held responsible for other people's lives and said, "Xtisha, we not gonna be able to let Lil Goose stay no more. It don't have nothing to do with him, it's just that we already over our limit and don't want our license taken away."

When Xtisha heard that, she smacked Lil Goose so hard, his eyes flew open in surprise. Quita and Kimi jumped back, due to the violence she displayed. They didn't see it coming. "What the fuck you did to them where they saying you can't stay here? Huh? I'm sick of people throwing you out! You gotta get it together, boy!"

When she pulled her hand back, her long nail knocked his cap off by mistake, revealing a scar which ran from the front, to the back of his head. It was shiny and long, and his hair appeared to avoid growing on top of it. They never saw his hat off and wondered what happened to the kid. Lil Goose looked at his mother, picked his hat up off the floor and said, "I'm sorry, ma. I'ma be better."

"Sorry ain't good enough! You 'bout to make me lose my good job!" She stomped her ashy foot, in her white thong sandal. The backs of her heels were so dry, they were white. "I been told you this shit gotta stop, Goose! You gonna be just like your damn father, dead on death row! You trying to send me to an early grave!"

"Xtisha, we didn't say he did anything to us," Kimi suddenly felt bad for the kid. Looking at Lil Goose she said, "Go downstairs to the Kiddie Club so we can talk to your mother." With his head down, he left the adults alone.

When he was gone Xtisha said, "I'm sorry ya'll, but I can't afford to take him nowhere else. This really is it for me. Beat his ass if he cuts up, I give you permission."

"I can't do that."

"But you gotta help me!"

"But he's been kicked out of six day cares," Kimi said. "And he doesn't get along with the other kids. If he's not hitting somebody, he's stealing somebody's food." She looked at Xtisha's hand. "As a matter of fact where is his lunch? You know we provide snacks and dinner for the kids who stay later, but lunch is your responsibility."

She looked surprised. "We told you that, Xtisha, so don't even fake like you don't know." Quita added.

"Oh my, God!" She said placing her claw fingers on her forehead before looking up to the ceiling. "You sure did tell me to bring his lunch. I be forgetting like shit."

"That's what I'm talking about. It's expensive to run a center, and we need you to purchase his lunch like you agreed, but you can't even do that." Kimi continued. "It's like you don't give a fuck! And what happened to his head?"

"He bust it open when he fell down the steps," she looked away and guilt spread across her face. "Look," she reached in her purse and grabbed six hundred dollars with her knuckles. "That's for two weeks." She handed it to Quita. "Please let him stay here, ya'll." She looked as if she were about to cry. "I ain't got no man to help me out, I'm a solo act. His father was injected years ago for murdering a cop, so understand I'm all alone. I need help. Please." She looked at Kimi and when her eyes told her she was uncompromising, she focused on

Quita. "Ya'll can't be believing Evanka and them up the street. That bitch think she better than everybody because everybody be bringing they kids to her and her mother. But they be lying on Lil Goose just because his father helped me out before the state killed him. Evanka is just jealous of a bitch that's all. She trapped the nigga Doo-Man in a pregnancy and she still tripping. I felt like killing her when she told somebody Goose not fit to be around animals but I don't pay that shit no mind. She wanted to put him out in a doghouse in the back of her house! My son is a good *chow*." They hated the way she made the word *child* sound like *chow*.

"We heard he does a lot of shit, but we talking about what he does here. Had we listened to them other chicks up the street, we would not have taken him the first time." Quita said. "I know they hating sometimes and want to get a bitch's center closed down. So that's not what this is about. It's about his behavior and what we see with our own eyes. We don't just watch kids here, we try to teach them too, but Goose don't be listening." Quita didn't like the idea of Kimi throwing him out, but she would lend her support.

Angry, she stomped her extra long feet again. "He does get along with other kids. That's what I'm trying to say! I'm telling ya'll they just jealous." She kept talking about other people, when it didn't have anything to do with the shit. "For one thing, one of them bitches who watched him tried to steal his iTouch and I caught her ass. She was about to steal from a chow! Who steals from a chow?" She looked back and forth at them. "And for two, they just jealous because Lil Goose stay fresh, while them other kids be looking a hot ass mess. But don't worry, Quita, he'll be fine here. I can already tell, he likes you. He likes both of you. Please ya'll?"

Quita was on the side of the money so Goose was fine in her book, but she knew she couldn't give the go ahead without Kimi. She hated that running a legal operation, forced her to rely on other people for decisions. Although she fronted the money for the bills necessary to run the day care, Kimi's name and good background were on the license, so in the law's eyes, that made her boss. She just wished she thought about the purpose first always…getting paper.

Lately Quita's attitude took a change for the worse because she was so greedy all she thought about was money. She barely saw Demetrius believing when she was with him, she would miss the night care appointments she provided for parents who were on the go and loved to club hop. Her personality was shining through in an ugly way, and she even shaved off the thirty percent profit that she was supposed to give to Kimi. She wanted all the money, all of the time, no matter what.

"It's not up to me," Quita said. "You have to talk to her." They both looked at Kimi and waited on her answer.

Kimi looked at Quita, folded her arms and looked at Xtisha. "I guess he'll be fine," she replied in a sarcastic tone. "But if he don't get better, you gotta come get him." Quita could tell she took pleasure in being the one who had the final say so.

"Thank you so much, girl!" She gave them both hugs, and one of her nails got caught in one of Quita's French braids. After working with Kimi to get herself separated from Xtisha's monster claw, she said, "I'm so sorry, Q." She put her hands behind her back, to prevent messing up anything else. "I really appreciate both of you though! Bye!"

Xtisha ran out and sped off before they changed their minds. Quita locked the door and said, "I appreciate it, Kimi. She got her shit with her, but she pays whatever you want her to and she don't buck. I know she work down at the Suicide Hotline, but I think she fuck with Stinky Micky from Southwest who sling and be pressed for rap."

"Whatever, Quita. I'm sure you do appreciate it." She paused. "I just wished you thought about the other kids instead of yourself."

"Kimi, every kid we take is bad. It ain't like he the lone ranger. That's what we do here! Handle the misfits."

"Yeah but he's worse and you know it! But you don't care do you?" She laughed. "I mean...how many more Gucci purses do you need? You got six! If we gonna do this we have to consider the children! It ain't all about the money!"

Quita grinned and shook her head. "What I buy with my money is my business." She didn't care if she had a problem with her purpose or not, she was serious about earning her paper.

"You right about that." She held out her hand. "Where's my cut?"

Quita peeled two hundred from the stack to give her the agreed upon thirty percent. She slapped the money in her hand and said, "Here. Take your measly money!"

Kimi was about to tuck it in her bra until Quita said, "Hold up, gimmie back twenty dollars. Your cut is only one eighty, remember? That's a little more than thirty percent, baby girl, so you owe me."

Kimi shook her head, reached in her pocket and handed her the money. "You are so fucking petty." Quita switched down the stairs and ignored everything else she had to say. She was changing for the worse, and people had better get out of her way. When they were in the Kiddie Club, they saw Lil Goose coming out of the bathroom, with a guilty look on his face. "What were you doing in there?" Kimi asked.

"Nothing!" he bopped his head to the music always playing in his ear. "Why?"

"Because we asked you that's why, little bad ass fucker!" Kimi yelled, in his face. "You too fucking grown! That's your problem!"

"Kimi, stop! He's a kid." Quita knew she was about to fuck with her money if she kept intimidating him. "Just chill out."

She rolled her eyes and Lil Goose said, "I don't like it here! I wanna go home!"

"Like somebody give a fuck!" Kimi continued.

"You don't know me, bitch!"

"Awww," Quita crooned, in a sympathetic tone, while bending down, placing her hands on her knees to address him face to face. "Don't worry, baby, she didn't mean to talk to you like that," she placed her hand gently on his arm. "There's nothing to be afraid of, you gonna have fun here. Just like last time."

"GET OUT MY FACE, BITCH!" He yelled. "Your breath smells like dick and you fat too! I hate fat girls!"

Quita looked down at his oval shaped body and frowned. "Not sure if you really got room to talk about nobody else, Goose. You look like you ain't missed a sandwich yourself."

Quita turned around and looked at Kimi who was behind her laughing to the point of tears. "Don't look at me...you wanted him, so there he is." She walked over to the Cot Room to get it prepared for the naps later. Quita rolled her eyes at her. "He won't make it a week."

"I'ma tell my mother you called me fat! And she gonna kick your ass!" She could hear the old rap group NWA blasting out of the headphones. "I don't wanna be here! I don't wanna stay in no funky ass daycare with you and that other old bitch! Just leave me alone 'fore I start punching people!" Quita saw there was something in his eyes that said he was scared. So she decided to shower him with kindness. Her mission was not to get him to like her, but to get him to believe that she liked him. And she would stick with her plan as long as the money flowed.

Fifteen minutes later, the rest of the misfits arrived. First on deck was seven-year-old Joshua, who kept a fresh patch of ringworms for his itching pleasure in his scalp and a sack of shit in his drawers for his ass. He whined so much, that after a while, people didn't hear him anymore because the noise blended in with everything else. He was a miserable child all the time and nobody knew why.

Then there was thirteen-month-old baby Axel, who cried so much, one day a fly flew into his mouth and almost choked him to death. Baby Axel hated human beings and he hated to be picked up, which was only discovered after he lured you to him with his eyes. He was so stunning, with his deep brown camel colored skin, his head full of curly hair and shiny brown eyes, that you wanted to hold him. The moment you did, he would cry so much that people couldn't wait to put him down...even if they had to throw him on the ground.

Then there was five-year-old Zaboy, who was extremely irritating. He asked for things because other people wanted it, hogged food that he'd later throw away and lied like no other. To make matters worse, Kimi nicknamed him Mr. Show Tunes, because he sang songs he learned from the Glee Club at his school, even if people didn't want to hear his irritating ballads. Zaboy also kept a case of strep throat or pink eye, which gave people another reason not to be around him.

When the doorbell rang, Quita went upstairs to answer it. When she opened the door, seven-year-old Miranda was standing outside with a dude she never seen before. "Hi, Miranda," Quita looked at the man and then back at her. "Who's this?"

In a low voice she said, "Uncle Charlie."

"Oh…Where's Uncle Dice who dropped you off last time."

"He's gone. This my new uncle for the hour."

Miranda walked into the house and the dude walked away. Born from a black mother and a white father, Miranda was often very quiet and extremely nosey. She was kicked out of the last day care center after discovering that the center's owner, was growing weed in her backyard, which resulted in her getting major time in prison. If something was going on, she was on the case and the chances of it getting solved were high.

Because of her sneakiness, nobody wanted the nosey girl roaming around their house, so for her mother Vonzella, Quita's spot was it. To top it all off, she was a fighter who would bite chunks out of your skin if you got in her way. The thing which most people didn't realize, was despite her violent nature, she had an above average intelligence. The school board said that she would be as close to a genius as a kid could get, if she could get her behavior under control.

"Where was your mother?" Quita asked, looking down at her. "Why she ain't drop you off?"

Miranda shrugged and fanned the air. "I guess she don't have to do anything, if she got uncles to do it for her." She took her long black ponytail, which fell down the middle of her back, and swept it over her shoulder.

They both walked downstairs and Quita helped Kimi prepare the Kiddie Club for learning time. Quita had her shit with her, but she was determined to teach the kids a few things along the way. It was a tribute to her mother, who always stressed the importance of an education.

When baby Axel started crying after being transported from his carrier to another side of the room, Kimi placed him in the crib as he screamed at the top of his lungs as if someone bit him. She thought about giving him something to cry about, but she left it alone. The children's irritation was evident, as they shifted their bodies and rolled their eyes at the screaming baby.

"He cries too much!" Lil Goose screamed.

"He's fine!" Joshua said, pointing at his forehead. The kid was straight weird. "Leave him alone."

Speaking loud to be heard over Axel's squalling, Kimi said, "Okay, today I'm going to read from Mother Goose and we'll pass the book around so everybody can have a chance to read the next chapter." Kimi held the book in her hand, and smiled. "Who's ever read this story before?"

"I can't understand nothing you saying!" Lil Goose screamed. "That baby need to shut the fuck up so I can hear!"

"Lil Goose, I'm tired of you talking sideways." Quita said. "Stop cursing like you grown because you not. Anyway, you got headphones on, how you know what you can hear anyway?" She was done with his ass for today and decided to start all over tomorrow.

"Whatever! You don't tell me what to do. Don't nobody tell me what to do." Miranda rolled her eyes at him. She hated him from the first time she met him and hoped it would be the last. She now saw it was not.

When Axel settled down to catch his breath, before screaming round number two began, Zaboy stood up in front of everybody and said, "Can I sing my song, Ms. Quita? You said I can sing after the baby stopped crying. I'm ready for my show!" He looked at Valencia and said, "What you call me that one time, Ms. Valencia?"

He had no idea the name she tagged him with was not meant as a compliment, but an insult. "Mr. Show Tunes." She rolled her eyes.

He grinned and said, "Mr. show Tunes reporting for duty!" He gave a salute and they couldn't help but to glance at his hard light brown leather shoes that were laced so tightly, they looked like somebody tried to pull him up by his shoe strings.

When Quita made that promise, it was when she was sure the baby would never stop crying. But since she was certain Axel cried all the way over to the center, she figured he was tired and needed a break. Quita looked at Zaboy standing before them in a hideous pair of dark blue corduroy pants, despite it being hot outside, and his sandy dirty brown Mohawk and felt sympathy for him. So she said, "Go 'head, Zaboy. But don't sing too long. We have to start our lessons."

"Man, I don't want to hear him! He sound dumb." Lil Goose said.

"Well nobody asked you now did they?" Quita responded, as she focused back on Mr. Show Tunes. "Go 'head, Zaboy."

He hopped out of the yellow chair. With his arms raised high and in the most horrible voice a child could have he sang the Annie classic, *"The sun will come out, tomorrow, bet your bottom dollar that tomorrow! They'll be sun. Tomorrow...tomorrow...I'll love you...tomorrow. You're only a day away!"*

Miranda shifted in her seat and rolled her eyes. While Goose just flat out said, "Man, fuck this nigga! My ears hurt! Make him stop!"

"Mine too!" Joshua whined as he walked in the Silent Corner, as if he were on punishment. It was his favorite place in the center, because he could be alone. "My head hurts when he screamed that loudly."

When Quita saw Joshua's face distort, and his fists ball up, she knew exactly what he was about to do. Take a dump on himself. "Oh no you don't! I'm not fucking with your funky ass right now. I don't have time for all of this shit!" She walked over to him and gripped him by the wrist, pulling him in her direction. "You not gonna shit in your clothes today. Let's go to the bathroom."

The kids burst out in laughter, and for the moment, Quita felt badly for doing it in front of them. But it was better to catch him early then to smell him for hours later. When she opened the door, and saw the condition Valencia's bathroom was in, she wanted to faint. The soft pink toilet cushion was ripped off and thrown in the bathtub and the word 'BITCH' was written using a red magic marker on the carpet, walls and the sink. "Joshua, go upstairs and use the bathroom on the first level." She said in a low voice as she examined the damage.

"But I don't think I can make it," he whined. "Plus Ms. Valencia told me if I ever took my funky ass upstairs again, she'd kill me."

"Go up there anyway!" She pointed. When he left she yelled, "Lil Goose, get in here right now!" Ten seconds later Lil Goose strolled into the bathroom bopping his head to the song, *'Fuck Da Police'*. He leaned against the sink and grinned. When he saw how mad she was about the damage he caused, he laughed uncontrollably. "Why did you do this?"

"Because I can." He bopped his head to the music harder. "Anything else?"

"I want you out of here!"

He wasn't grinning anymore and it was evident, that for the moment anyway, the rejection hurt his feelings. He stood up straight and said, "Okay, let me call my mother. Maybe she can come get me and find me another day care lady. But she'll want her money back too."

Quita already spent the money in her mind, so she said, "I didn't tell you to get out of the house. I meant go back to the Kiddie Club." When he left, she spent twenty minutes trying to get the bathroom together but she knew Valencia would still flip. She would use her money to make the repairs but charge Xtisha for it later. He was getting on her utmost nerves.

When she walked back into the Kiddie Club, Kimi saw the irritation on her face. She walked up to her and said, "You see how much greed costs?" She paused. "I told you he shouldn't be here but I guess you want money more than anything else don't you? The boy needs help we can't give him here and having him around will cost you more and more each day. Eventually you'll see," Quita looked at Lil Goose and Kimi continued to talk in her ear. "Mark my words."

Quita shook her head and they both walked back to the Kiddie Club. By now Stone and Jensen were home and had joined the crowd. When the phone rang, Quita answered and it was Charlene's voice on the other end of the line. She'd been avoiding her ever since she learned she was HIV positive and now it was time to deal with her. Quita picked up and said, "Give me one second, Charlene."

"No problem. Thanks for answering the phone."

Placing her hand over the handset she said, "Kimi, I have to take this call. It's Charlene. I'll be over here if you need me."

Kimi didn't know Charlene and had never seen her before, despite the fact that she'd gone to the same doctor's office she worked at for years. But she did know Quita felt bad for her illness and cared a lot about her so she said, "Hurry up. We 'bout to start learning time." She could have given her a harder time, since she kept saying it was her center, but she let it slide.

Stepping away she continued to cover the handset, took a few deep breaths and said, "I'm sorry about that girl. I have a whole lot going on over here." She continued, as if Charlene wasn't HIV positive, pregnant by her husband's father and miserable.

"I understand…I'm just glad you answered the phone."

"I been meaning to call you. Sorry I haven't gotten around to it yet."

"Quita, why won't you talk to me?" She paused. "I feel like you're hiding from me and we've always been such good friends. Maybe not as close as you, Valencia and Kimi, but close all the same."

"It's not even like that."

"Good...because I have to discuss something with you that's very important."

"Okay...I'm kind of busy right now with my new day care center, you think it can wait until later?"

"No...it can't."

The phone shook in her hand, as she tried her hardest to be strong for her friend. But what could you tell a person, who in Quita's opinion, would soon die from an illness. She didn't take into consideration that people lived for years with the disease, when they took their cocktails. "I got a few minutes now, are you okay?"

"Not really." She said in a low voice. "I do know I'm tired of crying though. I just want to be strong for my family right now and do the right thing. But I need your help."

"You got that," she said softly. "How's Flex handling everything?"

"He still doesn't know about the rape, the illness or my pregnancy." She laughed akwardly. "You know, I always had the hardest time getting pregnant and when I wasn't even trying, it finally worked. God has jokes doesn't he?"

"I'm sorry."

"Don't be. Please...I'm sorry enough for everybody."

"Don't you think you should tell Flex?" She paused, looking at Axel who was crying so hard now, his face was red. "So you won't infect him?"

"I haven't slept with him since I was raped." She paused and took a deep breath. "Quita...I really need you to come over here. I need to talk to you about something that must be done in private. I wouldn't hit you with this, if it weren't serious. Please."

"I think I can work something out," she smiled, in the hopes that Charlene would think she really wanted to be there for her. "Maybe I'll come over next week."

"It has to be today."

If Quita wanted, she could have made arrangements with Kimi, left a few hours early, and came back just in time to serve snacks. But who wanted to hang around someone who would probably cry, whine and be sad about the condition of their life? Not Quita, especially when there was money at stake. "I can't really come today, Charlene. Maybe tomorrow?"

"I really need you to be there for me. Please."

"I'm really sorry, Charlene. But I can't do it today. I wish I could."

Silence.

"I'll get in contact with you later tonight or maybe tomorrow." Charlene continued. "Don't be scared when I do, just do what I ask you. Okay?"

"Okay." She promised, eager to get the call over with.

"Do you promise me, Quita? Do you give me your word?"

"Of course!"

"I'll talk to you later." She paused. "I love you."

"Bye."

Quita ended the call happy she'd spoken to her and hopeful that she wouldn't hear from her for at least another few months. Charlene hated to be a bother, so she was positive she would not reach out again until she felt Quita was ready to talk.

When the kids got rowdy again, to keep them busy, Quita poured a bucket of colorful wooden blocks on the floor, so they could work on their colors and shapes. The kids dove in to grab a few with the exception of Miranda. She was uninterested in such childish matters.

When Zaboy reached for the same blue block as Goose, Zaboy snatched it so fast he scratched his hand. Lil Goose frowned and said, "Nigga, that was my shit! And you hurt my hand! Fuck wrong with you?"

Zaboy's eyes widened. He pointed his irregularly long finger in his face and said, "My mama said you can't curse in front of me. My mama said my ears are for God's purposes only. And that if some- body cursed at me I should tell her."

"And you a snitch too!" Goose ranted. "Suck my dick, gay boy!" Goose's words were so harsh, that Zaboy didn't have a come back. He wasn't use to kids acting like that around him because his mother spoiled him rotten and kept him sheltered. "I don't give a fuck about your mother! My mother will kill yours!"

"Goose, stop acting like you don't have no home training!" Quita yelled. He rolled his eyes but remained silent for the moment. She was already mad about Valencia's Smoke House, and didn't have room for any more of his shit. She was certain that the moment Va- lencia saw that bathroom, she would lose it and threaten to close down the operation. She would have to grease her palms majorly after this one.

In an attempt to regain order, Quita grabbed one of the blocks and said, "Calm down, kids!" they did a little. "Now everybody sit down." When they were settled she said, "Good...now who can tell me what color is this?"

Trying to steal all of the attention as usual, Zaboy jumped up and sang in a voice similar to a cat being hit by a car. "Bluuuueeee."

Quita and Kimi frowned and said, "You're right. But keep your voice down before the baby starts back..."

Right as the words exited her mouth, Axel started screaming at the top of his lungs again. Everybody looked at him, the kids included and shook their heads. "I'll get him." Quita said, rolling her eyes at Zaboy. The first peace they had for the evening and he ruined it. "I told you to keep your voice down."

"I'm sorry, Ms. Quita." When she took him out of the crib and he continued to howl, she made a promise to never have children of her own.

"Ms. Quita, where is Joshua?" Miranda asked, stuffing her ears with her fingertips.

Kimi's eyes widened. "You betta go check on him, Quita. You know how Valencia feels about the kids being upstairs in her house."

"I'll go check." Miranda offered, popping up. A weird smile spread across her face. "You have the baby."

Not wanting to walk upstairs anyway she said, "Okay. You can go find him but hurry up. I don't want to come looking for you both."

She smiled and said, "No problem."

After about fifteen minutes, Joshua walked back into the center funkier than ever and without Miranda. "Where is Miranda?" Quita asked, trying to rock the baby to sleep who was having none of it. "I thought she went upstairs to get you."

"I don't know." He shrugged, holding his hands behind his back.

"Well did you use the bathroom?"

"Kinda."

The moment he said that, a strong odor of shit knocked her in the face. The kids held their noses and yelled all kinds of obscenities at him. "Joshua, why didn't you use the bathroom on the toilet like I asked? What were you doing up there for so long?"

"When I left the bathroom down here, it was too late, so I went in my drawers." He held his head down. "I'm sorry."

"Did your mother bring you a change of clothes?" Quita continued, trying to hide her anger. He nodded. "Well go wash up and change in the bathroom upstairs." When he didn't move she yelled, "Go! Now. I'm tired of smelling your ass, Josh! Damn I wish you stop doing this shit! You too old to be using the bathroom on yourself."

"I'm sorry." He repeated.

"Don't keep saying that shit if you don't mean it."

Right before he made it up the stairs, Miranda came back down and said, "There's a man in the house, Ms. Quita. He's got a gun and he's asking for you."

ON CLOUD NINE

"Did you get my food?" Valencia asked Kimi, as she propped her legs up on the counter, crossed them, and polished her nails. "You been gone to lunch for over forty minutes." Now that she was boss, she carried shit like she was a star. The doctor's office was in total disarray, appointments weren't put on the books, people waited for hours and uncensored rap music blared from the CD player as if they were in a concert. Some people weren't fit to be bosses and Valencia was one of them.

"Yes. What you think took me so long?" Kimi sighed, rolling her eyes. She had to beg to come back to be placed on the schedule because she found it too hard to work with the children. Valencia was doing her best to make her grovel. "You asked for six chicken wings with extra mumbo sauce and fries right?" She sat the bag on the counter. "So there it is."

"Yep," Valencia asserted, never taking her eyes off of her hot red nails before blowing them. "Fried hard though. You did remember that didn't you?"

"No because you ain't say that shit," Kimi paused. "But I did get everything else you asked for so if you want them fried hard, put them shits in the microwave and burn them," she continued walking away. "I'm done being your runner for the day."

Terry held her stomach and said, "She got your ass right there."

Valencia stood up, pointed at her and said, "Get back to work before I fire you." She threatened people with termination so much, nobody cared anymore. Walking up to Kimi she said, "Are you okay, missy? Cause for months you been acting like you got four dicks up your ass. I mean you been gone for three months...what's wrong now?"

"Let's talk about what this is really about, Valencia. You mad because I been helping Quita for three months and already got a new car outside." She placed her hands on her hips and walked closer to her. "You also probably mad because as long as my name on that license, whether I work here or not, I'm gonna stay paid in full."

"Why the fuck should I be mad about that? Who house do you think it is? She watching my kids for free. So I'm good over here with the arrangements. "

"Yeah…okay." Kimi smirked, walking to the file cabinet. "You can think you have that much control if you want to. You and me both know that at this point, Quita gonna do what she wants at that center and in your house."

Valencia really did think Quita's daycare idea was brilliant. Why would she not? She would be saving over seven hundred dollars a month in childcare expenses and she could still do what she wanted at night if Quita was at home. All the extra meals stopped and Quita didn't allow her to boss her around like she use to, but so what? It was a win-win situation for everybody. Stone and Jensen were happy, healthy and cared for. It was the first time Valencia allowed Quita to do something constructive for herself, provided she got more out of the deal.

Letting the day care run out of her home was her idea of taking the psychic's advice and being good to Quita. The moment the idea was presented, Valencia cleared out her basement, helped Quita make it bright and colorful and kicked back to reap the benefits as she drove off the lot in her new used candy apple red Range Rover. Which was courtesy of the three thousand dollar deposit Quita gave her. Although the agreement didn't call for her getting any more money, just as long as she watched the twins, all would be cool.

Everything was looking rosy for Valencia to hear her tell it. Tech was back in the picture, although sporadic, she had a live in sitter and she finally got the job she always wanted. Although she saw another psychic on a regular basis, and ignored her suggestions to dump Tech for good, she was positive as long as she stayed in charge, things would work out to her advantage.

"Oh but I'm serious, honey." Valencia added. "Why should I be jealous of you getting your little coins when your center, as you practically put it, is in my house?" She looked her up and down. "Please tell me this, because I'm not understanding why I'm not benefit. This shit is lovely if you ask me."

"You're probably right, V. You shouldn't be mad," she said taking a deep breath. "After all, you not taking care of your own kids." The patients tuned into their conversation hoping to take some real juicy information to the hood to gossip about. "Matta of fact, I heard Stone and Jensen call Quita their real mama the other day." She giggled in her face. "You shouldn't have even been allowed to have kids, bitch! You don't know what to do with them."

In a low voice one of the patients said, *"That's a shame she don't take care of her own kids."* She shook her head.

Valencia was so embarrassed, her face was hot to the touch. "First off how you gonna tell me about kids when you can't have them?"

"You don't know what I can have."

"Yes I do!"

"When you raise your own kids, holla at me. Until then, get the fuck out of my face."

"What?!" She yelled moving closer to Kimi. "What the fuck did you just say to me? That I'm not a good mother? You got me all the way fucked up if you think that."

Kimi took two steps to her and repeated every word she said, "What I'm saying is clear...you shouldn't be allowed to have kids...bitch."

As the patients and her co-workers braced themselves for a good verbal beat down or if they were lucky, a fight, Valencia thought of what to come back with next. Everybody loved drama in the office and today was no exception.

Before Valencia could tear into her or think of a reason to fire her, Brooke Carmichael walked into the office causing all eyes to move toward her. Her bronze hair color was identical to Beyonce's and appeared to float as she moved. Her make-up was on point and she looked like she was ready for a video shoot instead of a doctor's appointment. "I have an appointment today," Brooke said giving Valencia a sly smile. "My name should be on the books. Do your job and check it for me, sweetie."

"Well let me see," Valencia responded with a snotty attitude. "Sometimes you patients get things mixed up and we have to put you in your place." She sat down at the computer and said, "Your name please?"

Brooke giggled, flung her hair again and said, "Yeah right, like you could ever forget my name, or my face. Let the record show that you think of my ass every day you wake up and every night you go to sleep. So stop wasting my time and check my shit."

Valencia's brow creased and she, through stiff lips said, "Either give me your name, or get the fuck out."

"Are you okay, Miss Valencia? You seem out of sorts."

"I'm better than okay, I'm perfect!" She shot back, giving off much attitude. "You're the one who's here to see the doctor, not me. You sure that fishy pussy of yours ain't in trouble?"

Valencia couldn't stand her and Brooke knew it. She was the main reason she had so many problems in her relationship, or lack their of, with Tech. High school sweethearts when they were younger, she would come in and out of his life, just so he wouldn't fall too deep in love with another. And Valencia could always tell when she was in the picture because he'd be gone for weeks at a time and would not answer her calls. Valencia was surprised she was even in town now, since she attended law school, in Florida and it demanded a lot of her time.

"Well trust me when I say I'm just here for a check up. The pussy is sweeter and never been better." She swung her hair and a few strands stuck to Valencia's red glossed lips. She angrily wiped it off, smearing it over her face. "You on the other hand should get that belly button cleaned, since I hear it smells…like…shit." Everyone laughed, Kimi included.

Humiliation squeezed her chest. "You don't know shit about me."

"I know more than you think," she placed her three thousand dollar monogram Versace bag on the counter as her diamond studded engagement finger glistened under the light. Who she was engaged to was beyond Valencia but she thought the worst. "Me and Tech are really good friends."

Upon hearing his name tears rolled out of Valencia's eyes and Brooke loved every minute of it. "Go sit down, I'll let the doctor know you're here."

"Sure," she grabbed her bag and said, "And Valencia, tell Tech I'll call him later about what he asked me. He says the cutest little things when I talk to him on the phone."

Her teeth clenched. "Why so you can ruin my relationship again?"

She stepped back, leaned in and said, "How can I ruin your relationship, when you don't have one?"

"Fuck you!" she yelled, spit escaping her lips and falling to the counter. "You been jealous of our relationship for the longest!"

"You wish you, rusty ass bitch," she walked away, took her seat and crossed her legs. Everyone was, "Ooooing" and "Awwing" in the background.

If I ever catch her on the street, she dead!" Valencia thought. Turning around, she decided to take her frustrations out on Kimi since Brooke got the best of her. "Back to you, if you ever talk to me like that again in this office, you will be fired. And trust me, I can make that happen. Or have you forgotten that I am your manager? A.K.A your boss!"

Her cheekbones rose as she smiled brightly. "Don't get mad at me because Brooke carried the ut-most fuck out of your ass."

"I'm not thinking about that tired bitch. This is business."

"Oh is it, Valencia," Kimi laughed, as her co-workers giggled. "Or is it that once again, somebody has reminded you that Tech was never yours to begin with?"

"Kimi, you have been wanting to be me since the first day I met you." She paused, as she appraised her with her eyes. "Keep it real. It's okay, boo boo."

With no teeth, just a smile she responded, "Actually, sweetheart," Kimi stepped closer. "You don't have anything I want, this job included."

"You sure about that? Because I know it burns you up to no end that Quita cares more about me than she ever could about you."

She was right but Kimi refused to let her know it. "Quita will find out who you are before long and I won't have to say shit else."

"Are you sure? She didn't believe your little lie about why she got fired."

"It's cool though." She winked. "Because I have every confidence that it will happen." She paused. "You a sneaky, evil, bitch and now that you got this little promotion, you've really let your true colors shine. That's probably why Tech's fine ass don't want to be bothered. And you know what," she giggled. She grabbed the bag off the counter. "You can take this food," she dumped it out of the bag and poured it onto the floor, "And shove it up your ass because I quit, you bum ass, bitch!"

SLIGHTED

Quita had a lot on her mind and didn't feel like dealing with Xtisha as she approached the door to pick up Lil Goose. Kimi had proven to be right about the situation all along and Quita wished she never agreed to keep him when she first asked. Besides, after losing someone she considered a close friend, to suicide, her patience grew slightly shorter.

A month earlier, the cops showed up at the door, to tell her that Charlene committed suicide after she talked to her. And in the letter she wrote she mentioned her name. The officer didn't tell her exactly what she said, out of respect for the family. They just wanted to know if she had any information on what would make her take her own life and leave her family behind. Reluctantly she let them know about her HIV status and the rape and they left the house on a mission. If only she had been there for her when she asked. The guilt stabbed at her and she often drank to get Charlene's voice, begging her to come over, out of her mind.

At first Quita was relieved to see that the man in the living room was a cop, since Miranda told her whoever was there had a gun until she found out the purpose. She knew it looked bad that she didn't go to the funeral but she needed to stay busy to keep her mind off of life's drama. Right now her focus was money and her mother, in that order. Her daycare center was sought after, so dealing with Lil Goose and Xtisha's extreme lateness wasn't a priority anymore.

The daycare center was closing for the day but the night care center was opening and Quita was ready for Xtisha to take Lil Goose and get out of the house. She didn't want him coming any longer, neither of them were worth it. Besides, she earned so much money that her client list was always full.

When Xtisha opened the screen door with her knuckles and slid inside, she saw the look on Quita's face. Making assumptions as usual, that she knew what the problem was, she said, "I'm telling you I packed Lil Goose's lunch this time, Quita!" Quita remained quiet and walked into the living room. Xtisha was right on her heels. "It was in his book bag so if you don't have it somebody stole that shit. For real!"

Quita looked at her extra large feet, her curly ass nails and the ridiculous short-tiny braids on her head. She was irritated all over again. "Xtisha, I have a few things to talk to you about. In terms of the lunch, if it was here then where did it go? I didn't even open my mouth about that, yet you knew one of the things I wanted to rap to you about was his food. I mean you bought the boy an iTouch to listen to music on, the least you can do is pack his lunch. Music not gonna feed him and he's a thief."

"My son ain't no thief!"

"Trust me when I tell you he is!" She paused. "He had dinner and lunch on me and I'm sick of pitching in. I'm not his father."

Xtisha leaned up against the wall and looked at the ceiling. Then she ran the palm of her hand over her hair and said, "I know you don't believe me because of the past, but I'm telling you the truth this time."

When Quita saw another parent coming to the door to drop off a child she said, "Can you go sit on the couch? I gotta talk to this parent right quick." Xtisha marched to the sofa and picked up a magazine with her knuckles.

Quita walked over to the screen door and opened it so Wondrika could walk in with her son Joshua. Wondrika was short and dark skin. She always shaved her head bald and it appeared to have a shiny glow. It was rumored that she was actually a man but since she apparently gave birth to Joshua, no one could be sure. "Hey, girl!" Wondrika yelled entering the house. "I love your shoes! They are so fucking cute!" Whenever Wondrika was confronted she would talk about how nice a person shoes were, even if they weren't wearing any.

Quita looked down at her bare feet, wiggled her toes and said, "I don't have on shoes, Wondrika. So what the fuck are you talking about?"

The smile on her face turned downwards. "Well your toenails are real cute. Real fly! At first I thought they were shoes."

"Wondrika, your check bounced and the money order you gave me the other day to cover it was no good either. If you can't pay the vig, you gotta watch your own kid. You know my rules. I'm serious about my money!" She could smell the fart easing out of Joshua's ass and said, "Go downstairs, Joshua."

"Are other kids down there?" Joshua asked. "I mean Zaboy?"

"Naw...Lil Goose down there though," When he walked away she said, "Why does he keep using the bathroom on himself? It don't make any sense. Did you take him to get some help?"

"That boy don't need no help. He just need to be smacked when he acts like that and you have my permission to do it." Quita shook her head at her trifling attitude toward her son. "Don't worry, I'm working with him really good and it'll stop in a little while."

Quita didn't like her response but she refocused on the purpose at hand, her money. "Quita, I'm really sorry about the bounced checks. I don't know what's happening. The money be in there when I give it to you. You got to deposit it right away."

"What's happening is I'm not being paid."

Wondrika rubbed her baldhead and said, "Let me give you cash." She reached in her bra and pulled out some money from up under her little bitty breasts. "That's five hundred for the bounced check and money order," Quita took the damp money from her hands and stuffed it in her pocket, "and I'll pay you two hundred and fifty dollars tomorrow. I need a sitter though...so you can't do this for me now?"

Quita's jaws were so tight, it felt like her teeth would crack. "Wondrika, if you don't have my money, he can't come back."

"I know, girl. That's why you gonna have your money. But I gotta go right now, I'm late for work. I'ma holla at you later." Wondrika rushed out before she could change her mind. The parents were getting on her last nerves.

Quita walked over to talk to Xtisha again. She was growing irritated. She smelled shit all day, listened to angry kids yell in her face, bought pampers for babies she didn't give birth to, because their mothers didn't bring enough, and yet they consistently broke the rules. Things were gonna have to change.

"Before you say anything, Quita, I'ma bring his lunch next week when I drop him off. I understand ya'll don't have time to be paying for his food. I promise, I will bring Lil Goose's lunch from now on. You won't have that problem anymore from me."

When Quita saw Lil Goose come upstairs she said, "Go get your things so you can go home. I have to talk to your mother for a few more minutes. My assistant, Essence can help you down there."

Lil Goose stomped back down the stairs because he hated when Quita told him what to do. Not only was Xtisha notorious for not bringing his lunch but she was also world renown for being up to five hours late ninety percent of the time. It was getting to the point that although they closed at six o'clock pm, on the nights she didn't provide evening care, she would have to stay behind to watch Lil Goose anyway.

"Xtisha, you really have to start picking up Lil Goose on time. I'm tired of your excuses and the money isn't worth it anymore."

"I'm doing the best I can, Quita, *dang*! Them people about to fire me on my job! And if I don't stay over a little bit when they need me, I'm gonna be unemployed. You don't know how that is because you run your own business! Them white people don't be playing with me!"

"I understand, Xtisha, but it's not fair to us when you come late. I mean look at what time it is now. You're the reason I started providing overnight care to begin with. I figured I'm here anyway, I might as well earn some cash in the process."

Xtisha glanced at her watch, saw it was six fifty-eight, took a deep breath and said, "I'll try to get here on time, Quita. That's all I can tell you right now."

"Trying and doing is two different things," Quita advised. "If you can't get here on time we're not gonna be able to let Lil Goose come no more. Unlike the last time, there's not gonna be any appeals from Kimi because my word will be final. Get here on time, bring his lunch, or you on your own. We clear?" Xtisha looked at her in a conniving way and laughed. "What's funny?"

"You."

"And why am I humorous?" Quita inquired. The moment she asked that, Kimi appeared in the doorway. Quita and Kimi already discussed Xtisha and she was there to see how things were going. Ever since she quit the doctor's office, she was on full time duty at the center. At first she bucked the system but after she realized she was truly earning more money than she ever had in her life, she started to understand the error of her ways. The day care center was a gold mine, so she needed to pitch in.

"Is everything okay?" Kimi asked, placing her purse on the table by the sofa. She was asking Quita but looking at Xtisha. "It feels kind of tense in here."

"Everything is fine," Xtisha responded. "But I wonder if the Office of Child Care services know how many kids ya'll got in this daycare? My friend said she saw your listing on Maryland's site and ya'll only qualified for eight. Including my chow, it seems like ya'll be having about twenty up in here at any given time. Now if I add the high ass fees you charge us by the week, you gotta be making at least twenty thousand dollars or more a month. How much are your taxes?"

"Are you threatening us?" Kimi asked. "If you are you can take Lil Goose's fat ass somewhere else! I don't care who you call cause we not tripping! It don't make us no nevermind, we don't give a fuck no more."

Xtisha looked at them and realized she'd gone too far. If they didn't watch her kid, no one would. He had a rep on the streets as being a monster. "I'm just messin' with ya'll dang!" she chuckled hoping they'd laugh too. When they didn't she said, "I'll try and be on time okay? So stop being so serious. At least my checks cash unlike Wondrika's man looking ass."

"Xtisha, either come on time, or keep your son at home. All that other shit you spitting is mute." Quita responded. "*Trying* to be on time not gonna fly with us anymore. The next time you late, you're gonna keep your own kid for good. Now before you leave, where are my late charges for the past week?"

She reached in her purse, handed her the money and with her eyes glued on her, she yelled, "Goose! Come on! It's time to go home." Lil Goose came running up the stairs, bopping his head to the music. "Later, ya'll." She looked at them both. "I'll see you next week."

When she walked out the door Kimi asked, "Who you got for evening care?"

"Right now it's just Joshua. Essence down there with him though."

"Anybody else coming? That you need help with? I can stay if you need me."

"We good. No last minute appointments right now."

They walked toward the kitchen. "I'm telling you I don't like that shit Xtisha just said." Kimi said, shaking her head. She never missed an opportunity to bash Xtisha. "We gotta watch her because she gonna be trouble."

"You telling me something I already know." Quita responded while walking to the refrigerator to get a Coke. "I planned to tell her to keep his ass home, but now I don't think it's a good time. She trying to get a bitch late!"

"Well we can't keep watching him either. Valencia went the fuck off on you when she saw her bathroom downstairs after he vandalized it. She not gonna keep letting him destroy her property. And Xtisha may have given you the money, but I don't feel like her talking to us like we kids just because this is her house."

"You think we should close down? Maybe open up some place else?" Quita sat on the stool next to the sink and when she crossed her legs, the soles of her feet were black.

"For what? Because she saying dumb shit?" Kimi was becoming more comfortable with the idea of doing whatever they needed to keep the business running. "I don't think we should close, we just gotta get rid of him. For now we good and don't have to worry about her reporting us because she don't have no where else to take him."

"But what if she do something else sneaky? Outside of telling OCC? Like some real slick shit? You gotta watch bitches like her."

"What else could she do? She needs somebody to watch his bad ass! That's what I'm trying to say."

"I guess so." Quita sighed. "I don't know if you heard but OCC making Valencia get a background check again. Somebody reported she had a record and be smoking around the kids. Even though she doesn't operate the center, it's still her house. I'm trying to think who the fuck would say something like that?"

"I think Brooke and Evanka had something to do with it. You know she had words with Brooke at the doctor's office the day I quit. They probably on some get back shit now. But if she come back dirty, since this her place, we assed out, Quita. We got to come up with a backup plan now."

"Maybe we gotta close for a few weeks." She sighed. "I wanted to pay my mother's nursing home up for a year. If this bitch slow me down, I might be liable to kill her."

"You ain't the only one." She paused. "I didn't give up my job for you, but I don't have a job now all the same. So if you think something gonna happen, I say we make moves now, so we can be ready. This my only source of income and I don't wanna go back to working for nobody else. Bitches is too caddy."

Quita grinned, nodding her head in approval. "Finally my girl is with me!" She clapped. "Now this the mothafuckin' Kimi I know!"

"I'm serious! I hate kids, but I love money. So we gotta do what we gotta do to make this shit work.

"So what's your plan?" Quita inquired.

"On the low, I say we be scouting for another place. When we get it, we set it up like our center here and open for business without telling the parents we don't want to be bothered with. And that includes Valencia."

"Valencia?" Quita frowned. "Why we can't tell her?"

"You still don't get it! That bitch is shiesty! After all this time you still can't see it? Open your eyes and look, girl!"

"Kimi, it's not about that. If I take the operation out of her house, what about Stone and Jensen? I'm responsible for them right now. They got appointments set up for the next six months and everything. And Jensen may have to wear glasses because she keeps bumping into walls. I need to take them to the doctors."

Kimi shook her head. "Listen at you. Them not even your kids, Quita. Those are Valencia's children not yours. You so busy with them, you don't even see the boy Demetrius anymore and he really care about you."

"He still around."

"For now," Kimi paused. "You gonna lose him unless you get some act right up in you."

"But the twins." Quita shook her head. "I can't do them like that."

"What about the twins? She'll have to find another sitter. She use to have Evanka watching them, until she found out Evanka's boyfriend and Brooke was cousins. She'll find somebody else, trust me. Either way don't lose no sleep, you not responsible."

Quita thought about what she said and she knew she was right. It was just a matter of time before they shut the center down and the twins were not hers. "You right." She sighed. "It's about my money and its time to make power moves. But if we do this, we can't make it legal. No paperwork, no advertising, no tracks leading back to us. And I'm the boss of the new spot. Your cut will still be thirty percent, nothing more and nothing less. Can you deal with it?"

Kimi laughed. "I don't have a problem with any thing you said, just as long as you give me *all* of my money owed. Don't think I don't know about all the cash you got coming up in here that never sees my palms. I didn't say nothing at first because you were doing most of the work, but all that's about to change. I'm full time too and I want my money to be right just like the next bitch."

Quita grinned and said, "You got it." She extended her hand and Kimi shook it. "Deal."

When the phone rang, Kimi walked over to answer it. But when she saw Psychic Advisor on the caller ID, her eyes bulged. She picked the cream handset up and said, "Hello?"

"Yes, is Valencia available?"

She looked at Quita. "No she isn't but can I take a message?" ·

"Yes, if you can tell her I won't be able to keep our appointment this evening, that'll be greatly appreciated. There was an emergency in my family and I'm leaving the office now." She paused. "Thank you for your time. Have a good day."

Kimi got off the phone and sat at the kitchen table. "Well?" Quita said, as she scanned her for a clue as to what information had stolen her interest. "You looking all wild eyed and shit. What happened?" She grabbed her soda, got up from the stool and sat at the table with Kimi.

"Girl...do you remember a while back, when Valencia said something about a friend going to see a psychic?" Quita nodded, yes. "Well that was the psychic on the phone just now. She was calling to reschedule an appointment with Valencia."

"Get the fuck out of here!" She slammed her hand down on the table and her drink moved a few inches.

"Dead serious! What the fuck is wrong with her? Don't no black person go to no fucking psychic! Valencia in this bitch lunching now! That girl needs help! Tech got her straight tripping!"

"Leave it to her to be the first black bitch!" They continued to laugh at Valencia's expense, until she walked into the kitchen.

Quita and Kimi were so quiet that it was obvious they were talking about her. "When I walked up the steps, I heard ya'll laughing, like you were watching a movie and now that I'm here, ya'll not saying shit. So what's so funny?"

"How come you always want to be put in on the joke?" Kimi asked. "If we wanted you to know we would have told you. We grown ass women over here."

"You know what, I'm not gonna even go there with you." Valencia grabbed a beer from the refrigerator. "This my house and I don't have to deal with your shit."

Kimi sighed. "People who always have to tell people they the boss, or they own this and that, are really trying to prove it to themselves. If this your house, live in it, don't make no announcements to me."

Valencia was growing heated and it bothered her that Quita didn't come to her defense. "You know what I notice, whenever you're with Kimi, you act differently. You never take up for me. That's fucked up and don't think I'm not taking note."

"Not true, but I'm not gonna argue with you about it either." Quita responded. "Anyway you a grown woman. Why I gotta come to your rescue?"

"Where are the twins?" Valencia asked with an attitude.

"They upstairs taking a nap," Quita couldn't look at her because the psychic thing was still funny to her. "You may want to wake them up though because they gonna be up all night, if you don't."

Kimi snickered in the background. "What's so funny, Kimi?" Valencia asked. "I told you I don't want you in my house unless it's for business anyway. So what are you doing here?"

"What do you think I'm doing here?" Kimi snapped back. "We have night clients and Essence is downstairs with one of them now."

"So what's so fucking funny then? If you scared to tell me bitch just say it. You laugh more than a fucking clown."

Kimi wiped the smile off of her face. "There's nothing wrong with me," she said coldly. "But if you go to see a psychic there's gotta be something wrong with you."

Valencia looked embarrassed. "You know what, you swear you know so much about me don't you? I don't see no mothafuckin' psychic, so whoever told you that shit lied. You are so enamored by me and what I do with my life that it's killing you. What you wanna do, eat my pussy or something?"

"What is up with you and this obsession with bitches eating your pussy? I don't go that route, sugar foot." Kimi laughed. "I mean, don't be mad at me because you're the one part crazy. As a matter of fact, I thought you said your friend went to see the psychic? So what we really finding out was that it was you all along." She paused. "Just be true to yourself and stop bullshitting."

"What I do is my business, Kimi."

"Exactly, and if you didn't ask us a question, pretending like you were talking about a friend, I wouldn't be in your business now. You lie about everything, Valencia and for no fucking reason. I even found out that unlike what you told everybody at work, you not back with Tech. He dumped you for Brooke and you were in the streets on your knees, begging him back. Are they still sore, sweetie?"

Valencia paced the kitchen floor as she tried to think of what to come back with. "What are you talking about?"

"You know exactly what I'm talking about. Anyway I saw him with Brooke the other day at the mall. So you see Valencia, your little world is not as perfect as you make it seem. You're washed up, irritating and all alone."

"Kimi, that's wrong," Quita interjected. Valencia deserved a taste of her own medicine but Kimi was giving her the entire bottle. "If you saw Brooke in the mall with Tech, why wouldn't you tell her before now? We beef all day long, but we're still friends."

"Because she said if it ain't about business, she didn't want to talk to me. Plus you and me both know, if I would've told her Tech's broke ass was cheating on her *again*, she would not have believed me, or left him alone. She's a glutton for punishment." Kimi looked at Valencia. "She ain't no fool though, she just loves to act like one. So let her."

"You got so much mouth don't you?" Valencia responded. "Since we wanna kick business and talk about niggas, what about Cash?" Kimi's eyes popped open. "Oh yes, baby girl, you not the only one who knows a secret or two. Unlike you, before now, I wasn't on a mission to blow up your spot, but allow me."

Remembering the brutal rape and the last time she saw Cash, in a low voice she said, "What about him? I don't fuck wit' Cash no more."

"I know you don't, honey bunch." She grinned. "That much I'm positive of. But what I'm not sure of is the real reason." She walked up to the table. "It's not because you dumped him like you told Terry and the rest of them at work. It's because he took your pussy...and didn't give it back."

"What the fuck are you talking about?" Quita asked, hearing the incident for the first time. "That didn't happen right?"

"Sure it did, big baby!" Valencia giggled. "And he told everybody about it too."

"Well the shit is not funny!" Quita interjected. "Who told you that bullshit anyway?"

"Apparently his mother just died and left him that run down ass house in Palmer Park." Valencia continued, enjoying the tears rolling down Kimi's face. "And he kicked it to a couple of people I know that was there. He thinks the shit is hilarious because he says she liked to be fucked, even did it a few times in his bathroom at his mother house when he thought she didn't know. So he gave her what she wanted. Kimi ain't nothing but a freak who likes it anyway she can get it!" She paused. "Don't you, baby girl."

Kimi almost choked on the juice she was drinking. She hadn't shared what happened between her and Cash with anyone, not even Quita. She had plans to take that secret to her grave, with the same diligence she was going to take the secret about her dead baby.

Kimi stood up and smacked Valencia so hard she spun around. Quita moved to separate them as quickly as possible but they were already entangled in each other's hair. Kimi managed to pull Valencia to the floor, as she smacked her repeatedly in the face. Quita was doing all she could to separate them but every time she tried, Kimi would fight harder. When Valencia took note from Miranda and bit her in the arm, Kimi screamed out in pain. It wasn't until that point that Quita was finally able to pull Kimi off of Valencia's body. On their feet, Quita and Kimi, fell against the refrigerator, rocking it a little. Wanting some more action, Valencia leaped off of the floor, and jumped on Kimi, in an attempt to gouge her eyes out. Some kind of way Quita was able to separate them again and she abruptly escorted Kimi out of the house by way of several rough pushes.

"What in the world is wrong with you, Kimi? I know ya'll beefing but I think you took shit too far tonight!" She looked back at the house to make sure Valencia wasn't coming. "You know how crazy she is about that nigga Tech. You were outta line!"

"Ain't nothing wrong with me!" Kimi responded, as she stomped quickly and angrily to her car. "She had that shit coming, Quita and you know it! You can't keep doing people wrong when they don't deserve that shit. It's time for payback!"

Kimi almost made it to the car when Valencia ran outside, throwing eggs in her direction. One smacked Quita on the side of the face, while the others crashed to the ground. "Valencia, stop!" Quita pleaded, wiping yoke off her cheek. "Ya'll are supposed to be friends! You giving your neighbors a show too!"

"That jealous bitch ain't my friend!" She cried. "She ain't never been my friend!" She continued, on a mission to empty the entire carton. "I want that bitch off my lawn and out of my life! I don't care what you say, Quita, she not allowed in my house no more! So find another partner!"

"I don't want to be in your raggedy fuckin' house anyway you, bum bitch!" Kimi yelled before getting in her car and slamming the door. "But if I catch you out on the street," she pointed in her direction, "I'm fuckin' you up on the spot! Know that shit is true because I ain't speaking lies! You don't know shit about me! I can snap if pushed!"

"I be back, Valencia." Quita jumped in Kimi's car before she sped off and closed and locked the door.

"Where you goin'?!" Kimi asked. "Since you so concerned, you can stay with your little friend."

"I know you don't think you leaving me in that house!" She opened her glove compartment and grabbed a napkin to wipe the remaining egg off of her face. "Especially after all that shit you just caused. What the fuck got into you anyway?"

"What about Joshua? And the twins?"

"That's what Essence is for. And like you said, Stone and Jensen her kids, not mine. I'll be back later when she cools off."

"I see you're finally coming around." When Valencia rushed toward the car throwing more eggs, Kimi sped off pushing a fuck you sign in the air with her middle finger. Quita allowed her to drive in silence before asking one of the questions she had to know.

"Was she telling the truth? About what she said Cash did to you?"

Kimi looked over at her and said, "I don't want to talk about him. There are some secrets I take with me so I don't put my burden on nobody else. I'ma leave it at that."

Quita nodded and said, "Well, did you really see Tech with Brooke at the mall? You can at least tell me that."

"Naw...I just wanted to fuck up her world."

"You are such a damn liar." She giggled.

"I know," Kimi laughed. "But so is she. That's why she believed every word I said."

PISSY ATTITUDE

Today Quita had 13 kids with 23 different personalities and she was doing the best she could to make things work, *without her partner*. Kimi had called off of work yet again, which happened a lot after the fight with Valencia. Because of it, she had to hire two young girls. She was in the kitchen making herself a cup of coffee, and her new assistant's Essence and Pooh were downstairs with the children.

Pooh was Kimi's cousin, far removed. She was an over the top and loud high school dropout who she recently hired. But she was licensed to drive the van Quita purchased to pick the kids up from school or their extra curricular activities, and was always on time and eager to make money. She was as greedy as Quita and because of it, they got along just fine, most of the time.

Quita continued to run a profitable center with little help from Kimi. Although Valencia said Kimi wasn't allowed in her house, Quita was sure she knew she was there every now and again anyway. Just as long as Kimi wasn't in the building, when Valencia got home, things were calm.

For the first time in Quita's life, she was making more money than she'd ever dreamed. She managed to save over eight thousand dollars in the bank and was preparing to leave in a month, to purchase her own house, which meant more space and privacy. She hadn't built up the nerve to tell Valencia she was leaving, but she was trying her hardest. Part of her reason for moving out was that Valencia failed the drug and background check OCC required and the other part was she was tired of being a slave. So *Teach Them To Grow Child Care Center* was officially closed for business, and *Quita's Day Care Center*, was born in its place.

It wasn't enough for Quita to get paid, she had to push her get rich quick schemes to another level. She discovered that there was a demand for convicts, on probation, who needed fresh urine. She couldn't fulfill their needs because she smoke and drank liquor on a regular basis, but her kids could. She had already supplied ten felons and her client list was growing more by the day.

Quita leaned up against the bathroom door and asked, "Why are you taking so long, Goose?" Since Goose pissed like a Russian racehorse, she used him for the supply, and he got on her nerves every time too. "It doesn't take that long to go to the bathroom."

"I'm trying! You gotta wait!" He huffed.

Quita shook her head and tried to be patient by tapping her feet. Luke from southwest was upstairs and she knew he was growing irritated by her keeping him waiting. "Lil Goose, are you done yet?" Quita asked again, after banging on the door two more times. "All you gotta do is piss in the cup and give it to me. It ain't surgery! I mean damn, are you taking a shit too?"

"Why I gotta do this anyway?" he bucked. "I'ma tell my mother you making me pee in cups."

"Your mother know already!" She lied, hoping he'd drop the issue. "She the one who tells me to have you do it!"

"I'ma tell her anyway! When I get out of the bathroom I'm gonna call my mother! I don't believe shit you say!"

Quita wasn't trying to deal with Xtisha now or never. But she also wasn't going to let her stop her from earning her coins. "I don't know about all that, but I do know this, if you don't do what I ask you to, I'ma come in there and fuck you up!"

"No you not! If you put your hands on me I'ma stab you! I'ma cut your throat and stab your stomach! I'll kill you just like my daddy killed that man!"

Quita backed up and thought about what he said. Goose was getting out of control and would be gone already, if Xtisha didn't blackmail her a few weeks back. Still, she couldn't let him know his threats had any affects on her so she said, "Well I'm gonna tell your mother I can't watch you no more if you call her." She paused, focusing on the pearl doorknob. "And you know what's gonna happen when I do that?" She paused, looking into the wood. "She gonna beat your ass like she did the last time! Now hurry up and piss in the cup."

"Like when she hit me in the head with a bat?" He asked, in a low voice. "And busted my head open?"

Quita placed her hand over her mouth and backed up. She always wondered what happened to him and how he got the scar on his head, and now she was hearing it in such an unexpected way. In her opinion, it now made sense why Goose was so bad; his mother was not in her right state of mind. Feeling bad about the situation she said, "Look…do it for me this last time, and you don't have to do it anymore. Okay?"

When she heard his urine being entered into the cup a few seconds later she exhaled. She was starting to learn more and more about the kids and their parents as the months passed. She looked at the kids who were in the Kiddie Club watching a movie and grinned.

"So here's my plan…we gotta find these aliens and make them our slaves." Zaboy told Miranda, as he sat next to her in the chairs. No matter how much she tried to get away from him, he would morph next to her and was there wherever she turned her head. Quita knew he liked her, but because he was so weird he was unable to show it. "Then we can make them do anything we want them to do. I'm gonna make my alien sing. Like real good. Like how I do."

"First off you can't sing." Miranda laughed, shaking her head. "Second of all there ain't no such thing as aliens! So stop saying that!"

"I believe in them." Joshua said in a low tone.

"You would. You believe everything Zaboy says." She rolled her eyes, sat back in her seat and folded her arms on her chest.

Quita shook her head as she waited for Goose to finish up. Normally baby Axel would be there but his mother called and said he had an appointment. On days like this, she could throw a movie in, schedule her assistants and go about her business.

"All three of ya'll shut up." Pooh said. "Before we make you take a nap early." The three of them huffed and remained quiet, despising naptime more than anything. The rest of the kids hoped they didn't ruin their fun.

When Quita saw Zaboy pull at his lash, which was laced with mucus from a pink eye infection, she knew he was up to something. Five seconds away from sticking his finger in Miranda's face Quita said, "If you do that I'ma fuck you up."

Zaboy turned around and looked at Quita. "I wasn't 'bout to do nothing."

"When Goose gets out of the bathroom, go in there and wash your hands."

"Yes, mam." He said, focusing back on the TV. Miranda looked at him trying to decide if she should drop him or not.

Quita looked at Essence who was preparing the Cot Room for their naps, and saw Pooh who was on the cell phone texting and said, "What are you doing, Pooh? Did you just see that shit? He was about to stick his finger in that girl's face. Trying to give her that shit."

"I'm sorry, Miss Quita!" She stuffed her phone into her jean pocket. Pulling a chair next to them she said, "I'm gonna keep an eye on them now. My boyfriend just wanted me to know he was taking me to the movies when I get off of work." Quita shook her head. She had a feeling Pooh was going to cause a problem in the future, she just didn't know when.

When Lil Goose walked out of the bathroom angry, he pushed the piss cup into her hand and a few drops splattered on her fingers. "You make me sick, Ms. Quita!"

Just like that, the empathy she felt for him went out the window. "Shut the fuck up and take your little bad ass over there and sit down! You getting on my nerves with all that talking back and shit."

Goose stomped over to where the rest of the kids were and threw his body into the seat. "Little bastard." She trudged upstairs knowing Luke from southwest was probably beyond mad now. He had a meeting with his probation officer in less than an hour and waiting on Quita was making him late. She grabbed the Styrofoam cup, walked upstairs and into the kitchen.

She placed a lid on the cup and wiped the sides, strolled into the living room and said, "Sorry it took me so long. He was having a hard time producing for you."

He stood up from the couch and said, "You trying to get a nigga locked up or something?"

"You know that ain't the case." She paused, as she trekked toward him. "Some things take time." She smiled. "Got my money?"

He dug in his jacket and handed her the cash. "Thanks, ma. I thought you were about to stand me up at first." He took the cup. "Now you were down there for a minute, you sure this shit is clean?"

"Come on...don't insult me. I'm a businesswoman. I told you the kid had a problem going...you just make sure you tell your friends

I'm here." He walked to the door and she followed him. "Good luck with that situation." She opened the door and he walked out.

"Later," he said, nodding at Evanka who was slithering up to the stairs with a pregnant belly.

The moment Quita saw her she knew there was going to be a problem. Mainly because Quita refused to give her back the money she paid for fake pregnancy papers. When she first asked for the money, Quita was too broke to give it back. And now that her pockets were fat, it was the principal. Whether Evanka was pregnant or not, was not part of the arrangement. Quita agreed to give her the documents she needed to fool Doo-Man, so as far as she was concerned, their business was over.

"Can I talk to you for a moment?" Evanka bombarded her way inside and plopped down on the sofa. "I didn't know it was so nice in here. I'm surprised to see that Valencia keep a fly crib. Since ya'll don't have the center no more."

"You know she don't want you in her house," Quita said, leaving the door open so she could exit just as smoothly as she entered. "Now what do you want? I'm busy!"

"I paid you a hundred dollars for a forged pregnancy test. As you and I both know, I was pregnant anyway, so I'ma need my money back." She rubbed her belly for affect. "I'm tired of hearing you say you gonna pay me later when the shit never happens. What's up with the cash right now?"

Quita had one hundred dollars in her pocket but refused to hand it over. She didn't like her attitude and she didn't appreciate the fact, that she kept pressing her out. "Naw...I can't do nothing for you, man. A deal is a deal. I don't have nothing to do with you being in the family way. You wanted the papers and I risked my job to get them for you."

She shot up off of the sofa with borrowed might. "You not just gonna take my money, Quita! You gave me something I didn't need and I want my cash back! Fair is fair!"

Her lips curled into a semi smile. "Are you seriously that broke, where you gotta come over here and bother me about one hundred bucks? I know you not getting the money the way you use to at your center, but even you must admit that this is a little ridiculous."

"No...are *you* seriously that broke," she pointed a finger in Quita's face, "where you gotta hold on to my money!"

Quita walked up to the door and said, "Get out, Evanka. You pregnant and all, but I'm five seconds from raising up on you."

"Are you serious? You putting me out?"

Quita tapped the door and said, "Bring it on this way. I got shit to do and don't have time for all of this."

When Evanka heard the kids voices grow loudly downstairs she said, "Are you still running a daycare center out of your house? Because I heard Valencia got pulled up because of her background. As far as I know, ya'll shouldn't be doing shit here but sleeping and eating."

"Why are you so worried about what we do?" She laughed sarcastically. "Everybody know you called OCC, so move on."

"If you not licensed, why are you watching kids?"

Before she could answer Miranda ran upstairs and said, "Ms. Quita, Lil Goose took his pants down and sat on Zaboy face! They 'bout to fight and everything!"

"What the fuck!?" Quita said with widened eyes. Lil Goose made it his life's work to cause her havoc. "Give me a second, I'm coming now!"

Evanka laughed and said, "So you are watching kids without a license. And you took one of my kids too." She paused, shaking her head. "Damn, Quita, you just love digging into my pockets don't you?"

"Evanka, get your dumb ass out of my house," she pushed her out the door. "I gotta go!"

She slammed the door in her face and Evanka banged on the wood and said, "You gonna get what you deserve...and real soon too! Trust me!"

Quita ran down the stairs toward the basement and almost fell back when she saw the scene. Pooh was holding Zaboy who was flailing wild arms and crying. Blood dripped from his arm and one of his ugly shoes lay a few feet over from where he stood. Essence kept Goose back but, he kicked his bare legs awkwardly in an attempt to get away. His pants were on the floor and he was naked from the waist down.

Quita walked up to Lil Goose and yelled, "What were you doing?! What the fuck is wrong with you? Why you always gotta be starting shit!"

"He tried to give me pink eye! My mother said if he touched me to make him kiss my ass! So I made him kiss my ass!"

"Where is the blood coming from?" She asked frantically. "From his arm?!" She looked at Pooh.

"Ms. Quita, he tried to stab him too." Pooh looked down at the knife in the middle of the floor. "I don't know if it's a good idea to have him here anymore. The other kids are scared and to tell you the truth, I am too."

THE COOLEST KID ALIVE

It was cold outside, the winter breeze rattled the windows and whisked past the house, on the day she met the little boy who would change her life. Her assistants were there and Quita needed both of them today because she had a meeting with some parents. Joshua's mother Wondrika, Cruella, Zaboy's mother and Clarkita, baby Axel's mother. She already cut Xtisha and Lil Goose off, stating the center was closed for business and she could not legally have them in her home. She derived so much pleasure out of telling them to get the fuck that tingly sensations ran through her body on the day she let Xtisha know. She hated Lil Goose and she hated Xtisha even more.

When someone knocked at the door, she walked to it and saw a man she hadn't seen in awhile. Charlene's husband, Flex. Standing by his side, was the most attractive kid she'd ever seen in her life. He looked just like him. Flex was tall, lean and neat cornrows ran to the back of his head in an intricate pattern. He was very respectful. However, it was rumored, that he was the most murderous person to ever roam the face of the earth. Although he could be violent when it came to his money, he was extremely loyal to Charlene and believed in the spirit of family. He wasn't always faithful but after cheating on his wife many years back, he vowed never to make the same mistake again. And he kept that promise, until the day that she died. He adored his son, worshipped his mother, and treated his grandmother with the respect other grandchildren could only imagine.

His son, seven-year-old Cordon, stood next to him, with a blue knit hat pulled down over his head, which introduced his large brown eyes. He was kind, an honor roll student who respected adults with the swag of a southerner. People always said how they wished most kids could be like Cordon, and center owners would kick other children out of their program for a chance to have him in their care.

Not only was he smart, kind and a joy to be around, he was full of love and Flex paid triple the center's fee, so that Cordon would get the attention he needed. To some it felt like robbery since the child never got in the way, but they took the cash all the same. Cordon was certainly not a problem child, so Quita wondered what he was doing at the door of the woman, who specialized in misfits.

Quita opened the screen door and said, "Flex...I haven't seen you in forever." She thought about the funeral, and the fact that she didn't go. "I'm sorry I couldn't make it to Charlene's..."

"I understand. I didn't want to go either." He held his head low before looking directly into her eyes. It was as if he gave himself two seconds to grieve in her honor, but not a second more. "Let's just leave it like that."

"Well how are you?" She was trying to engage him the best way she knew how.

"Can we come in?" He asked, looking down at his son Cordon. "It's kind of cold out here. I don't want my boy to get sick."

"I'm sorry," she opened the door wider and they walked inside. Cordon immediately removed his hat and held it close to his body. After shutting the door she said, "I must be tripping, it's just that, I'm surprised that you are here. And looking at you reminds me of..."

"I know." He paused, stuffing his hands into his coat pockets. "You don't have to say it. Look...can we talk in private? I need to rap to you about a few things."

"Of course." She shook her head. "Cordon, why don't you go downstairs. It's a little busy but I'm sure you can find something to get in to. My assistants can help you if you need anything and there are other kids down there."

"Yes, mam." He walked away and left them alone.

"Quita, this is kind of hard for me, but I needed to come anyway." They walked toward the living room. "When my wife committed suicide, she killed me too. I didn't understand why, until the cops told me what you said about what happened to her. I can't even imagine her having to deal with that alone." He paused, looking into her eyes. "Is it true?"

Quita's throat felt dry. "Can we go into the kitchen? And drink some coffee?"

"Sure."

When they were inside the kitchen she poured two cups of coffee. "How do you like yours?"

Standing in the middle of the floor he said, "Black."

She preferred sugar and cream, but at the moment it seemed unimportant, so she didn't bother. "You can sit down." Flex took a seat and she sat across from him. "What exactly are you asking me? I don't want to tell you more than you need to know."

"I need to know everything." He was assertive. "About my wife."

"Well, she was raped by your father." Quita could see his jaw flexing and the vein on the side of his head pulsating, yet his overall facial expression remained the same. "He got her pregnant and she contracted HIV."

He clasped his hands together on the table and looked down at them. The table rocked slightly because his left leg wouldn't stop jumping. Yet his facial expression did not change. "When did this happen?"

"Not sure when." She swallowed the bitter coffee. "I think it happened when he was dropping off your son home one day."

"So you saying he raped my wife," he stood up and walked toward the stove, "are you telling me, that he raped my wife while my son was there? Got her pregnant and gave her HIV?" Quita nodded. Talking to himself he said, "So that's why she wouldn't have sex with me."

"I'm sorry, Flex." She looked down at her hands. "She asked me to meet with her…on the day she took her life, and I never got over it. I had so much going on, and all she wanted was a few minutes of my time. I still feel bad about that shit, to this day."

"Do you know," a tear rolled down his face but he didn't bother to wipe it away. She knew at that moment that he was more man than any she'd ever seen in her life because he was strong enough to allow it to remain. "Do you know…why she didn't tell me? About what my father…I mean…what that nigga…did to her? Why didn't she let me know? Why didn't she let me defend her? We always had the kind of relationship that we can talk about anything."

This conversation was heavier than she felt like dealing with, but she knew she had no choice. Charlene was a good woman and he deserved to know what kind of person he married. "Because she wanted to be strong for you. She wanted to love you and take care of your family, like she promised the day she decided to be your wife." She heard him weep but he silenced it by placing his hand over his mouth. He walked away, so that his back was in her direction. "She didn't want you to worry, Flex. She just wanted to be a wife and a mother to your son."

Flex turned around and looked at the floor. "You've probably heard a lot of things about me. You probably heard a whole lot of lies too." He looked at her and leaned in. "Have you?" She nodded. "What kinds of stuff have you heard?"

"That you were a cold blooded killer." She smiled, hoping he'd deny the accusations. The man standing before her looked like any-thing but a murderer. "Stupid shit like that."

"That part of the rumor is true. I kill...but only when I have to."

Quita stood up to pour herself another cup of coffee, even though it was already full. It spilled out of the cup and splashed to the floor. Flex grabbed a mop in the corner and cleaned it up. When he was done, he pulled the chair out for her and said, "Have a seat." She appeared stiff. "Please." She sat down. "I didn't mean to scare you, because you don't deserve that shit. Sometimes who I am, and who I can be, comes out at the wrong time and at the wrong place." He swallowed. "I'm here, because my wife said she trusted you, in the letter she wrote to us before she took her own life. She asked me to bring Cordon around you, for whatever reason. Said you would even-tually know why. I see you run a daycare center and I didn't know that. My son use to be at Evanka's, up the street but I don't want him there anymore. I gotta respect my wife's wishes."

He reached in his coat pocket and pulled out a manila colored envelope and sat it on the table. With one finger, he slid it into her direction. "That's three thousand dollars. That's what I usually pay each month. If you want more I can give it to you." He paused and looked at the dough. "I want you to look after my son, and make sure he's taken care of. He's a good kid, but he needs love. Can you do this for me? Like my wife wanted?"

Quita was so concerned about the money that she didn't hear *the way* in which he asked for her help. "Yeah! I can do that! No problem at all." She went to grab the money, when he placed his cold hand on top of her warm one. "I need you to be sure."

"Trust me, I can handle it." She was thinking about how well mannered he was. In her opinion if she dealt with Goose, she could deal with anybody. "It won't be a problem at all."

"Quita, if one hair is harmed on his head, it won't be good for you. So think clearly before you take my paper."

"I can do it!" She said, licking her lips, ready to stuff the money into her pocket. She already calculated that with him paying her three thousand dollars a month, she would earn thirty six thousand a year. On one kid. Essentially by watching little Cordon, she would be making the money she earned at the doctor's office…tax-free. Quita looked up at Flex and said, "He'll be safe here."

Flex removed his hand from hers and said, "I'm gonna hold you to it."

THE MOTHERS

After talking with Flex, Quita still had to speak with two parents. First up was Cruella. She was sitting in the living room with Cruella and Zaboy, preparing to tell her how things were going, since she had been caring for her son. Cruella's gold lace front wig was so far down on her forehead that it was dangerously close to connecting with her eyebrows. Zaboy was wearing a brown pair of corduroys and leather shoes pulled so tightly, they looked like they would fold in half. He was sitting on her lap as if he were a baby, with his head resting on her shoulder. Cruella's extra glossy lips, smiled at him, and her mustache was so thick, it looked painted on.

Cruella's body was frumpy and she had a bad case of cankles, which was the merging of the ankles and calves together. She had gastric bypass surgery last year and excess skin hung everywhere on her body. To conceal her body's condition, she wore colorful muumuus every day of the week, which did nothing for the skin flapping on her arms like a turkey's neck.

"Did Zaboy tell you he won sixth place in the glee club competition for singing *Somewhere Over The Rainbow*?" She didn't pause for Quita to respond. "Well he did," she hugged him tighter and kissed him on the lips. "He's such a great child. Isn't he?"

Silence.

"How 'bout you sing for Ms. Quita, baby."

"Oh no!" Quita held her hand out. "That won't be necessary..."

Zaboy hopped up anyway and eerily screamed, "SOME-WHERE...OVER THE RAINBOW....WAY UP HIGH...THERE'S A LAND THAT I HEARD OF...ONCE IN A LULLABY."

"That's enough!" Quita jumped up and screamed. She looked at both of them and said, "I heard all I want to hear! Please! No more!" She dealt with his wretched voice on a daily basis, and she needed a break.

Zaboy jumped back in his mother's lap and hid his face in her breasts. Cruella angrily stared at her. "You didn't have to scream at him like that. He's just a baby, Quita. All he needs is a little love. You best be remembering that while you're spending my money."

"He's not a baby, Cruella." She pulled her weave over her left shoulder and rubbed her neck. "That's why I wanted to talk to you."

"He *is* a baby!" She pointed at her, before her fingers formed a tight fist. Quita was worried now. "He's *my* baby." She gripped him tighter and rocked him in her arms. "Plus he's only 60 months old. He's not this grown ass man you making him out to be."

"60 months makes him five years old." She held her hand out and spread her fingers. "Like I said, he's not a baby." Cruella appeared to have tapped out on the conversation.

"When my son was stabbed, by that kid named Goose, I never reported you to the police. I accepted your answer as truth and left the matter alone. You said they were fighting, and I knew boys would do what boys would do. But if you want to be rude to him, then maybe I'll let the authorities know you're operating a daycare center."

She hated how parents loved to threaten her with the police. If somebody came down their jobs, and threatened their places of employment, they would lose it. "Cruella, that situation was out of my control and I appreciated you not calling the police. I even gave you two free weeks of day care service, and trust me it was not easy. But Zaboy had a part in that incident too. Had he not tried to give the other kid pink eye, none of that would've happened."

"That's not what my boy says."

"That's not what happened, mommy." Zaboy lied, looking into his mother's mustache. "He was just picking on me."

"Cruella, do you mind if he goes downstairs with the other kids so we can talk alone? This is really very important."

"Mommy, I want to stay up here with you. I don't want to go downstairs yet."

"Please, Cruella. A child shouldn't be up here, while we discuss these types of matters."

"Actually right now may not be a good time anyway. He's hungry." She continued, looking down at her son. "You mind if I feed him before he goes there? He ain't ate all day."

At this point she would give her anything she wanted, to be done with the meeting all-together. "I guess not." She shrugged, wanting him to eat so Cruella could leave as soon as possible. Quita stood up and moved toward the kitchen, where his bags sat on the table. "Where is his lunch? In the bag?"

"No...I have it right here." Before Quita knew it, Cruella whipped out her titty and Zaboy greedily sucked on it, as if he were trying to draw blood.

At that time, for the moment anyway, the meeting was officially over.

A FEW HOURS LATER

After waiting for Cruella to finish breastfeeding Zaboy's grown ass, which in her opinion was a hot mess, she told her to get his behavior in order, if she wanted her to continue to watch him. Zaboy loved to show off, yell out answers he thought he knew during class, and take bites off of snacks, after claiming he was hungry, only to throw them in the trash. In the end, Cruella promised to help Zaboy get it together knowing that if Quita threw him out of her center, it would be a wrap and she'd be taking Mr. Show Tunes with her everyday at work. And that would be a problem since he was banned from there too.

After meeting with Cruella, she spoke with Clarkita Kemp. Clarkita, a 42-year-old woman, despite her grey Jerri Curl, was beautiful, single and alone. She had Axel after being inseminated in a fertility clinic and he was her only child. Unlike some of her other clients, she was a board certified surgeon who pretty much wrote her own ticket. She was kind, willing to give her all and that went for everybody she met. Quita couldn't count the number of times Clarkita would stay late to help the girls clean up the center, since her baby was sometimes the last to go home. The only problem Quita had with Clarkita was Axel's fussiness.

"Clarkita, you know you're one of my best parents," she said, surprised he wasn't crying at the moment. "But Axel cries nonstop. It's very distracting and it disturbs the other kids."

"I know…it's so sad. I'm a doctor, yet I can't even help my own baby." She looked down at him and he smiled. The only time he was silent was when she held him in her arms. "Pediatricians tell me he's healthy and just a little cranky. I even had one who told me I should let him cry but I can never do it." She sighed, but when he smiled at her, she grinned. "As crazy as my baby is, I love him so much. He's all I got." She looked at her and a tear fell down her face. "They told me I couldn't have any kids, and we proved them wrong. Didn't we?" She took his foot and placed it in her mouth. Axel let out the cutest laugh Quita ever heard him create. For the moment, he was human. "But he doesn't allow me to leave him with other people. I can never understand why."

Quita looked at the stunning baby and his beautiful mother and said, "I don't know what to do. You're one of my favorite parents. It's just so hard to care for him because he never stops crying."

Clarkita placed her hand gently on Quita's knee. "Work with me a little longer. Maybe we both can find a plan together. If after two months, we can't find an answer, I'll take him out of here for good and pay you for the month. Fair enough?"

There was no way she'd tell her no, especially after she dealt with Little Goose for months. "Fair enough." She paused, nodding her head. "But I have to tell you something else that might change every-thing."

"I already know." She looked at her. "Your license was re-voked." She paused. "Guess what, I don't care."

She felt a short jolt of unease, pierce her stomach. "How did you know?"

"He may be a noisy baby, but he's mine and I love him. I need to know everything and everybody in his life and that means you too. So I found out on the net, that your business license had been re-voked." Quita smiled, because she still trusted her. "You're a good kid and I never told you this, because I didn't want you to only watch him because of it, but I knew your mother before she got sick. We went to grade school together and remained pretty good friends for years. She talked about you all the time and how smart you were." Quita's heart warmed in surprise at this information. Quita saw her mother once a week, no matter what, and would love to have told her that she met one of her friends, but she knew she'd never understand a word she was saying. Dementia held her mind and her memories.

"I know you love money and there's nothing wrong with that, Quita. It gives you motivation to push harder. Hell, getting paid was the reason I became a doctor. But there ain't nothing you can say, that will convince me that a person who chooses to deal with the worst kids money can find, would do this for so long, accept for the fact that they are an angel from God. This is your calling, Quita. You handle the misfits and the children forgotten. And whether you know it or not, you were put here to help parents like me. Just don't let your heart harden over time, where you forget that. Okay?"

Quita was emotional as she listened to the jewels dropped in her lap. Clarkita was right. Money was taking her by the hand and ruling her life. She was around children most of the time, moved by the beat of money and she'd even been avoiding Demetrius. She decided to do a little work to repair the relationships in her life, starting with Kimi.

"Okay, Ms. Kemp. You got it."

She smiled and said, "Well…I'm off for the rest of the day from work. I'd love to stay and help you with the kids if you need me."

"Ms. Kemp, I would love it."

FIRST CRUSH

Miranda lay on the cot, in the dark, a few feet over from Cordon, who at the moment, had his eyes closed. She remembered the day she first met him, and couldn't explain the feeling in her heart. He seemed nice and different from the other kids at the center. She wanted so badly to talk to him and be his friend. But she didn't know what to say, and didn't want to sound stupid, so she ignored him all together.

Turning her head to look at Quita, who sat in a corner at the computer station in the center, she watched her count a bunch of money in her hands. Miranda wondered how much she could steal from her, and how far she could runaway. She hated her life, and she hated her mother Vonzella, but what could she do while broke? She had to think of a plan and she had to think of one soon. It was just a matter of time, before the latest uncle would sneak in her room and fondle her at night. Although she hadn't been penetrated yet, she knew that if she didn't runaway, that it would happen soon.

"Why you looking over there like that?" someone whispered. "You 'spose to be sleep."

Miranda turned her head to the right and saw it was Cordon. He barely talked to her, so she wondered what changed. "Why you worried 'bout what I do? I thought you were sleep too."

"Naw...I can't sleep when I'm not home." He looked up into the dark ceiling. "I been woke the whole time."

"Well leave me alone." He laughed softly at her response. "What's funny?" She whispered.

"The way you say, leave me alone" He continued, rolling over to his side, to see her clearly. "If you take that lady's money, you gonna get caught. So don't do that."

Miranda's heart began to beat fast, as she wondered how he knew. Did she really look that guilty? "You don't know nothin'. So mind your business before I tell Ms. Quita you being fresh with me."

"She won't believe you."

"Why not?"

"Cause that ain't my style." Miranda liked him immediately. He said the cutest things and she loved to hear him talk. "You wanna go upstairs? And eat some snacks? My pops brought me Popeye's chicken earlier. My favorite."

"Ms. Quita not gonna let us go." She whispered. "We 'spose to be sleep. So shut up 'fore you get me in trouble"

"You wanna go or not? 'Cause I'm about to ask."

"If she let you," She shrugged. "I guess I'ma go too."

Cordon popped out of the cot, swaggered over to Quita and said, "Mam, do you mind if I go eat my chicken? With Miranda upstairs?"

Quita looked at them and whispered, "You're not sleepy? After all that running around in the park we did today?"

"No mam." He stuffed his hands into his pockets, like he always saw his father do. "I sleep when I get home."

"Go ahead. But let me know if you need anything."

"Thanks, mam."

"I'm going too!" Zaboy morphed into the conversation as usual. A few of the children moved a little who was sleep when they heard his voice, but luckily no one got up. "I want some chicken."

Quita frowned at him. "First off keep your voice down," she pointed in his face. Out of all of the kids, she truly couldn't stand his ass the most. "And your mother didn't bring you no chicken so you can't get none. So unless you want the titty juice in the refrigerator upstairs, that she squeezed out for you, go back to fucking sleep."

Zaboy's eyes fluttered. "That's not nice, Ms. Quita."

"It wasn't supposed to be. "Now take your ass back to bed."

"It's okay, Ms. Quita." Cordon smiled, looking at Zaboy. "If he wants, he can have some too."

"You sure, Cordon? 'Cause you don't have to do that shit."

He nodded yes. "It's cool. My pops bought me a lot."

"Please, Ms. Quita, can I go." Zaboy continued, moving in place as if he had to pee on himself. "I can sing you a song if you like."

"Please don't, Zaboy. I am not a fan." Quita shook her head at him and looked back at Cordon and Miranda. "Okay, let me know if you need anything. Your food is in the kitchen on the table. Use paper towels instead of plates."

The three kids marched upstairs and Cordon pulled a seat out for Miranda like he'd seen his father do for his mother. She was shocked at first, but eventually she eased into the seat. Zaboy stood with his arms folded over his chest, as he waited for Cordon to do him the same honors. When he didn't he said, "I'm waiting. Please pull my chair out too."

Cordon looked at him and said, "I don't do guys. You gotta pull your chair out yourself if you wanna sit down."

Zaboy frowned, snatched a chair back and flopped into it. "I want some chicken…give me a piece."

Cordon grabbed a couple of pieces of paper towel and handed one to each of them before taking his seat. He pulled the box toward him, looked inside and asked Miranda, "Which one you want?" He tilted the box so she could see inside.

"I don't care." She shrugged, playing with her hair. She liked him and it made her nervous. "Anyone you give me."

He picked a wing for her, his favorite, and said, "You want a biscuit?" She placed the chicken on her napkin and nodded yes. "You want jelly too?"

"Naw," she pulled her ponytail again, and pulled it over her shoulder. "I'm good. Thank you."

Cordon grabbed a piece for himself and slid the box over to Zaboy. "I want you to get mine for me too! Like you did hers." He pushed the box back across the table and it almost fell to the floor. "Give me a wing like hers."

Cordon wasn't feeling him, but his mother and father taught him not to be rude. "Look, man, I'm not your girl. I'm a boy, and you are too. You gotta get your own food or people gonna think you sweet." He pushed the box back. "Here."

Zaboy frowned, snatched the box and grabbed four pieces of chicken. Miranda who was irritated by everything he did said, "Why you gonna get all that! You not gonna eat it anyway! You always do that shit!"

"I am too gonna eat it!" He took a bite off of each piece of chicken and said, "Uggh! I forgot I don't like fried chicken! It's nasty! I wish I never ate it!" He grabbed the food, hopped off the chair and threw it in the trash.

Cordon was mad but he was determined not to show it. His father warned him about showing emotions. "Why would you do somethin' like that, man? If you ain't want it, why you ask for it?"

"Because I want some biscuits instead." He snatched the half empty box, courtesy of him, and pulled out three biscuits. Following suit, he took a bite off of each and threw it in trash again. "That's gross."

Cordon looked at him and said, "If I ever give you something again and you don't eat it, after you asked for it, I'ma bust you in the nose."

Zaboy's eyes flapped wildly. "I'ma tell Ms. Quita on you." He pointed in his face. "My mama said my ears are for God's purpose only!"

"Man, I don't have nothing to do with all that. You heard what I said right?"

Zaboy walked up to him, pointed in his face and said, "I'ma tell my mother! You can't talk to me like that. Nobody talks to me like that! I'm a star!"

Cordon stood up and looked into his eyes. Slowly Zaboy put his hand down without Cordon having to say a word. He'd never been in the presence of a kid who was on the sure road to becoming a real man. Cordon, was the last of a dying breed and Zaboy's ridiculous behavior, although they were almost the same age, proved it.

"I'm going downstairs, to take a nap. I missed my beauty sleep! Ya'll shoulda left me alone! I didn't want to come up here anyway!" Zaboy said, backing up. "Bye." He ran down the steps and out of sight.

"I can't stand him." Miranda said, playing with her ponytail again. "You shoulda hit him in the nose like you said you would."

"Why hit him when I don't gotta?" He shrugged, pulling out his chair. "Anyway he probably don't have no friends. Or no dad. That's why he act like that. Like a girl." He sat back down, and scooted closer to the table. "You got a dad?"

Miranda left her hair alone and picked up the wing. "I got uncles. A lot of them. No daddy though." She seemed to zone out, as she explained her home situation in a few brief words.

When she said that there was a soft knock at the door. Miranda hopped up to answer it. "What you doing?" Cordon inquired. "Never go to the door unless you expecting company. Your mama coming to get you early or somethin'?"

"No." She rolled her eyes. "But I wanna know who it is."

Miranda opened the door and Xtisha was on the other side with Lil Goose. Cordon walked up behind Miranda and could tell by the look on the adult's face, that she wasn't happy to see them. "What ya'll doing here?" Her knuckles were on her hips, and her curly nails stuck out from the sides of her body. "She not 'spose to have no kids in this house."

"Why?" Cordon asked, standing in front of Miranda to protect her. "You don't know me so it don't make no difference."

"What's your name, lil nigga? I ain't seen you here before?"

"What you want?" His eyes told her he was not afraid, nor would he back down. And because of it, Xtisha didn't like him.

"You must want me to have my son kick your ass. He's your same age."

Cordon looked at Lil Goose, and the headphone stuffed in his ears and said, "He can try if he want to. I don't think it's a good idea. And then you gonna have to deal with my father."

"You gonna wish you ain't say no shit like that to me." She paused. "Is Quita here?"

"I'ma give her your message. What you want?"

Xtisha could tell the kid was from the streets, and even though she knew she could hurt him because he was still a child, she backed off. "Tell her that she better not be running a day care center out of her house no more. 'Specially since she told me my chow ain't welcome. If I find out she is, I'ma let the authorities know and all ya'll gonna get locked up." Cordon laughed and it angered Xtisha all over again. He was smart enough to know kids didn't get thrown in jail. "You better give her my message, lil nigga! Or else!"

LITTLE KIDS & HAPPY MOTHER'S DAY CARE CENTER

Evanka continued to rub her belly, as she waited for Flex to answer the phone. She was the type of bitch who wanted everybody to know she was pregnant, and would often go over the top to get attention. Ever since Xtisha told her that she found out the new boy over Valencia's house was Flex's son, she was enveloped in anger. She didn't mind Quita starting her little program, when it didn't impact her business. She didn't even mind Lil Goose going over there. But losing Cordon meant a bill wasn't going to be paid, and now she declared war. Not to mention Quita took the money for the fake pregnancy test and refused to give it back when it was discovered that she was actually expecting.

She was sitting on the sofa with her mother Ursula, Doo-Man's cousin Brooke, Xtisha and Lil Goose. When Flex finally answered his cell, she was flustered and almost forgot what to say. "Hello, is this Flex?"

"You called me." His voice was heavy with irritation, so she knew she had better get to the point of the call quickly.

"I'm sorry," she giggled trying to be calm and lighten the mood. "This is Evanka, I was calling to see if you were bringing Cordon back today. Or any time this week. We haven't seen him in a while and we miss him. He left his boots over here and everything."

"I told your mother I wasn't."

"I know. But I wanted to ask you to be sure."

"If your mother is your business partner, why would you have to ask me something you already know the answer to?"

Evanka stood up, because her underarms started sweating and she wasn't sure if they could smell them. Rubbing her belly again for affect she said, "I guess I'm calling to find out why."

"Look, I'm busy so I'ma tell you like this. I took my son out because I fucked his mother, made her my wife, and that makes me his father. Now I gave your mother six thousand dollars to cover our arrangement, so as far as I'm concerned we're done."

"You gave my mother six thousand dollars?!" She yelled, looking at Ursula. "When was that shit?"

Her mother was caught, green handed, so she walked out of the room, to find something...*anything*...to get in to so she could avoid her daughter's wrath. "I guess she ain't tell you." Flex said, tiring of the matter all together. Their problems didn't have shit to do with him.

"No...she didn't." Her nostrils flared and she was breathing so heavily, it sounded like she was about to go into labor. It especially made her mad because just last night she asked for three thousand dollars to buy a new car and Ursula cried broke.

"Look...whether she gave you your money or not, that's on ya'll."

"Well did you know they don't have no license? You shouldn't even be letting him stay over there. It's not safe."

"I was raised in a home by a woman I'm sure didn't have a license either and I'm good." He paused. "Now I consider our business done so don't call my fucking phone with all this female shit." He hung up in her face, and she took the phone away from her ear. Throwing it in the sofa she tried to consider, what made her angrier. The fact that Quita stole Cordon or the fact that her mother was too slick for words. As she thought about it more, she realized her mother was the winner. She was embarrassed at her thievery, and couldn't wait to talk to her when they were alone.

Waking her out of her thoughts, Xtisha said, "What he say? I mean...was I right? She is watching him ain't she?"

"Yeah...but I don't get it. Why would he take him out of my center, and put him over there?" She looked at them. "I mean...is he fucking her or something?"

"Fuck no!" Xtisha interjected as if she could talk. "Since she been running that center, she's gotten fatter than ever." Evanka and Brooke looked at her weird curly nails, the short braids on her head that were all over the place and her ashy kneecaps, and kept their comments to themselves. "She really should take better care of herself."

"The shit don't make no sense to me." Brooke said, taking a brush out of her purse to tame her long hair. "I wouldn't want a bitch watching my kid without a license. I'm just saying."

"Me either…but he said he fucked his wife so that makes him *his* son."

"All this is so ridiculous! She not fit to watch nobody's kids. I autta call the authorities and let them know about all that shit going on over there." She yelled pointing her extra long finger in her direction.

Evanka wanted war, but wasn't keen on the police. If Xtisha did hateful shit like that to Quita, she would do it to her too. "Naw…don't do that. I'll think of another way to get at her."

"I told ya'll I didn't have a reason to lie! Now will you believe me?" Xtisha had ulterior motives that Evanka wanted to avoid.

"But why would Flex send his kid over there? That bitch deals in misfits." Evanka paused. "Cordon don't deserve to be over there, he's so good. If them other kids were on a long bus it would turn short."

"What fucks me up," Brooke said swinging her hair for no apparent reason, "is that Valencia be getting high over there! She ain't even supposed to be running a center in her house. We called the Office of Child Care on that bitch and everything. So what gives?"

"It's illegally operated!" Xtisha offered. "I knew there was a reason I took my son out of that house." Everybody knows his bad ass was thrown out on the street, but they let her live. "I didn't feel comfortable with him being there." She shook her head. "You gotta let him come back here, Evanka. You hurting for cash with Cordon gone I know it. You know I fuck with Micky from Southwest so my pockets are right."

"You mean, *Stinky* Micky?" Brooke asked, looking at her as if she were a science project. There was never a nigga funkier than that dude, so she wondered why anyone would be bothered with him including Xtisha. "With the funky car and neck?"

"That's what people say," Xtisha frowned, "but it don't' bother me none. He a man...he be outside a lot."

Brooke and Valencia shook their heads. "How much were you paying Quita, and don't lie because I'ma find out.

"One hundred and fifty dollars." Xtisha lied, trying to maintain a straight face. If she could save some money from what she'd been paying Quita, in her opinion it was worth it.

"She only charged a hundred and fifty for his bad ass?" She pointed at Lil Goose who looked like he was waiting to get into something as they spoke.

"She's cheap." She shrugged, trying to move away from the topic of money. "That's how she gets all of them kids over there."

Evanka looked at her and said, "I'm 'bout to check my mother for this money she owe me. And then I'm going home to be with Doo-Man." She paused, wanting everybody to know they lived together, as if anyone really cared. "But if I let Lil Goose stay, he gotta stay out back." She pointed at the window.

Xtisha stood up and looked at the red shed. "Wait, you want my chow to stay in a shed?"

"You don't have a choice."

"Come on, Evanka!" She said throwing her hands up in the air. She looked out the window again. "That shit ain't right...he a chow!"

"If you feel that way, don't take my offer and you can take your *chow* home." She could care less. Nobody wanted to be bothered with the Goose, and she knew Xtisha knew it."

"But I need a sitter. Them white peoples on my job gonna fire me!"

"Well there it is," Evanka paused, looking at her seriously. "I guess it's settled. But you must know, my moms not letting him stay inside. You saw how she ran out here, when she saw you in the house with Goose. She was doing that shit to keep an eye on him," she paused, "until the money came up." She grew angry. "She got ghost then."

"But it's cold out there!" She looked at the window again, as if the shed would magically disappear. "You can't be serious."

"It may be cold outside but not in there! It may be a shed but we got central air and heating in there. And a TV too. Doo-Man be out there when he come over here sometimes to cut his coke." She continued as if she were talking about a legal project. "So you want it or not?"

"I guess I ain't got no choice."

Evanka smiled. "Good, and the rate is two hundred dollars. You not slick." Since it was still cheaper than Quita's prices she didn't buck. "And later this week, I want us to come back together. We gonna find a way to get them bitches back. And maybe Flex too!"

THE WALK

Quita was pushing baby Axel in a stroller while Miranda, Cordon, Joshua and Zaboy held hands in pairs following behind her. Although it was cold outside, they were bundled up well, and on their way to the park. Her assistants Essence who was always on point and aware of the children, and Pooh who was good for errand running, and texting on the phone, followed behind the kids to be sure they were safe. Although she had five with her now, her evening care client list had quickly filled up as it was New Years Eve, and a lot of people were going out. At first she was concerned about the load, but when Clarkita dropped off Axel, she promised to come back and help. Kimi finally reached out and said she was coming to work also. Quita figured she needed some money because since she'd been missing in action, she hadn't given her a cut.

"Did you know that your brain is more active at night, than during the day?" Miranda asked Cordon, as she held on to his hand, while swinging her arm.

"Naw. How you know that?" Cordon's steez was so much like his father's, if you put them together, they could be twins.

"I read a lot. Like real big books and stuff like that. You like to read?"

"Naw," Cordon shook his head. "I don't know what I like yet. I'm kinda young."

"But you real smart. And tough. You can be a judge. Or a cop."

Cordon frowned when she mentioned being a police officer. "Naw, I'll probably be like my dad. He makes a lot of money and he's real tough too."

She looked over at him and asked, "What your dad do?"

He looked away. "We don't talk about stuff like that. With strangers anyway."

"Well I'm gonna be a cop!" Zaboy interrupted, morphing into their conversation as usual. He broke away from Joshua's hand. "I'ma arrest both of ya'll too if ya'll be bad. I'm gonna be a good cop! Watch!"

"Zaboy, hold Joshua's hand!" Quita said, as Axel continued to scream at the top of his lungs in the background.

"But he stinks!" He looked at him, rolled his eyes and frowned. "I don't wanna hold it!"

No matter how badly Zaboy treated Joshua, he would always gravitate toward him. The assistants and Quita tried to get Joshua to befriend some of the other kids, even Cordon, but he felt like they didn't have anything in common. Zaboy was just as weird as him, in his opinion, so he decided to take his chances and be his friend.

"I don't care what you want to do." Quita responded, with an extreme attitude. "You're not the most likable guy either, but he doesn't say anything to you."

"But I don't doo doo on myself! He smells all the time and my head be hurting!"

"Yeah but you loud, ridiculous and you singing all the time. So how do you think he feels?" She paused looking over him briefly. "Now shut up and hold his hand. I'm not trying to lose none of ya'll kids." Zaboy snatched Joshua's hand, and did as he was told.

As everyone continued their walk, Cordon looked back at Zaboy and said, "You know, that's why people don't like you right."

"What you mean?" He said through stiff lips. "I ain't even do nothin' to him. It's not my fault he don't wash up!"

Zaboy was rubbing Cordon the wrong way, and he was trying to keep his temper at bay. His father always told him that a temper can't get you anything but trouble. "You shouldn't talk about people. That ain't nice." Cordon looked at Joshua. "He a nice dude, and he don't bother nobody. People can't say the same about you."

"Right! Because your singing is terrible." Miranda added, kicking a soda can off the sidewalk. "All you do is be rude and get on peoples nerves. That's why I don't like you."

"Well I don't like you either!" He lied, trying to hold back his tears. "You better leave me alone for I tell my mother."

"See what I'm saying. Why you keep saying you gonna tell your mother?" Cordon shook his head and focused on the people in front of him. "Not cool, man."

Zaboy looked at them and said, "But he stinks and I don't like him."

Joshua remained quiet, as they spoke about him as if he weren't there. "And you sing a lot. Some people don't like that. But do you like when people pick on you?" Zaboy shook his head no. "Well remember that when you mess with other people."

Zaboy thought about what Cordon said, and tried to understand what he was doing wrong. When he was home, he was praised for everything from taking a dump, to hitting someone if he said he was defending himself. Cruella's behavior, which was intended to make Zaboy dependent upon her, was ruining his social life. He didn't get the same reaction that he did with his mother, over every little thing, like he did around other kids. "If I don't pick with him, will you be my friend too? Like you are Miranda's?"

"Boys don't ask each other to be friends. I'm Miranda's friend because I think she's pretty."

"You think I'm pretty? For real?"

"Yeah," he shrugged, trying to avoid eye contact. "I guess."

Miranda blushed. She couldn't believe what he said. Cordon was rich, dressed cute and always had money. He even bought her gifts, when he knew she'd be there. Like the gold locket around her neck, with the picture of a piano inside of it, that he bought because she said she loved to play. It was the first piece of jewelry that she owned. So she knew he liked her as a friend, but never thought he felt she was pretty.

"Awww…ain't that cute!" Pooh said, looking up from her texting activities. "I swear he looks like somebody I know. With his fine self!"

"Yeah…he looks like his father." Essence added.

"You probably right," she paused, "But don't they look so cute together."

"Shut up, Pooh!" Essence interjected. "You getting in the business without even knowing what's going on. Leave them kids alone."

She waved her off and said, "I know the boy likes her, and she likes him. I bet you it's a love story in the making. Ya'll gonna see." Cordon and Miranda looked at each other and smiled. They knew they liked each other, but that was the extent of it. They were too young to see into the future.

At the moment, Quita was too busy thinking about the new house she was trying to buy, so she wasn't paying anybody any mind. She saved over twenty thousand dollars and was ready to make a move, at the right time. It would be her first home, and she couldn't wait to move her mother out of the nursing facility, and into her house. She was also thinking about Stone and Jensen, and how it was evident that Valencia was keeping them away from her on purpose. The friendship with Valencia she could part with without an emotional connection. But she loved the twins with all of her heart.

She wondered if Stone went to his dental appointment, and if Valencia took Jensen to her eye appointment, because she told Valencia she felt she couldn't see. It was taking her awhile, but she was finally understanding what Kimi meant when she said, they were not her children. She was just about to turn into the park, when Axel's cry grew louder and more irritating.

"What do you want now?" She asked looking down at him. She was about to pick him up when a yellow pitbull, off the leash, charged in their direction.

"Oh my, God!" Not thinking straight, and on instinct, Quita took off running with the kids while both of the assistants followed in her direction. The only problem was, she left the baby. The only one who tried to help Axel was Cordon. He had enough bravery to at least grab a branch, in an attempt to defend that baby. But when the dog finally got up on Axel, instead of chewing his face off, the dog licked his forehead, and the baby threw his legs up in glee. With his hands and legs on the dog's nose, the baby was in heaven. No more crying and no more tears. A moment later, a frazzled woman rushed up to the dog and said, "Killer, get over here! Now!"

The dog stopped licking the baby and obeyed his boss's command. "I'm sorry." She said. "Really." She put the leash around the dog's neck and ran away.

When Killer was pulled away, baby Axel started crying hysterically again. When Quita, her trifling assistants, and the kids rambled back over to the baby, an idea came to Quita's mind. She had plans to put it into effect immediately.

AT THE HOUSE

When Quita and the children arrived back at the house, a man in a black North Face coat was standing on the porch. A red Lexus was parked on the curb, and Miranda's mother Vonzella was sitting inside of it. She was striking to look at and it was no wonder why men fell all over her. "Hey, Quita! We're here to pick up Miranda early. A friend of mine is throwing a New Years Eve party, and the kids can be there too."

Quita looked at the strange man, who was staring harshly in her direction. "Is he with you?"

"Yeah, girl. That's Miranda's uncle Mike." She looked at her daughter. "Say hi, Miranda. Don't be rude." Vonzella was grinning so hard, she looked artificial.

Miranda held her head down and in a low voice said, "Hi, uncle Mike."

"What happened to the other uncle?" Vonzella wiped the smile away and said, "What other uncle?" She looked at Mike, "You must be mistaken, I don't have no other uncles around her." Clearing her throat she said, "Miranda, get in the car. We got some place to be."

Miranda separated from Cordon and said, "Bye. And thank you for the necklace." Her eyes told him she didn't want to go, and she looked as if she were about to cry.

"No problem." He waved, hating that she had to go home so soon. He was gonna ask his father to bring them over some chocolate ice cream later on that day. He loved it so much, he ate it every chance he got. "I'll see you later. Right?"

"Hold up," Vonzella craned her neck out of the window, "ain't that Flex's son, Quita?" She grinned again. "With his cute ass self!"

Mike's eyes widened, upon hearing the news. "You talking about rich Flex from southeast?" Mike looked at Cordon as if he were a bag of money, and Quita immediately felt uncomfortable.

"Yeah...that's him." Vonzella smiled harder. When Miranda eased in the car Vonzella said, "So that's the little boy you can't stop talking about." She looked back at Cordon. "Snag him, Miranda. He's cute and rich."

"Vonzella, can I talk to you please?" Quita asked as she looked at Mike. She didn't want anything they talked about to be said around him. His energy was dark and it made her uncomfortable. Something about him was off. "In private?"

"Can it wait? I really got somewhere to be."

"Please. I'll be quick."

Vonzella begrudgingly got out of the car. Her light skin reddened the moment the cold air smacked against her face, and her long hair flew everywhere. The blue sweater dress she wore hugged her curves and her ass was so perfectly round it looked fake. When she got closer, Quita saw bruises on her neck. She figured Mike was beating her.

"Essence, come get baby Axel and take him in the house." She paused, giving her the stroller. "And Pooh, take the kids to the Kiddie Club…I'll be down in a minute." The kids followed the assistants, and Quita and Vonzella walked into the house and into the living room.

"I don't have long, girl. Mike be tripping when I keep him waiting."

"Don't you mean uncle Mike?"

Vonzella put her hands on her tiny hips and said, "That's my business now ain't it? Now let's get this over with. What you want with me?"

Quita wasn't sure what she even wanted to talk to Vonzella about. Based on her own rules, they didn't have any business outside of her watching Miranda and getting paid. Vonzella always paid on time, so there shouldn't be a problem. She couldn't even bring up behavioral issues, because since Cordon had arrived, Miranda was a model child. But there she was, emotionally involved and worried for the child's safety. She didn't even know how she got there. "I wanted to talk to you about the uncles."

Vonzella frowned. "What about them?"

"For starters, there doesn't seem to be a shortage of them."

"And?"

"Well, since I been keeping her, I've met ten different men, and that's no exaggeration. Miranda seems like she has a lot on her mind, and I just want to be sure, you're watching who you bring around her."

Just when she said that, Kimi knocked on the door. She hadn't seen her since before she started watching Cordon and she was surprised to see how bad she looked. Evening care was about to be a madhouse, so she was glad she actually came. "Everybody is downstairs, Kimi. Thanks for coming."

She lost a lot of weight, and looked as if she had a lot on her heart and mind. "Okay. I'll see you down there in a minute."

When she left Vonzella said, "Quita...what do you want with me?"

"I thought I made myself clear, Vonzella. I think you should watch your little girl, and limit the men you have around her. You might give her the wrong impression."

Vonzella held her head down, looked at the floor and giggled. "Look at your body, Quita. You're fat...ugly and naive. The only thing you got going for yourself is your daycare center, but this ain't even your house." She paused to let the insults soak in. "You don't know shit about what it means to take care of a man, or how keep one." She pointed at herself. "But I do."

"Some of that shit you said may be true, but is that how you want Miranda to live?"

Vonzella walked up to her and said, "Give me your hand."

"Huh?"

"I said, give...me...your...hand."

Quita reluctantly gave Vonzella her hand and she pulled her closer. Quita could feel the heat from her body, and she could smell the minty gum on her breath. With a firm hold on her hand, she pushed it down, spread her legs, and placed one of Quita's fingers into her vagina. "You feel that," she paused, "that's my pussy." She removed Quita's hand and brushed it against Quita's nose. A little of her cream sat on her top lip. "You smell that, that's my pussy too. And do you know what that means?"

Quita was so stunned she could barely react. "No." Her pussy was odorless.

"Well let me tell you," she said placing her hand on her hips, "it means I decide what to do with my pussy and how to use it. Unless you wanna start paying my bills, which includes my rent, my clothes, my car note and your high priced ass day care services. Now I don't have a problem fucking with a woman, if that's how it gotta be, so are you gonna take care of me?"

"No."

"Then do yourself a favor, and stay the fuck out of my business. Are we clear?" Quita nodded. "Good. I'll call you later." She took Quita's finger, stuck it in her own warm mouth and said, "Bye."

Quita didn't know what was going on with Vonzella, but she knew there was more to the eye than what she could see. She could've never imagined that the quiet Vonzella from Southeast, could be so gutter, but she certainly knew now.

⬅————————————————➡

THE KIDDIE CLUB

After Quita touched her first pussy, she went downstairs. The funny thing was, because Vonzella wasn't nasty, she wasn't even grossed out. Her only concern was Miranda and she wanted her safe. For a second she was questioning her sexuality, until she saw her friend Kimi, who looked more frazzled than ever. Kimi just placed her phone in her purse, so she figured she'd just got off a call that made her upset. The kids were playing in the Kiddie Club, and her eyes were glued on them, as if they were aliens.

"Kimi, what's going on with you?" She asked, sitting in the chair next to her. "No offense but you look bad."

In a slow steady voice she said, "Nothing. Who's the new kid?"

"That's Charlene and Flex's son."

"Flex." Kimi repeated. "Cool name."

"It's alright." Quita said.

"What's his name?"

"Cordon."

"He seems sad."

"He is…his girlfriend Miranda had to go home. He's always sad when she isn't around."

"What happened with the rape. I mean...didn't his father rape Charlene, which caused her to kill herself?"

"Yeah...I saw Flex's father the other day. And I couldn't understand why, since he raped Charlene." Quita said.

"Maybe Flex didn't tell anybody."

Quita didn't want to talk about Charlene because the issue was still sensitive with her. "I don't want to talk about Charlene."

"I understand." Tears rolled down her face, and Quita wondered what their purpose was. It wasn't like Kimi was as close to Charlene, as she was. She didn't even know her. "But wouldn't you want a rapist to be locked up? Instead of roaming the streets?"

"Yes." She touched Kimi's hand. "Maybe Flex will handle the matter on his own time."

"But he raped his son's wife, she killed herself, and he still isn't in jail." Kimi looked at Quita. Her eyes were so red, Quita knew she was high. "He committed a crime."

"Maybe the police couldn't prove he did it, because Charlene didn't mention the rape in her suicide letter. I don't know, Kimi! But like I said, I don't want to talk about it!"

Kimi looked at Cordon. "Isn't he beautiful?"

"Yes." Quita said, glancing at him. "Just like his mother."

"He probably looks like his father too." She smiled weakly. "I can only imagine what Flex will do to his father, when he finally get's his hands on him though."

"Yeah," Quita looked at Cordon, "it won't be nice."

"Quita, if you found out I did something bad. Really bad, would you still be my friend?"

"Is it something you did or are going to do?"

Kimi looked away from the kids and said, "Does it matter?"

"What happened to you, Kimi? I wish you would just talk to me! I feel helpless!"

"Would you stand behind me, if you found out I did something wrong or not?" She cried. "Answer the fucking question!"

The kids jumped upon hearing her angry voice. And the assistants tried to redirect their attention at the game they were playing. "Kimi, please...tell me what's wrong."

"Either answer the question or say fuck you." She paused. "But I'm tired of you beating around the bush."

"Of course I would stand by you!"

Kimi breathed a sigh of relief. "When it's time, I'm gonna tell you something. And you gotta remember the day you made me this promise. Okay?"

"Does it have something to do with Cash? Or the reason you're always sad?"

"You'll find out in time," She stood up and walked to the stairwell. "I can't come back here anymore, Quita. At least not right now anyway." She looked at the kids again and back at Quita. Tears ran down her face but she wasn't audibly crying. "I'm glad you have them to help you out around here." She nodded toward the assistants. "It makes me feel better for abandoning you." She walked away and for the time being, out of her life.

BACK TO THE FUTURE

Valencia couldn't believe she was back at Bula's psychic office. She tried to talk herself out of it on more than one occasion, yet there she was in the parking lot. The moment she walked inside and saw the receptionist's face, she ran back out. Leaning up against the wall, she vomited everything she ate earlier that day. She realized that it was becoming essential to have her future displayed before her and was overwhelmed. Wiping her mouth, she pulled herself together and walked back inside. Instead of seeing the receptionist again, she was greeted by Bula with a warm smile. "Come on back, Quita. Or do you prefer me to call you by your real name?" She paused, after winking one eye. "I've been waiting on you."

Valencia followed and took the same seat she usually did and Bula sat across from her. She admired how pretty she was once again, with her sharp bob complete with a Chinese bang. "Are you gonna tell me why you lied the last time I saw you? And why you told me your name was Quita?"

"I don't know." She paused, shuffling in place. "But this time is different, I'm not here to get my palms read. I'm here to apologize for how I treated you the last time we met."

"Is that right?" Bula smiled, again. "You really don't want me to predict your future?"

"Yes."

"Where do you live?"

She cleared her throat and averted her eyes. "Palmer Park."

"Well Palmer Park's a long way to come just to apologize. You sure you don't want to tell me something else? Or are you sure I can't help you with something?"

Valencia looked around the room. This was the first time she'd focused on the decorations, outside of the soft comfy love seat she sat in, and the beautiful cherry wood table that separated them. When she looked at the picture of a little girl on a table, she smiled. "That little girl is pretty. Who is she?"

"She's my daughter."

"I can see the resemblance," Valencia replied, trying to spark friendly conversation, hoping she wouldn't have to apologize again for the way she acted, before getting her palms read. "She looks just like you."

"Thank you. She's been dead now for two years."

"Oh," Valencia said in a low voice. "I'm sorry."

"It's okay. Diamond is with me now. Diamond is with me always."

"How did it happen?" Valencia interjected, wishing she could take her question back the moment she asked. "That is, if you don't mind me asking."

"I don't mind talking about my baby. She's love," she said softly. "I respect your candidness." She sighed, taking a long glance at the picture. "My child was abducted from our house after school one day. Witnesses said she walked willingly with a man she didn't know. At first everybody kept saying that a stranger took her, but I knew that wasn't the case. I knew in order for Diamond to go with him, he had to be somebody she trusted," taking a deep breath she continued. "I remembered a conversation she had with me, about one of her teachers. She went on and on about how nice he was, and how he was willing to help her finish her work, way after school was over. I was so happy a teacher was taking an interest in her education, that I ignored some very obvious signs. When she was abducted, it was as if she whispered in my ear and told me where to look. So I went to the police and told them everything I knew.

She stood up and poured herself a cup of coffee, before sitting back down. "He was an upstanding member of the community, so nobody really believed me. At that time, I was a young black stripper, and he was a forty-year-old white man who was also a teacher. But I decided to do some investigation on my own. I followed him from work and to his house everyday. For a while I couldn't find anything, but I knew if I stayed focused, that eventually it would pay off. And one night I was right. When I saw him bring out a large grey bag, that he was having trouble putting in his trunk, my heart stopped." When she began to cry Valencia started feeling very uncomfortable.

"I knew my daughter was in that bag. I saw her eyes, as if I could see right through the burlap cloth." She wiped her tears away. "I called the police, ran out of my car and approached him before he pulled off. I had to ask him why. Because without even looking in the bag, I knew my baby was in there. When I finally walked up to him he threw the bag in the trunk and looked me in the eyes. I can still tell you where every wrinkle was on his face." She appeared to go away for a second.

"He said to me…in a calm voice…that he killed Diamond because of me. He said that when he abducted Diamond, that she kept saying that my mother knows things. She told him I had a gift and that I would know he kidnapped her. He said after he killed her, she haunted him every night and that he wanted it to be over. He turned himself in willingly when the cops pulled up to his house. He's still in prison to this day." She sat her cup down on the table. "After that I decided to dedicate my life to my purpose, and that's why I sit before you now."

Valencia received the answers to the many questions she had about Bula, all at once. She knew why she read palms, and why she seemed no different than her. Now that she had the answers, she didn't know what to do with them. "Can you tell me about my boyfriend? I mean, I haven't paid, but I can give the money to you."

"So you don't think I'm a fake anymore?"

"I never thought you were a fake." She paused, clasping her hands together. "I was just scared."

"Okay give me your hands." When she observed her palms, her face became distorted. It was like she was reading a horror story of Valencia's life. "You're dating a man who isn't right for you. He'll suggest something, and you'll go against it at first, but eventually you'll agree. And when you do, your life will change forever."

"Do you see what it will be?"

"No, Valencia," she said taking her eyes off of her hands to briefly look into her eyes. "That's not how this works. I give you the information, and you'll take the advice and figure out how it applies.

What you have to do is try to be a better person. You don't have to be perfect, nobody is. Just try your hardest to always do the right thing. When you do that, you'll avoid danger, because it won't be able to find you."

"So Tech really isn't right for me?"

"If that is his name, not only is he not right for you, he's the total opposite. If you don't cut him off, and keep him away, your life as you know it will go down the drain. He'll ignite some evil things in you, you never knew existed. My advice to you is to stay away. Far, far away from him."

WHY CAN'T WE BE TOGETHER

Tech and Valencia were in her room, on her bed and she was on the verge of a mental breakdown. Although she was happy that he at least decided to show up this time, she still wondered if he loved her or not. Most times she'd call and beg him to come over her house, he'd claim to be on his way but he'd never show up. He was famous for standing her up lately.

"Tech, I know you don't really love me. I get that, but what I don't understand is why you don't tell me the truth. If you want to fuck other bitches, just stay out of my life. But every time you give me hope that you gonna do right, you fuck with my mind and my heart! So when you gonna stop bullshitting and be real wit' me?"

"What you want me to say, Valencia? That I'm gonna marry you when I'm not?" He paused, waiting on an answer he hoped would be brief. "That's the only reason I don't come over here like you want me to because I'm tired of telling you the same thing. You just don't wanna listen." He stood up and walked toward the middle of the room.

"But why don't you want to marry me, Tech?! When you asked I said yes and you took the proposal back!" She asked, as she kicked off her shoes and walked toward him. "You were gonna do it at first remember? Everybody around me got a ring on they finger but me. And then…that bitch Brooke had the nerve to come down my job a few months back, and talk shit in my face about you. On top of that Kimi tells me that she saw you at the mall with her," Valencia sulked. "All I want is you. All I ever wanted was you…but I want you to want me too."

"Valencia, I ain't got shit to do with them cat fights you be participating in. If you want to let a bitch get you all messed up in the head 'bout me, then that's on you." He said, walking over to the window, to see where the children's laughter was coming from. "I ain't dealt with her in the longest. It's over between us…but that's all I can say."

"Do you still care about Brooke or not?" She paused, as her breaths grew heavier. Losing him was causing her extreme unease. "If you want to be with her, let me go and stay out of my life. That's all I'm saying. You fucking with my head and my heart and I can't take it anymore."

"You the one who keep breaking up with me."

"Because you keep cheating!" She screamed. "But I do want to be with you." She touched his arm. "I just want you to want to be with me too." He sighed. "So were you with her at the mall or not?"

"I told you I wasn't. But you keep believing that shit because you want to. I fucked her in high school and haven't dealt with her since."

"That's not what she said, Tech." She cried, wiping her tears away with the sleeve of her shirt. "And how come you get into your feelings every time I mention her name?"

"How come every time *you* bring her name up you get mad when I answer your question? How I know you ain't the one trippin' off of that bitch? You sure you don't want to fuck her, and you just putting it on me?"

"Don't get slapped, Tech!" Valencia warned, her face heated with jealousy. "Look at you," she continued, throwing the top off a bottle of water in his direction. "You can't even talk about her without looking away from me. Or blushing! I see how your eyes light up when I say her name."

"Man, please cut the bullshit!"

"I will when you tell me the truth! I can take it! It's better than people talking behind my back. You don't want to marry me…you don't want to be with me, but you'll take my money and fuck me."

"Well I guess I'm getting ready to leave you after all, because I ain't come over here for all this shit!" As Tech walked toward the door Valencia blocked his path. "Move, Valencia." He tried to walk around her but she blocked him again. "I don't want to hurt you but if you don't get out of my way, I will."

"Well marry me! That's how you don't hurt me! I bought this house for us and now I'm in it by myself."

"No you not. Quita live here don't she?"

"I'll put her out if you want me to." She paused, to see if she was getting through to him. "Come home to me, Tech. Please! It ain't like we ain't been together forever. I'm ready to start all over and start a family with you. Don't you want kids?"

"Not really."

"Well I do! I'm ready to take care of you. You don't even have to pay no bills, if you don't want to." His eyes widened. Now she was talking his language. Broke Bastard 101. "I need you to come back because I can't live without you." He walked away from the door and approached the window again. It was obvious something outside inspired him and held his attention.

"Valencia, do I have to marry you, for you to take care of me?"

"Yes, for me, Tech!"

"Well I can't do that now."

"Why?"

"Shit different, since I moved out. I been in the streets and I like my freedom. When I was up in here I felt like a kid wit' a curfew." He paused, remembering how needy she was when they lived together. "But it's obvious I'm still feeling you, otherwise I wouldn't be here at all!"

As Valencia was trying to put her life together in the bedroom, she could hear the children playing as if life for them couldn't get any better outside. The daycare center had grown larger than she expected, and she saw all the money Quita was bringing in. As a matter of fact, that very day, Quita pulled up in her new red Escalade, fully loaded. "What you got going on downstairs?" Tech asked, as the children's laugher overpowered their conversation. "Who all them kids belong to?"

"Oh that," she responded as if he should have known. "That's a daycare center I own." She lied as usual. "I thought you knew about it."

"*Your* daycare?" he walked over to her. "When you open a daycare center?"

"The moment Quita moved in. Why you think I let her live here," she giggled. "Rent free at that."

"Where the twins?"

"They been staying at my mother's house," she said in a low voice. Not wanting him to know that she was trying to hurt Quita, by keeping her away from them, since she knew she loved them so much. She was being evil all because she was jealous of Quita's bond and love for Kimi.

In addition, Valencia heard the rumors that she wasn't taking care of her own children, and that Quita was their honorary mother. Instead of stepping up, she stepped back, by moving them to their grandmother's house. But in that instant, she realized in her evilness of trying to hurt Quita, she was getting the short end of the stick. Since her twins were with her mother, Quita was living there and working there rent free. She didn't have the responsibility of taking care of the twins anymore and she wasn't paying rent. She made a mental note to start taxing Quita immediately.

"You know how my mother is. She has to be around her grand-babies at all times." She could see the daycare center interested him for whatever reason so she said, "I don't tell you everything that goes on, Tech. You ain't here enough, but I wish you were. I am making good on my center though. It's good money."

"Maybe I can be here a little bit more," he responded looking out of the window. "How you run the daycare, when you work a full time job?"

"Just like I run shit at the office," she walked over to him and threw her arms around his waist. "It's called delegation of responsibilities. I let Quita do what she gotta do, and I take the money. A lot of it too."

He looked at her and kissed her lips. "Well how come she has a new Escalade and you don't?"

"Because I bought a Range."

He looked out the window. "Naw, that joint she pulled up in is a late model. Looks like she's making more paper than you are to me."

Valencia was insulted. "Well I do make a lot of money! This my house and that makes it my daycare center. I just don't need to floss on cars."

He raised his hands up and backed away. "Okay...okay, ma-ma." He chuckled, after lifting her chin, to look into her eyes. "When you say a lot of money," he pulled her closer and kissed her softly on the lips. "How much we really talking 'bout?"

"Enough to make your problems go away!" she bragged, step-ping closer to him. "If you come back to me. I can even buy you a new car. I know you getting tired of that run down shit you driving now. That's the kind of shit real bitches do."

His dick got hard. "Prove it." He said gripping her ass. "Hit me off with a few bucks now."

"Okay. It's not a problem, Tech. Whatever you want I will do." His face went from happiness to anger. "What did I do?" She asked. "I mean...did I just say something wrong?"

"I'm just remembering something you told me when I first came over."

"What?"

"Earlier when I asked you for some money, you said you was broke. How come you lied then?" She forgot about her fib. The only reason she told him about the daycare, was because she saw the inter-est in his eyes, and she knew she was about to lose him. If money was what she needed to keep Tech, then he was about to be paid in full.

"I'm sorry I lied." she said sitting on the bed, and reaching for her purse. "But how much do you need now?"

"Enough to put a deposit on a new car." He paused. "About five thousand dollars."

She put her purse down because that kind of cash was not in there. "I don't have that kind of money, Tech. It's expensive to run a center and we still in our early stages. I got a Range and she bought a Caddie"

"You just said you were makin' a lot of cash with the daycare," he complained as if she owed him something. "If you don't want to give it to me, just say that shit! Look who's playing games now!"

Now that she lied, she would have to eat her words and give him the money that for real, she didn't have. She knew she wasn't the owner of Quita's daycare center, but now it was too late. They we-ren't even that cool anymore, so she wasn't sure if she could even ask Quita for the money. "I'm not playing games. You know I'd do anything for you," she pleaded. "I proved it already." She swallowed. "I just have to find a way to get it."

He grinned. He had her heart, and that meant he had her purse too. Like the male prostitute he was, he immediately got on his job, and removed her jeans and panties. Then he began to massage her feet. "I know what you doing, Tech, but I'm gonna need a little more from you than that this time," she said in a low voice as his fingers continued to massage her toes. "If I pay you, you're mine. No more fucking with Brooke or other women."

"If you take care of me, I'ma take care of you." He got on his knees, put her toes in his mouth, and circled them with his tongue. She lay on her back, and allowed Tech to do his business. When he seduced her with his soothing foot massage, he moved up her thighs with warm tongue strokes. She moaned as she readied herself for the real treat...hardcore pussy and asshole eating, courtesy of Tech. Pushing her legs apart, he bent down and sniffed her womanly scent. She was soak and wet.

"Valencia," he whispered, looking up at her. "How much do you know Flex?" He flicked his tongue over her clit.

"What?" She frowned, wishing he continued his business. "Not good...why?"

"They say he loves his family...a lot too."

"I guess, baby. But can we talk about that later?" She grabbed his ears and pulled him into her warm mound.

"Look...I have a proposition I want to talk to you about." She was so horny that she would've sold her twins to him if it meant he'd continue to make her feel good. "If we plan right, we can get at least a hundred thousand."

"What?" She lifted her head. "How would we get that kind of money?"

"I gotta plan, that is fool proof."

"Okay...but do we have to talk about this now?" She wanted him to shut up and continue about his work.

"No...after I finish, but it involves something you never did before."

She thought about the psychic but was ready to sell her soul to the devil anyway. "Okay...kiss it for me again, and we'll talk about it later."

"Before I do it, I need to know that you'll do anything for me."

"Tech, I'll die for you." She said seriously. "Let me show you by staying in my life."

"That's all I wanna hear."

YOU SHOULD LET ME LOVE YOU

Quita and Demetrius were sitting on the porch, watching the children play outside in the front yard. Her assistants Essence and Pooh, were facilitating game play time with the kids. The weather was slightly warmer than it had been in the past, so she decided to sit outside with them.

"What is it about me that you're not feeling, baby? And be honest, I can take whatever you dish." Demetrius responded, trying to get through to her mind and heart.

"What you mean?"

"Ever since the day I bought that picnic basket over here, months ago, you've been acting differently. Not like the girl I fell for at Dave N Busters."

"Who said I'm not feeling you?" Her eyes avoided his. And at that moment, the children running around, and the fact that she hadn't seen Miranda in weeks, were the only things on her mind. Suddenly she wondered if approaching Vonzella about the men in and around her life was a good idea after all. She could tell she wasn't the only one worried about Miranda, because Cordon seemed unhappy since she'd been gone also. "I care about you a lot. It's just hard for me to show it right now."

"Every time we make love, you act as if it's surgery. Almost like you don't want to be bothered with me or something. Not to mention, you don't wanna see me outside of this house. I can't take you out, I can't show you a good time, and I can't be the man I know I can be, and take care of you."

"That's not fair, Demetrius. You know I have these kids, and I have to run this center. What you want me to do, take them with us when we go out?" She looked at him and hoped he wouldn't say yes.

She could feel his desperation and knew he was willing to do anything to get through to her. "I work seven days a week, with maybe three hours of sleep a day. My life is hectic right now."

"And that's normal?"

"It may not be normal, but it is my life." She said. "And I'm choosing to live it like this."

"With the money you making now, you can get somebody else to look after these kids. I see you have Essence, and the other little girl, but maybe you need more help. Nobody can function off of working everyday, with only three hours of sleep."

"How you know how much I'm making, Demetrius?"

"Let's see, you have a red Cadillac Escalade parked on the curb, when it use to be a Honda. You have on a different pair of shoes every time I see you. You have an abundance of Gucci and Louie bags...I mean...I got eyes, babes. I can see."

"That's it?"

"No...not to mention whenever I come see you, I have to hear you remind me, that you can finally take care of yourself, and you don't need a man for nothing. Like I want to take your independence away from you. That's not the kind of man I am, Quita. I believe in making my woman better by adding to her, not taking from. But you aren't realizing that a part of making you better, is demanding that you take care of yourself. Which you aren't right now."

"I am taking care of myself."

He looked her over. "Are you sure?" He lifted her chin when she tried to look away.

She moved away. "What the fuck is that supposed to mean?"

"Nothing." He looked at the kids. "But I am tired of you making me feel like I'm not a real nigga. You even tried to pay for dinner that one time we did go out, and that was very disrespectful. I have a full time job as a biologist, for one of the biggest hospitals in the world. I don't need to take money from a woman, especially one I'm falling for. I don't care how many daycare centers she owns."

"Demetrius," she said taking two deep breaths. "I know we don't get out much like you said, so how about we do this, let me work a few more weeks. I have a plan I'm sure you'll love and it involves leaving this house, and being in a place of my own. When I do that, I'm gonna hire more people and we can go out anytime you want."

She made him a promise, but for some reason, she didn't feel like keeping it. Her heart told her he wasn't the one, but she couldn't understand why. He was tall, handsome, employed, and head over heels in love with her. Yet there was something about him that pushed her away.

Demetrius looked at her, leaned back and said, "Are you serious? You're really moving out?"

"Dead serious."

He nodded his head. "That's a hell of a start." He looked at her again and asked, "When you move out, and you get settled, will you be my lady then?"

"You mean on an exclusive basis?"

"That's the only way I want you. All to myself."

Quita was silent, as she looked at the children playing. The cold concrete underneath her thighs, felt hot. She smiled as she continued to look out on the children, who were all there as a result of some misfortune or another. Now that they were with her, she wouldn't trade them for anything in the world. Unless a parent was stupid enough to not pay her...then it would be a whole different story. Over time, she learned that she got far more from them, than they did from her.

Although Demetrius' anticipation of her answer burned a hole in her consciousness, for a moment, her eyes fell upon Cordon. His personality was as mesmerizing and as suave as his father's and she wondered what life was like for him, when he wasn't under her care. She could see depression in his eyes, when a few of the mother's picked up their children from the center. She knew he was missing Charlene for sure when he cried the day Cruella's heavy mustache wearing ass, kissed Zaboy and told him she loved him. Nobody but a child missing his mother, could cry from that scene. She knew he needed his mother and she wished her friend hadn't taken her life. Still ever since he came, there was something in the air that told her things wouldn't be right, but she could never place her finger on why.

"Demetrius," she said realizing she kept him waiting too long. "I do care about you. I mean, I never met a man who was as attentive, kind and understanding as you are, to me." She looked at her gloved hands. "Sometimes I don't even feel deserving."

"Then what is it? Another man?"

"No!" Quita responded, rubbing her hands on her jeans, for warmth. "If I don't have time for you, what makes you think I have time for someone else?"

"Do you want to be happy?"

"Yes," she looked at the earth beneath her. "I want happiness more than I ever realized, until recently. But you have to understand where I'm coming from. I'm tired of rushing into things, and getting bad results. I want to take my time."

"You got to explain, baby."

She sighed and said, "I lost my job, Demetrius. I lost it unexpectedly and wasn't sure if I would be able to find another to take care of myself because of my past. Shortly after that I lost my apartment, my car and almost couldn't afford the nursing home my mother is staying in. That shit was scary to me. To not be able to support yourself, and the people you love, is depressing. I never want to experience that kind of emotion again. So I hustle and hustle hard. That's my life right now. So if I come off strong about my independence, you got to forgive me. With a little time, I'm sure I'll feel safer and things will get better. Maybe then I'll let my guards down."

He rubbed her leg. "Okay, what can I do, to make you understand, that I want to be with you? And that I want to make things easier? I'm willing to do anything."

"Hold on, Demetrius," Quita interrupted. "Yo, Zaboy, keep your hands to yourself. I'm tired of you messing with Joshua." She looked at her assistants. "Why aren't ya'll watching them? He just hit that boy in the face!"

"I'm sorry, Ms. Quita." Essence said rushing toward them. "I was playing ball with the other kids. But I'll break them up now."

The other assistant felt froggy so she decided to jump. "Quita, look at all these kids out here! We got like twenty!" Pooh bucked. "It's impossible for us to watch them all at the same time."

"Maybe if you stay off your phone you can do better."

"I wasn't even texting this time." She continued, placing her hands on her hips. She had a crush on Demetrius and loved showing off whenever he was around. "I just listened to a voicemail. It's not that deep."

"Pooh, if you can't watch all twenty kids at one time, then what am I paying you for?" She took her hands off her hips and tended to the situation. "That's what the fuck I thought." Quita paused. "She's a mess!"

Zaboy was so angry that Pooh yoked him up and took away his toy, that he kicked the innocent grass beneath his feet and threw himself on the ground. When he did, Joshua quietly walked over to him, and brought him another toy. For some reason, as bad as Zaboy treated him, Joshua felt he was still his friend. Some people were use to being treated badly. By looking at that scene Quita saw that accepting what you didn't deserve started early in life. In his mind Zaboy protected him from the other kids, so it was best to stick with him, despite the abuse.

"Sorry, Demetrius," Quita said, directing her attention back at him. "That boy gonna make me ring his neck out one day. His mother told me the other day, that this was the longest daycare he'd ever been in before. Sometimes I can see why."

"What's up with that kid over there?" Demetrius asked, zeroing in on him with his eyes.

"Who?" Quita asked, fanning a fly out of her face.

"The lil man next to your truck. Who looks like he lost his girlfriend."

"Oh," she smiled. "That's Cordon, he's a loner. Every now and again he'll kick it with the other kids, but mainly he's stays by himself. Unless he's playing with Miranda when she's here." She grinned. "His little girlfriend."

"His clothes look fresher than mine."

"Me and Pooh said the same thing. I don't know too many kids, who wear Gucci scarves and gloves to school. I tell his father all the time, to bring some play clothes for him when he drops him off, but he says those *are* his play clothes."

"He must make some serious cash," Demetrius said, as his eyes implied something Quita didn't like. "If he can dress a kid like that for play he must be paid. Must be nice...real nice."

"He's doing something right," she responded, wanting to get off the subject. People were often too concerned with Cordon, and it made her uncomfortable. "But his father pays in advance, Cordon doesn't give me trouble, so they're both cool with me."

"Quita, I saw how you avoided my question, about being my lady. So I'm gonna ask you again. Are you gonna be my…"

"I can't do it." Quita blurted out. She looked into his eyes so that he would know she was serious. "I'm sorry."

"What exactly are you saying?"

"I'm saying," she swallowed, "That I can't be with you, Deme-trius. I don't love you and I don't want to force it anymore. It wouldn't feel natural."

He stood up, brushed the back of his jeans off and said, "Where did that come from?"

"The heart. And I think we should step back from one another for right now. I need enough space to get to know who I am."

He looked at her and said, "You know what, the crazy thing is, I respect that shit. It may have taken you an hour to beat around the bush, but you finally came around." He bent down and kissed her on the lips. "Let me give you a piece of advice though. When I first met you, you were fine as hell in the body department. But you picked up a little too much weight, and now your body is dumpy. You may wanna push back from the table."

He walked away, and she knew immediately her decision was right. He was all wrong for her.

BABY AXEL

Baby Axel, sat in a swing, screaming at the top of his lungs, as Quita walked into the room. A beautiful yellow lab stood on her side, and she kept him closely to her, by tugging on the leash. "Hey, Axel, you see the doggie," Quita asked, as she crept to the swing. "We bought this dog, and he wants to play with you." Axel was quiet for one moment before he activated his vocal cords and screamed louder than before.

"Why are you crying?" She asked, wishing the baby would re-lax and go with the flow. "You like dogs remember?"

Quita knew he stopped crying when the pit-bull approached him, but she wasn't going to bring, what she thought of as a killer, into the house. So the lab would have to do. Axel looked at the dog, back at Quita, and screamed some more.

"What the fuck does he want?" Pooh asked, rolling her eyes at the child. "His little ass got lungs of steel."

Essence was downstairs in the Kiddie Club, watching the other children.

"I don't know, but pick him up and put him in the crib." Quita ordered, staring at her. "Make yourself useful around here before I fire your ass." She was tired of hearing her complain as if she weren't being paid.

The crib was white and had orange and green balls embedded along the sides. It blended in perfectly with the yellow designer wallpaper, which decorated the small space. The room use to belong to the twins when they were babies, and Quita only used it for Axel, when Valencia wasn't home, and she was trying to put him to sleep.

When Pooh sat the baby in the bed, Quita took a seat in the soft green chair next to it. She picked up a white doll baby, and placed it inside of it, even though Axel was a boy. Nothing seemed to work and Axel continued to wail which caused the lab to bark louder. "Come on, Woody," Quita said, patting the dog. "Cut all that barking out."

Since Axel had refused to stop screaming, Woody continued to bark in his face. When the phone rang Quita told Pooh, "Watch the dog and the baby." She looked at the phone she was texting on and said, "Do not text in here. Eyes on the dog and the baby. You got it?"

"Yes, Ms. Quita...dang!" She sighed, placing her phone in her jean pocket.

Quita walked out the door, to get the phone in the kitchen. When she answered, she was shocked to hear Terry's voice on the other line. She hadn't heard from her since the night they went to Dave N Busters, and to be honest she didn't care. She always felt Terry was more Valencia's friend than she ever was hers, and Quita didn't lose a minute's sleep worrying about it either.

"Hey, girl! What you been up to?" Terry asked, as if they were best good girlfriends. "I ain't heard from you in months. How was your New Years?"

"I can't talk right now. I'm kinda busy. So what's up?"

"Okay…"

"Not trying to be rude but I have a lot going on right now." The dog and baby Axel continued to compete for the, *'Who Can Be Louder'* contest, so she knew buying the dog was an epic fail. "And I can't hear you, so you got to speak up."

"I see, what's up with all that noise in the background? I hear a dog and baby."

"Terry, what's up?" She tried to refocus her attention.

"I just wanted to see if Valencia gave you my message."

"No…is she at work?"

"Yeah…but she at lunch now. She should be back any minute though."

"She didn't give me any message, Terry. And to tell you the truth, although I live here, I hardly ever see her anymore. Or the twins." She tried to envision their faces.

"That's fucked up. Anyway, I just wanted to tell you that Kimi was put out on the streets. I drove up there the other day to go see her, and all her stuff was on the sidewalk. Her TV, her couch, her clothes, everything." She paused. "I picked up a few things myself, because I figured she'd want me to have them instead of everybody else, but it was so sad. Do you know where she is?"

"No!" Quita couldn't believe what she was hearing. Her friend didn't have a home and she didn't call her? What the fuck was up with that. "Are you sure, Terry?"

"Quita, I been over her house many times. Those were her things on the sidewalk. Trust me, she got evicted and I don't know where she is now."

"Is Valencia there yet?"

"Yeah…she just walked in. Wanna talk to her?"

"Yes." As Quita waited on Valencia, she noticed the dog wasn't barking and the baby was laughing. She reasoned that maybe her plan worked after all. A minute later, Valencia got on the phone with her usual attitude.

"What the fuck you want?"

"Can you tell me why you didn't tell me Kimi was put out?"

"Why do I have to tell you anything? She's your friend... shouldn't you know already? Plus I don't recall me having to answer to you. You live in my house, not the other way around."

Quita rolled her eyes. "Valencia, I'm serious!"

"And so am I, Quita. Kimi is not my problem anymore. She's yours!"

"Can you at least tell me if she's called me? When you answered the phone?"

"You're at my house more than I am. So how the fuck should I know?" She paused. "Now I have to go, because unlike some people, I have real work to do. I'll rap to you later."

When Quita got off the phone, she decided to get in her truck and look for Kimi. Whatever was going on with her, had to be worse than Quita originally thought. It was time for them to have a serious conversation. Walking back to the baby's room, she was mad to see Pooh outside the door texting on the phone. "Why you texting out here! And not watching the baby like I asked you to?"

"Because you said no texting in the room. So I'm texting out here."

"If you don't get it together, I swear to God, Pooh, you will be gone. I really am tired of warning you. And why didn't you tell me your cousin was set out?" Quita grilled.

"I ain't know. I think her cell off cuz I ain't talked to her in a minute."

Quita shook her head at Pooh and walked into the room and the moment she did, baby Axel stopped laughing and started crying again. Seconds later, the dog started barking in his face, as if they were a team. When she closed the door, the crying and barking ceased and Quita had her answer. The baby didn't like humans, and the dog didn't like crying babies. If they were alone, they were fine.

If their union worked for them, it would work for Quita too.

CRAZY DRIVER

Pooh was driving Quita's van with Cordon, Zaboy and Joshua inside. They were coming from the movies and since their parents were the only ones who payed for them to go, Quita stayed home to watch the rest of the kids who couldn't go. Plus, Axel was there, even though he was locked in the room with the dog, Woody, the baby's real sitter. Pooh was talking on the phone, and not paying the road or the children any mind.

"Bitch, I'm telling you, I saw the nigga Doo-Man in the club with another chick! Evanka swear he loves her ass. I don't even think that's his baby she pregnant with." She paused so the caller could speak. "And they have a nerve to be talking about how we treat the kids at our daycare center! I heard they put Lil Goose in a dog house and everything! I bet OCC don't know 'bout that shit!" She laughed, taking her eyes off of the road, to change the CD player. "I'm for real! It's almost sad how they treat his bad ass."

"Can you stop cursing?" Zaboy said, stuffing his fingers into his ears. "My mother said my ears are for God's purposes only! I don't wanna hear all that."

Pooh put the phone in her lap, turned around and said, "Shut your faggy ass up!" Zaboy's eyes popped open. "Always getting in people's conversations...you ain't fuckin' grown! When I'm on the phone, keep your comments to yourself."

Zaboy looked at Cordon and he looked away. He warned him about talking when he didn't have to. Truthfully he was tired of Pooh's mouth too, but he realized he was a kid, and it was not his van. "You don't talk to me like that! I'ma tell my mother! And I'ma tell Ms. Quita too." Zaboy retaliated.

Pooh was heated at the mentioning of Quita's name. She didn't care about him telling his mother, but she was concerned about her boss. She specifically warned her about using her phone when around the kids. So if Zaboy told her she was driving and talking without a headset, it could mean her job. And if there was nothing else she feared, being broke was it.

"I'ma call you back, girl. Zaboy's gay ass 'bout to make me unleash on him again!"

When she hung up Zaboy said, "You not the boss of me! I hear you talking about me. I'm telling, mama! I'm telling my daddy too."

"You ain't got no damn daddy! You a bastard!"

"I got a daddy! He went to the moon, so he can make me a lot of money when I get older. He gonna come back and get me later. I'ma be rich!"

Pooh laughed so hard her stomach hurt. "Who told you that dumb shit?"

"My mommy!"

Pooh took two quick breaths and said, "Boy, shut your dumb ass up! Everybody know that father of yours is in Florida, because he don't wanna be around you. He ashamed that instead of being a real boy like Cordon, you choose to run around DC singing like a faggy!" She laughed. "And if you tell Quita anything about me on the phone, I'ma knock your ass on your back. Or get Lil Goose to do it for me." She grinned, knowing he was scared of him.

"You can't get The Goose! He don't go to day care no more!"

"I'ma take you to the park and he gonna be there waiting! And soon as he sees you, he gonna stomp your ass out! And your mommy...God or even your daddy on the moon, won't be able to do shit about it."

Zaboy sat back in his seat and looked at Cordon, for help. Cordon turned away again because he tried everything he could to get him not to be so extra, but nothing he seemed to do worked. Zaboy was just one of those kids who loved to call attention by snitching, singing and the like. As far as Cordon was concerned, it was over for the kid, besides he had his own problems to deal with anyway.

His mother was dead and he missed her dearly. The one person he looked forward to seeing these days seemed to have disappeared off the face of the earth too. He was going to ask his father to help him find Miranda, knowing he would, but he tried to be a big man, by doing the work himself. It had been weeks since he'd seen Miranda, and he needed to see her, so he could feel a little better. If only he wasn't a kid, he could get on a bike, go and find her, himself, but that wasn't the case.

"What's that on your wrist?" Joshua asked Pooh as he did his best to hold his bowels. He was sitting in the front seat next to her. The last time he shitted on himself, and they were stuck in traffic for hours, everybody yelled at him, including Cordon.

"Oh," she grinned, taking off her coat, so she could show him the entire pattern. "It's my new tattoo." Once out of her coat, she showed him the rose vine running up her arm that started at her wrist. She was so busy showing off, that she didn't realize the cops were sitting on the corner, as she drove past the stop sign, without breaking. "My boyfriend wanted me to get this when he came over last week. So I…"

WOOP…WOOP! The police pulled up behind the van, and Pooh was so scared, she started swerving. The kids were nervous at first, thinking she was about to crash. "Oh, my God! Oh, my God, they…they pulling me over!"

The kids turned around and tried to look out of the back window. But because they were little, it was difficult to see what was going on behind them. Pooh got it together and pulled over on the side of the road. The officer got out of his car and approached the driver's side. "License and registration please." He said looking at the children, before focusing back on her.

"Sir, what did I do?" She immediately began crying. "I didn't do nothing wrong."

"You ran a stop sign, mam. With kids in the car at that. Sure you did something wrong."

Pooh turned around to see what he was talking about. She stared at the kids as if she didn't know they were there, and then the stop sign, and a look of surprise spread across her face. She was doing her best "Puss in Boots" expression of sad eyes, but no one was buying it, especially the officer. "License and registration please." He repeated.

She dropped her head then looked up at him and said, "Sir, I don't have a license. Please…don't be mad, I'ma lose my job."

He leaned into the window and asked, "What you mean you don't have a license? Whose children are you driving around?"

"My boss'."

"And she allowed you to drive these kids without a license?"

"I showed her a fake one, but I don't have it on me. She didn't know I wasn't supposed to be driving. I needed a job, my mother got mad at me because I was running up my phone bill. And cuz I dropped out of school." She cried harder and her words were almost inaudible. "I was going to go back, but my boyfriend was gonna kick my ass because I crashed his window. So I was scared." She dipped into deliria. "Please let me drive home and I'll never drive again after that, I promise."

"Mam, step out of the van." He opened her door. "And put your hands on the hood."

"Oh my, God! You actually about to arrest me?" She damn near fell out of the van. "Oh my, God! You can't be serious! I didn't do nothing! Them not even my kids! Please don't do this! I can't breathe." She held her chest. "I can't breathe."

"Well try harder," he paused, "*after* you put your hands on the hood." The officer said, uninterested in her performance. He'd seen this type of thing a million times before. "Now, who can I call to come get these children?"

"I don't remember the..." Pooh passed out, and was unable to provide the officer with any more information. He grabbed her before she hit the ground, and her tattooed arm drooped over his shoulder.

The officer put his hand on his head, looked into the sky and said, "You got to be kidding me." He looked at his partner. "Get an ambulance out here, man. This girl done fainted."

He looked into the car at all of the kids, and since Cordon looked the most reasonable, he said, "You know your parent's number? Because we have to have them come pick ya'll up."

QUITA'S DAY CARE CENTER

Quita was so indebted to Cordon, that she didn't know what to do. She hadn't realized that Flex made him memorize the names, numbers and addresses, of every place he was allowed, in case of an emergency. Flex stressed the importance of always knowing his surroundings so he wouldn't have to depend on others. To make things even better, instead of calling Flex, like the officer requested, Cordon elected to call her. As soon as they came back to the center, in Cordon's honor, Quita gave everyone ice cream. A lot of trouble could've kicked off with the parents, and the authorities, had Cordon not been thinking on his feet. Although Joshua and Zaboy were in heaven, because of the ice cream, Cordon seemed to be in a world of his own.

"You okay, Cordon?" Quita asked, placing a hand softly on his back. The children downstairs were playing extra loudly, so it made it difficult to hear him, but she was use to it now. "I was hoping I put a smile on your face."

"I'm fine, Ms. Quita. Thank you." He picked over his treat with a spoon. "Guess my head kinda hurt."

"Why you not eating your ice cream? It's your favorite. Chocolate."

"Not really hungry I guess." He shrugged.

"That's sad." She said softly. "Because I was hoping you would want to enjoy a bowl with an old friend." When she said that, Miranda came upstairs with a smile on her face, wearing the locket he bought. He didn't fake cool like he normally did. Instead he hopped out of the seat, ran up to her and hugged her tightly.

"Where you been?" He asked, releasing her. "I been looking all over for you." It was so cute Quita giggled. She could really imagine the little guy, roaming the world to find his first love.

"I been at home. I couldn't come over no more." She looked down at her feet. "But Ms. Quita came and got me today, and told my mama she would watch me for free. So my mama let me go so I can play with you."

"You want some ice cream?" He asked, trying to stop the smile from spreading across his face. He was losing his cool by his father's standards, and was trying to pull it together.

"Yeah...I'll have some." When she said that, Zaboy jumped up and pulled out her chair for her. She looked at him in shock, before finally sitting down. "Thank you." She told him.

"You're welcome." He grinned.

Cordon gave him some grown man dap, before taking a seat himself.

Quita watched the kids laugh and eat ice cream for twenty minutes, before realizing she was wearing a smile on her face. Cordon and Miranda had found love, and she was reminded that she was alone. She wondered how Frank was doing, and if her crush Bricks, ever thought about her.

Now in a solemn mood, she decided to go downstairs and talk to Essence about her new responsibilities, since she was firing Pooh's ass the moment she came back to get her things. She couldn't believe she lied to her about having a valid driver's license, or the reason she was pulled over. Of course Zaboy gave her the full details, without missing a beat.

Right before she walked downstairs Zaboy yelled out, "Ugggghhh! Not again!"

Quita knew immediately Joshua defecated his pants. "Joshua, please tell me you didn't." He held his head down and looked into his empty bowl. She wasn't about to yell at him, because it was obvious he couldn't help himself. "Your mother bring you extra clothes?" He nodded. "Go get them and meet me upstairs. I got to check on baby Axel, but I'll see you in the bathroom."

Since Pooh wasn't there, and Essence was watching the younger kids downstairs in the Kiddie Club, she had to bathe him. When Joshua walked into the bathroom, she felt sorry for him, and she wished there was something she could do to help him. The water was running in the tub, so she could give him a bath. He looked so sad and her heart broke, despite the smell steaming from his body. "Joshua, why do you keep doing this, baby? I don't understand."

He shrugged and said what he usually did, "I'm sorry."

She shook her head and said, "Ease out of your clothes, honey." When he did, her heart pounded in her chest, when she saw his underwear was covered in blood and stool. She turned him around, and saw bite marks on his inner thighs, buttocks and stomach.

"Joshua," she was shaking so hard she couldn't stand still, "who did this to you? You gotta tell me okay?" He shook his head no. "Baby, please...I'm gonna get you some help." He started crying and so did she. Now his behavior at her center made sense, someone was abusing the child.

"Joshua, please. Please, talk to me." He cried harder. She wasn't concerned about the smell, or his feces anymore, so she pulled him to her body and held him tightly. His naked body shivered under her fingertips and she knew he was beyond scared. "Joshua." She pushed him away softly. "Look at me."

"Okay," he wiped the tears from his face.

"I'm not gonna let nobody hurt you again. Do you hear me?" He nodded his head. "Do you believe me?"

"Yes."

"Good now tell me who did this to you. So I can help."

"My daddy."

Quita nodded, happy she got something from him. "Okay...now who is your daddy?" She paused. "Where is he baby?"

"My mommy."

She frowned. "I'm confused. What are you talking about?"

"My mommy is my daddy."

The bathroom felt like it was spinning and she held onto the sink for support. "Wondrika, is your dad?"

"Yes." He nodded. "And he hurts me every day."

WAITING ROOM

"Hey, Demetrius! You came so quickly!" Quita said as she ran to the front door to greet him. She had Axel on her hip, and the yellow lab moved everywhere the baby went, as if it were his protector. "I'm so glad you could come. I would not have called you if I didn't need your help so thanks for dropping everything."

"It's not a problem, but is everything okay? How's the kid? And what's wrong with him?" He paused. "You didn't tell me much over the phone."

At first Quita felt it was a bad idea to have him come over to watch the kids, but she didn't want to bother the other parents, by having them pick the children up early. Besides, most of them didn't get off until later that evening. Quita's mind was all over the place after seeing what Wondrika did to Joshua. Her heart said she had something to do that day, but she couldn't remember what it was. The good thing about it was, Essence was still there, so Demetrius wouldn't be with the children alone.

"Demetrius, everything is happening," Quita responded, while trying to ignore her thumping headache. "I feel like I'm running around with my head chopped off."

"Well what's going on, Quita? I hate when you talk in circles." He said, looking her over. "And are you okay?"

"I'm fine…I just gotta go to the hospital." She paused, waving the air. "I can't say too much of anything right now. I just need you to stay here with Essence, until Valencia gets home. Can you do that for me?"

"No doubt. Do what you got to do, that's what I'm here for."

She grabbed the baby's bag and said, "Thank you. The kids are all downstairs. You can turn the TV on to keep yourself busy."

"Slow down, Quita." He said, rubbing her shoulders. "And look, I'm sorry about that shit I said the last time I saw you. About your body." He continued. "I was just mad that you didn't want me, so I started saying stupid shit."

"I know, Demetrius. So don't worry about it, there is no need to apologize" She moved in and kissed him on his cheek. "I really have to go. Joshua is in my truck waiting on me."

"Where are the kids?"

"Downstairs," she ran out the door and yelled, "Thanks again!"

THE HOSPITAL (THREE HOURS LATER)

Quita was pacing the floor until a police officer approached her. Baby Axel sat in the stroller and Woody stood right next to him as always. She was surprised at how good he was being, despite other humans being in his presence. She thanked God for small blessings. "Are you Quita Miles?" An officer asked, approaching her. Quita stood up.

"Yes." She shifted her weight form one side of her body to the other.

"How is he?"

"He's gonna be fine." He paused, shaking his head. "Well…he's going to be fine now anyway."

"You know…I have never seen anything like that shit. He had bite marks on his stomach, back and everywhere else. Who could do a child like that? He's so sweet and doesn't deserve any of that shit! I feel like I let him down!"

"Take it easy." He paused, looking her over. "Look…what is your relationship with the child? He told me you watch him sometimes, but I'm not really sure what that means. It seemed like he was trying to protect your or something."

"I'm a good friend of the family." She lied, not wanting to alert them of her illegal daycare center. "Well…I thought I was a friend of the family. And Joshua is right, I do watch him every now and again."

"Well, we're glad you were smart enough to bring him here. And we're happy that you came into his life when you did. This is amazing."

"Why you say that?"

"Wondrika is a convicted pedophile, Ms. Miles. He's done things far worse and it's a wonder the child is still alive. We believe it has something to do with his calm spirit. He must've gotten too comfortable, thinking the boy wouldn't tell people who he was, which he didn't until today."

"I'm totally confused right now."

"Me too," the officer said, trying his best to explain. "Let's just say that he kidnapped that kid years ago from Houston, Texas. In the middle of the night." He shook his head. "His family has been looking for him for years. As a matter of fact, he was missing two years ago to this day. It's almost too real to be true. On the same day he was abducted, years later, he was discovered by you."

Quita stepped back. "What do you mean?" She asked placing her hand over her chest. "I don't understand what you're saying. Wondrika wasn't Joshua's real father? Or mother?" She paused, as a nauseous sensation took over her. "I feel so sick!"

"The young man that you know as Joshua is actually Joey Kennan. We believe Wondrika, who's real name is Wallace George, named him Joshua so he would have a name close to his own when people called him. Anyway, Wallace kidnapped him from his home, on the day he was released from prison for child molestation. The young man's family never gave up on him. Today they were in a church, praying for his return, like they do on the evening of his kidnapping every year. The moment service was over, they got a call from me, because of you finding their child. Their prayers were finally answered."

Quita was so scared, that she backed into her seat and flopped down. She stared out in front of her, and slapped her hands into her face. All those times Joey cried, and whined, she didn't help him. It was his way of expressing himself, and crying out for help, yet she ignored the signs. She could only imagine what he went through every night he went home to Wondrika. Quita was overwhelmed and cried her eyes out. The baby sat up in the stroller and waved his hands to get her attention. Quita continued to weep.

"Mam, your baby wants you." The officer said, looking at the child. "He's a handsome little guy too."

Quita wiped her eyes and was surprised that Axel wanted her attention. For the first time ever, he wanted her. She picked him up, wiped her tears and the baby cooed loudly in her lap. "See, that's what it's all about…love. Your baby loves you a lot mam."

She smiled, wondering why the baby had a change of heart. "He ain't mine."

"I could never tell. He sure acts like he belongs to you." He laughed, shaking the baby's hand. "Look…I know you're upset, and I understand why." He paused, looking down at her. "But you had no way of knowing what was going on with that child. Don't put that kind of pressure on yourself. It'll make it hard for you to sleep at night." He continued, so she could digest his words. "Look at all the good you have done."

"What good?"

"You saved that boy's life, while simultaneously giving him back to his family. Wallace is on his way back to prison where he belongs, and Joey has a chance at a real life. Give yourself some credit, Ms. Miles."

She looked up at him wanting so desperately to believe his words. Yet at the end of the day, she felt responsible for not finding out what was going on with him sooner. "Thank you for the encouraging words." She told him. "I appreciate it."

"And I appreciate you. If we had more people like you, who cared enough to take the extra step for the love of a child, the world would be a better place."

VALENCIA'S HOUSE

When they got back to the house, Quita felt something was off, the moment she stepped out of the truck. For starters, instead of having to use her key, the front door opened with a twist of the knob. Once inside, she noticed all of the kids were gone, so she walked to

Valencia's room. With Axel on her hip, and Woody by her side, she knocked softly on the door. "What?" Valencia screamed. "I'm busy right now!"

"It's me." Quita said, hoping she'd open it up. "It'll only take a second."

"What do you want, Quita?"

"Do you know where the kids are?" She asked, speaking into the door. "Nobody's here."

Valencia stomped to the door before snatching it open. "Do I know what? I couldn't fucking hear a word you said."

"Do you know where the kids are? They were here when I left and now they're gone."

"If it's *your* day care center, why aren't you running it properly?"

"Valencia, please!" Quita snapped. "This is serious. Now it's a little too early for them to be gone...so if they not here, where could they be? They not supposed to be leaving for another hour."

"I don't know, Quita. When I got here, Demetrius was sitting in the living room. He got mad at me because I wouldn't fuck him, so we got into a fight. The next thing I know, I came upstairs. I think he got mad and left. That's the last time I saw him."

"Valencia...what about the kids?"

"I just told you I didn't see any kids! Aren't you listening? What the fuck is wrong with you? Now leave me the fuck alone! I got problems of my own!" She slammed the door in her face.

Quita looked at the baby and Woody and said to herself, "What is going on?"

She crept downstairs to her daycare center again, to make heavy observations. Everything was neat and in place, so she was starting to feel a little comfortable. Organization meant Essence cleaned up before she left, so everything must've been fine before she went home. Instead of calling her first, she decided to call Demetrius, since he was supposed to be there. But every time his phone rang, he didn't answer. Finally she walked back upstairs to the living room, and sat on the sofa. A few minutes later, Clarkita came through the front door and Quita was shocked. She hadn't realized she didn't lock the door until she walked inside.

"Hey, honey." She walked in, picked up the baby, and landed kisses all over his face. The baby started playing with his mother's nose while smiling from ear to ear. "I see he wasn't crying before I came in. As a matter of fact, it looks like everybody is getting along. Maybe our plan worked after all."

"The dog." Quita said flatly. Her mind was elsewhere. Something wasn't right and she knew it.

"Huh?" She giggled, looking at the beautiful animal. "I don't understand what you mean."

"The dog." She repeated, dryly. "Axel loves dogs. If anyone has one, he won't cry anymore."

Clarkita looked at the beautiful animal and a smile spread across her face. "Are you serious? After all this time, this was all I needed to do?"

"Yes." She looked at Woody. "You can have him if you want to. I only bought him for Axel."

"Quita, you may have saved my life!" She said cheerfully. "A dog!" She pats the animal on the head. "I can't believe it! Why didn't I think of that?" She kissed the baby again. But when she saw Quita's face, and felt her nervous energy, she knew something more was going on. "Honey…are you okay?"

"I came home, and the kids." She tried to prevent from crying. "The kids…they're…they're not here."

The color appeared to drain from Clarkita's face. "Where were you? I mean, what happened to the children?"

"One of the kids I was watching was being abused. So I took him to the hospital, and when I came back, they were gone."

"Did you call the young ladies who help you? The assistants?"

"One of them was fired, for lying earlier today. And the other one I haven't called yet."

"Well let's start there first." Clarkita walked into the kitchen, and brought the cordless phone to Quita who was unable to move. "Here…make the call."

Quita took the phone out of her hand and called Essence. Luckily she answered on the first ring. "Hey, Quita! You need me to come in early tomorrow?"

"Essence, when you left," she ignored her question, "were the kids here?"

"Yes. Well most of them." She paused, as her nervousness was expressed through the phone. "Why…what happened?"

"Who was here with them?"

"Demetrius." She paused, as her tone got lighter. "He told me you called him to watch the children. So I left after most of the parents came and picked their kids up."

"So the parents did come?"

"Yeah…Vonzella got Miranda, Cruella picked up Zaboy and most of the other parents came and got their kids." She paused. "Why, what's wrong?"

"What about Cordon? Did Flex come and get him?"

"I don't know." She said, as her voice trailed off. "You're scaring me, Quita. What happened?"

"What the fuck do you mean you don't know?" She paused. "Did Flex come and get him or not?"

"When I left, Cordon was still there. So I figured since Demetrius was with him, and he was another man, that he would be safe and it would be fine for me to go home."

"I just took Joshua to the hospital because another man bit and raped him! So Demetrius being a man doesn't make Cordon safe now does it?"

"Quita, I'm sorry. I stayed until most everybody left but him, so I figured I could go. I had to go to school tonight so I can get the last credits for my degree. He told me that's why you invited him over."

"But it's not time for everybody to leave yet." Quita looked at her watch. "Not for at least another thirty minutes."

"Quita, we told all the parents to be there early, because you were going to see your mother for her surgery. It was to-day…remember?"

Quita had totally forgotten. That was the thing she had to do to-day that she couldn't remember. "But what about Axel, his mother just got here?"

"Maybe you forgot to tell her."

"I have to go, Essence."

She hung up the phone and Clarkita asked, "Quita, what's going on? Talk to me!"

Quita ignored her as she ran upstairs to approach Valencia, but when she knocked on the door, she didn't answer. Not caring if she got mad, she twisted the knob and looked around her room, but she was gone. When she walked over to the window, she saw her car was gone too.

Clarkita walked up the stairs, and into Valencia's room with Axel on her hip and Woody by her side. "What's going on, Quita? Please talk to me. I'm worried about you."

"He's going to kill me." She said flatly.

"Who?"

"Flex."

RAY THE RIPER

Quita sat on the couch alone, waiting on what terrible thing would happen next. The silence made her uncomfortable, because she was use to being around children all the time. She dropped the ball majorly, and because of it, Cordon may have been kidnapped. She thought about everybody…whoever had been around him. There was Valencia, Essence, Pooh and now Demetrius. Could they possibly have taken him, for hostage purposes?"

She looked at her watch and prayed that Clarkita would come back after she dropped the baby off to her best friend, like she promised. At first her best friend said no, knowing Axel cried non-stop with no signs of sleep. But after explaining how Woody would have to come too, and that it was an emergency, she agreed to let her drop him off.

Every time a car passed the house, Quita got scared thinking it was time, for life as she knew it to be over. When the door opened a few minutes later, and Valencia walked inside, for the first time in a while, she was happy to see her face. For the moment it meant that Flex wasn't there to kill, at least not yet anyway. "What's going on?!" She threw her keys on the table by the door, and walked over to Quita. "Why you sitting in here looking all crazy?

"Where were you? I knocked on your bedroom door again, but you were gone."

"I had to go take care of something." She paused, trying to avoid her eyes. "Now what's going on? You look terrible."

"Cordon," Quita sobbed, as her right leg began to tremble. "He's missing. And Flex is on his way over right now. He's pissed and I have a feeling he's gonna kill me, Valencia. I'm still trying to understand what happened tonight! He told me to take care of his son, and I didn't, and because of it, he's gone."

"I don't understand," she paused. "What are you talking about?"

"You heard me, Valencia! I came home today, and found out that all of the kids were returned to their parents accept Axel and Cordon. Clarkita came and got her son after a few minutes of me being home, but I don't have a son to give Flex. That means he's missing, and it means it's all my fault. Now can you please tell me what happened when you got home? Maybe something you tell me will help me find out where he is."

Valencia sighed. "Okay...Demetrius was here when I got home and I believe Essence was gone. I can't say for sure because I never go downstairs. I will say it was quieter than it usually is when people are in your center." She sat next to her. "The moment I came home, Demetrius tried to kiss and fuck me. I don't know what came over him, he was acting real different. I told him it wasn't like that between us, and he still wouldn't stop. I told you how he can be, Quita. He's a dog."

"Please go ahead." She said, not caring for the adlib, or the fact that Demetrius wanted her.

"Anyway, like I said, I went off on him. Cordon walked upstairs from the Kiddie Club, and I remember being surprised because it was so quiet down there, I thought everyone was gone. Since Demetrius was here, and I felt uncomfortable, I went to my room. The next thing I know you're knocking on the door asking where the kids were. I'm just as confused as you are. I can't say how much time lapsed from when I went upstairs and you came."

As Quita looked around the living room, she felt as if a Mack truck had hit her. She wanted this to be some kind of cruel joke but no one was laughing. All she kept thinking about was Flex, and how he would react once he got there. She wished she never accepted the money he slid across the table, but now it was too late.

"Where were you? I mean, why would you leave the kids alone with him, Quita?" She paused. "You don't even know him like that. You should've known something like this could kick off."

"Why you say that?"

"I mean, do you think he had something to do with him being missing?"

"I don't know." She shrugged. "I don't know anything."

"So why did you leave him here alone, with somebody else's kids? He's not one of your assistants. He's a grown man that the children's parents didn't know or authorize you to leave them with. I hate to say it, but this shit is really your fault."

"Joshua was raped by Wondrika." Quita said. She looked into her eyes to see if she cared. To see any signs of her being a human being, with actual feelings. She saw a glimpse of hope. "He was bitten, raped and abused. That's why he whined a lot, and that's why he kept defecating on himself. Wondrika had ripped his anal cavity apart, and he lost all control of his bowels. So it wasn't that I wanted to leave, I had to!"

She put her hands over her mouth. "What do you mean? How can a woman do that type of damage to his anal cavity?"

"She's a man."

"Are you kidding me?"

"Valencia, I had a rough day. I'm probably about to lose my life. The last thing I want to do is kid with anybody, including you."

Valencia stood up, spent a few moments in the kitchen, and brought back two beers. She handed one to Quita, which she gladly accepted. "When does Flex get here?"

Quita looked at her watch and said, "In about five minutes." She took a sip of beer and she wished she had vodka inside of it.

"Quita, I know we have our problems," she paused, "and I'm sorry about my part in all of this drama. But I just wanted you to know, that I never meant for any of this to happen."

Quita looked at her and said, "Why did you forge the documents to get me fired?" Since she was going to die, she might as well have the answers, to the things she always wanted to know. "I loved that job more than anything."

Valencia sat back in her seat and said, "I guess I thought I deserved the job more than you." She took a sip of beer. "It felt like since the moment I met you, I've always walked in your shadow."

"But you have everything…a car…kids…your own house and a good job. Why wouldn't that be enough? All I had was that job, Valencia. I don't even have a man!"

"I'm not happy I guess." She sighed. "I always want more, and sometimes I don't even know why." Quita didn't feel better. "I just wanted you to truly know, that I never wanted anything like this to happen to you. We had our problems, but you are still my friend, Quita." She paused. "When Flex gets here, just be honest with him, and tell him what you know. This is not your fault and could've happened to anybody. Maybe he'll understand."

She stood up and grabbed her keys. "Where are you going?" Quita asked.

"I have some place to be. I'll see you when…"

A second later, Flex busted through the door with three hard hitting niggas, all dressed in black. As the men ran through the house, without saying a word, Flex pulled up a chair and sat directly in front of Quita. He looked up at Valencia and said, "I don't know where you were about to go, but your plans are cancelled for the evening. Sit down." He pointed to the couch. Valencia slowly took a seat and placed her hands nervously in her lap.

His eyes were red, and Quita could tell he'd been crying. Placing his Ruger 9 millimeter handgun in his lap, he wiped his face with the back of his hand, and took a deep breath. Rubbing his palms together in a brief manner, he exhaled, and placed them on his knees. It was as if he were trying to find something to do with his hands, other than hurting someone.

"I couldn't get here fast enough. I tried, but it didn't seem like we were moving quick enough for me." He said to them. "I was hoping once I got here, that you'd tell me that you found my son and all this would be over." He looked directly at Quita. "Have you found my son? Is he here?"

"No," Quita sobbed, "and I'm so sorry. I really don't know where he is, and I would never fuck with you like this. I know how much you love him."

"So my son's still missing?" She could tell that he was trying with all his power, to speak to her calmly. His main purpose was to find Cordon, and if he could do that peacefully, that would be best for all parties involved. "I'm here, and my son's not waiting on me?"

"No…and I'm so sorry. I was going to call the police, but you told me to wait on you." She sobbed.

His men gathered back into the living room, with disappointed looks on their faces. "He's not here." One of them said. "What you want us to do to them?"

Quita knew it was over, but saw the frightened look on Valencia's face, and she felt awful. If he was going to kill her, she would have to deal with the issue, but she didn't want her to die too. "Flex, Cordon was my responsibility, not Valencia's. Can you please let her go?"

"Unfortunately not." He shook his head. "The only time that door is going to open, is if I'm going out or my son's coming in." He paused. "Now...what...happened?" Quita's body trembled so hard, she was forced silent. "Listen," he said again, taking three deep breaths, as tears rolled down his face. "I need you to calm down, and tell me what happened to my son. And in order to do that, I need you to get a hold of yourself and breathe."

Quita looked at the men who were standing around the house, in an authoritative manner. Their guns in full view, only added to the apprehension and tension in the air. "Quita, please tell him what happened." Valencia pleaded with her, as if she were holding back. "I'm scared."

She couldn't stop looking at the guns, and the way they hovered over the house. It was like her voice was trapped inside her throat, and couldn't be released. "Quita, they're not the ones you need to be worried about," Flex said in a slow serious tone. "I am. Now tell me...what happened...to my son."

"Uh...I took a child to the hospital...uh...because...uh...he was bleeding..."

"Quita," Flex advised again. "Remember I told you to calm down?" She nodded, and tried to steal several breaths to ease her mind. "You're stuttering so I need that to stop. Aight?" Quita nodded her head quickly again. "Now talk to me about my boy."

She took three more deep breaths and said, "Okay...okay...I went to the hospital, because a child had been raped. It didn't happen here, but I needed to get him help anyway. When I got there, I found out he was actually kidnapped by the person I thought was his mother. It's a long story, but it was the only reason I left."

"Okay..." Flex said, hoping she'd get to the part that involved him.

"When I got back home, the person I left to take care of him was gone and so was Cordon."

"Who is this person?"

"His name is Demetrius."

Flex snapped his fingers, and one of his goons stepped up. "Give me the address." The man pulled out a small pad and a pen to take the information. "I'm ready."

She looked up at the goon and then Flex. "I don't know his address."

"Fuck you mean you don't know the address!?" His brows were drawn so closely together, they looked connected. "You said you left the dude around my kid. Why wouldn't you know where he live?"

"He always came over here. I never been to his house before. I was always so busy."

Flex's jaw pulsated. "What's his telephone number?" She gave it to him. "Call him, man."

As the goon dialed the number Quita provided, Flex's eyes remained fixated on her. She could hear the goon talking to someone, and figured Demetrius answered the phone this time. When he came back into the living room, he whispered in Flex's ear. Flex appeared shocked before looking back at Quita. He stood up, and stole her in the face so hard, she dropped to the floor. "The number you gave us, was to a dead man. They said he was murdered in his house tonight."

"Murdered?" She yelled, holding her face. "That's impossible! He was here today! Or maybe he was killed after he left."

"The police answered the phone, they said he'd been there all night. They had a warrant out for his arrest because he'd been robbing banks or some shit like that. Apparently when they went in to get him, he was already dead."

"He was a biologist!" Quita corrected him.

"NO...he was a modern day stick up kid." He continued, rubbing his chin, before dropping his hands. "They said they tried to call this number earlier, but no one would answer the phone, and that they were on their way to talk to you." Quita remembered how Valencia went into the kitchen to get the beer, and how long she was gone. She must've turned the phone back on at that time. "If you ask me, it sounds like he's been dead for a while. So where's my son?"

Right when he said that, the phone rang. "Can I answer it?" Quita asked, pointing toward the kitchen. "Maybe it's about Cordon."

Reluctantly he said, "Go ahead."

Quita stood up and answered the call. From the kitchen, she could see everyone staring at her, waiting on the verdict. "Hello?" She paused and looked at Flex. Her eyes widened and she removed the call from her ear. The phone shook in her hand and she said, "They…said…put…put…the phone on speaker."

Flex walked over to her and whispered, "Then do it."

Everybody followed him and hovered in the kitchen. "Am I on speaker?" The caller said, using an altered voice.

"Yes." Quita said softly.

"Good…is Flex right there?"

In a gruffly voice he said, "Yeah. Who the fuck are you?"

"Perfect. I'm the person who has somebody you love. And I'm the person who controls whether they live or die."

"Nigga, I will kill you!" Flex yelled into the phone. "You don't know who you fucking with! I'm not some sucker ass nigga!"

"Okay…and I'm really scared," he chuckled, "if only you knew who I was you would know I'm about mine." He laughed. "I make the rules in this game." He paused. "Now, this is rule number one. You gonna gather up two hundred thousand dollars, and place it in a black trash can, on the side of the McDonalds off of Riverdale Road. The one next to the IHOP. When you do, I'll release him to you untouched."

"If he's hurt…"

"I told you what I want done." He interrupted, his voice stronger and more authoritative. "Do it, and you got three hours. Not a minute more. I'm not the one to fuck with."

When he hung up Flex looked at Quita. He walked up to her, and she backed into the refrigerator, for fear of what he was going to do next. "Who was that?"

"What?" She paused. "I don't know. I don't have any clue!"

"When you answered the phone, the first thing you asked was can you put the phone on speaker. How did he even know I was here?"

"I don't know. Maybe they're watching the house."

"You think I'm a joke don't you?"

"No, Flex!"

"We had an understanding, and you broke that agreement. You promised to take care of him before you took my money. Because of you my son is missing." He turned around to look at his man and said, "Do that for me."

The man stepped away, and made a phone call out of earshot. "What's going on?" She asked, looking at the man and back at Flex. "What you just tell him to do?"

With zero emotion he said, "I hope you said goodbye to your mother. If you didn't, it's too late now."

FROM WHENCE I CAME

The nursing home seemed to be normal when Quita got out of her car, and walked inside. If her mom had been murdered, like Flex said, she would expect more activity. Instead she bypassed a few elderly people, whose awkward smiles, seemed to be eerily out of place. She wanted to run away, and deal with this at another time. Perhaps after waking up in her bedroom and realizing everything was a dream. As she continued down the hallway, the lights turned off, with the only illumination coming from the front desk. She realized then that the residents were preparing for bed.

When she approached the front desk, a black woman with a kind smile stopped what she was doing to greet her. "Well hello there, Ms. Miles. I never see you here this late. How are you?"

"I'm fine...I guess."

"That's great," she moved a few charts to the side and said, "Well what can I do for you tonight?"

If her mother had been murdered, she figured the greeting would be totally different. Maybe Flex was just fucking with her mind, to get her to help him find his son. If that was his plan, it certainly worked. Partially relieved she said, "I was coming to see how my mother was doing...after the operation. I'm sorry I wasn't able to make it."

A brighter smile spread across her face that was so contagious, Quita couldn't help but smile too. "She pulled through the surgery with flying colors. After the anesthesia wore off, she even requested a big meal." She giggled. "That mother of yours is tougher than you realize."

"Did she ask about me?" Quita asked pushing the limit. She knew her mother suffered from dementia, but hoped for the best.

The nurse's smile dimmed a little but she said, "She didn't...but I know she wants to see you. She's resting right now though, and I don't think we should wake her up. She needs all the sleep she can get after the surgery. She's strong but she's still fragile at the same time." She looked at how distraught Quita looked. "Is something else wrong?"

"Are you sure my mother's okay?" She asked, leaning on the counter. "I mean...when was the last time you check on her?"

"I'm not only sure, I'm positive she's okay. And I just checked on her. Not even an hour or so ago. She's sound asleep, Ms. Miles and there is no need for you to be worried. The best doctors performed her surgery and everything went well. We tried to call the house, but nobody answered the phone. Are you sure you're okay?"

Quita smiled, and pulled her phone out of her coat pocket, when it vibrated. When she saw the number flash across the screen, she knew exactly who it was. "Excuse me," she said, stepping away from the nurse. Placing the phone to her ear she said, "Hello..."

"I thought you told them you were taking the trash out?"

"I lied." She paused. "I'm at my..."

"I know where you are, but why?" Flex asked. "I told you the status of that situation before you went. The only thing you need to worry about now are the funeral arrangements."

"But I needed to see my mother, Flex. You just told me somebody I love is gone! I need to make sure she's okay."

"And I told you she wasn't and hoped you said goodbye," he paused. "You were supposed to be at home, waiting on that officer so you can get rid of him. Any information about my son is gonna come through that phone at your house, and I need to be there. I'm gonna find my boy tonight, I don't care how many more people I have to hurt in the process."

Tears rolled down her face. "So you really did...you really did kill my mother?" The nurse looked at her strangely and she stepped further away. "Please tell me this isn't true!"

Silence.

She cried harder. "She was all I had. Why did you do this to me?"

"You got fifteen minutes to find out the answer to something you already know. Take any longer, and I'm coming for you next."

When he hung up, the phone rang again and she saw Kimi's picture flash across the screen. She thought her cell phone was disconnected, because whenever she called, Kimi never answered. It didn't matter at the moment, because Kimi wasn't a factor. She didn't feel like talking, and she didn't feel like being supportive to anyone but herself. Ignoring the call, and placing the phone back in her pocket she said, "Can you check on her again...my mother? For me...please." Quita needed the nurse to go in and look to be sure. She couldn't bare walking in her mother's room herself and finding out the truth first hand.

The nurse looked into her eyes and said, "If it will make you feel better," she continued in a calm voice, "it will be my pleasure."

"It really would. I had a bad dream and I want to be sure."

"Give me a second." She disappeared into the back of the nursing home, for what seemed like forever. When she didn't come back right away, her soul told her that something was up. This day was growing more horrifying by the second.

"Excuse me, mam." Another nurse said, bypassing Quita and rushing into the direction the first nurse walked in.

When she saw doctors and other nurses rushing in that direction also, she walked backwards toward the door. Her mother...her dear sweet mother was gone, and it was all her fault. As she continued to move toward the door, heaving heavily, doctors and nurses brushed past her on a mission to her mother's room. The worst thing that she could ever imagine happened, and her life would not be the same. And she had a missing boy to blame.

$\longleftrightarrow$

THE TRUCK

Quita sat in her truck, on the side of a road, and looked out into space. What was she going to do now? Her mother was her reason for living. She didn't have a man, she didn't have kids of her own, and she didn't have a purpose. Now that she thought about it, she didn't even have real friends. She couldn't believe it, after waiting outside the nursing home for thirty minutes, when a doctor actually told her, *'Ms. Miles, your mother is dead.'*

She thought about driving her truck off a cliff, or maybe a bridge, but she needed to bury her mother. If she didn't give her mother the proper burial, no one would. So for the moment anyway, she couldn't even take her own life. She thought about the chain of events leading up to this moment, and her stomach churned. Opening the car door, she leaned her head out and vomited on the side of the road. This was too much for her...too heavy for her to deal with. He actually did it. Flex actually murdered her mother, by having someone suffocate her while she slept. And it didn't matter that she had nothing to do with the situation, her daycare center or his son.

When the phone rang again, she removed it from her pocket and saw Kimi's face flash across the screen once more. With nothing else to lose, she answered the phone and said, "Hello, Kimi. What's up?"

"Quita...can you talk?" Kimi's voice was low and steady. "I been trying to call you all day."

"What is it?" She looked out of her window. "I'm kind of busy."

"You sound as bad as I feel." She paused. "Are you okay? Really."

"I'm worse than okay, Kimi." She said, looking at the cars passing by. "So what do you want?"

"Wow. I thought you'd be happy to talk to me. Especially since we haven't spoken in a while." She paused. "I figured you'd miss me as much as I miss you. I realized a lot about our friendship...we have our shit with us, but in the end, we were always there for one another."

"Kimi, that may be true, but being a friend to anybody, at this point, is the least of my worries. Besides if you cared about me, it would not have taken you this long to reach out."

"Whoa...did I do something wrong?"

"Outside of avoiding me, and making me worry about you." She said sarcastically. "Naw...you didn't do anything wrong."

"Then what is it?"

"My mother was murdered tonight, Kimi. The one person who gave a fuck about me, even though she couldn't say it to me anymore, was taken from me."

Kimi gasped. "Oh my, God!"

"I'm not done...I found out today, a child in my care was being raped, tortured and abused." She laughed. "And get this, the person I thought was his mother, wasn't even a woman! He was a grown man who kidnapped him from Texas years earlier! He took him from a family who prays for him especially hard once a year. That boy will never be the same!"

"Quita, are you fucking with my mind?"

"Am I fucking with your mind?" She laughed harder. "Bitch, you think too highly of yourself! I don't have time to fuck with your mind, or anybody else's for that matter, when my world is falling apart! The only person's head that's being fucked with right now is mine, and I'll be glad when it's all over."

Silence.

"I'm so sorry, Quita. I really am. I know how much you loved your mother, and I know you're dying inside. Murdered? I can't imagine who would want to kill your mother?" Quita choked back her tears. Besides, she cried for an entire hour after the confirmation that her mother was dead. And since it couldn't bring her back her tears were useless. "My bad, you don't have to answer all my questions. I know you are going through it. Please forgive me for calling right now with all my shit...I really didn't know."

Quita felt badly for talking to her that way because she could feel her apology was genuine. "I can't do anything but deal with it now, Kimi. And try to figure out my next steps."

"Maybe I should call you back...at a better time."

"My mother is dead. And she is not coming back to life." She paused. "There will never be a better time for me, no matter when you call. Tell me what's going on with you. I need a distraction right now...for the moment anyway." When she hadn't said anything Quita said, "I'm serious. Tell me what's up."

Kimi sighed. "I wanted to call you to tell you why I've always been out of it. I couldn't' talk to anybody about it before, but things have changed with me now."

"Go ahead."

"This is hard for me, so you gotta forgive me if I move slowly." She paused. "When I was younger, I was pregnant by a man I really loved. I wanted him so much, that I thought I loved him more than myself, and even my flesh and blood. But he was often weird. It seemed like he was three different people at the same time. One minute he loved me...the next minute he hated me...and the next minute he needed me. It's kind of hard to explain, but that's how I always felt."

When she didn't say anything Kimi said, "Are you there?"

"Yeah." she exhaled.

"Anyway, when I went into labor, I was hopeful, even though he said he didn't want a baby, that he'd change his mind. I figured once he'd seen the baby, he'd realize that getting rid of it, like we planned, would be impossible. I figured he'd love me too much to let him go. But he was serious, Quita."

"Wait...you have a baby?"

"Just listen...please." She swallowed. "When I went into labor, at a movie theater, I should've known it wasn't going to end well. After he drug me out of the movie theater bathroom, and outside, I gave birth to our baby in the back of his truck. He was beautiful, Quita. Perfect. As quickly as I could, I counted his fingers and toes and he had all of them." She wept. "He was so beautiful." She paused. "But the moment I gave birth to him, he took him away from me. I let him get rid of my baby, like he was a piece of trash!" She sobbed harder. "You can never imagine...ever...what it felt like to want to fight for your child, but feel too scared to try. I felt helpless! I actually gave birth to my baby in the back of a truck, Quita, and let him take him away from me. All because he told me, he didn't want any kids. I didn't think about what I was going to tell my mother, my friends and even my coworkers, when they asked me how was the baby. Or where the baby was. Can you imagine, having to walk out of your house, and dread being asked about a baby you didn't have anymore? A baby that wasn't in your life? All because you were too scared to fight back?"

"No...I can't."

"Well it was hard. The loss of my baby, caused me to hold resentment in my heart for other kids. That's why I couldn't stand to be around them, and when you first told me about the day care idea, I wasn't mentally invested."

"It makes sense now." Quita said softly. "I'm sorry I put you through any of that."

"It seemed like after that, every man I got with, the only thing on my mind was having a baby. Most of them would do the act, but not many of them, wanted to stand by me and help me raise a child. And you know what?"

"What?" Quita said, to assure her that she was listening.

"I really didn't care. I was focused and I knew what I wanted. To have another baby, just as beautiful as the one I lost." She paused. "So when I got with Cash, my mission and focus did not change. If you had a dick and could stick it in me, that would do. It wasn't until getting with him that I realized that I did have limits. And that there were some things I was not willing to do. I chose wrong when I let him into my home, and he raped me for it. Quita, he raped me and threw me away like trash...just like Thomas did to me and my baby."

"Who's Thomas?"

"My son's father." She replied. "I felt resentful...and I never got over it. So I had to get revenge."

The hairs on the back of Quita's neck stood up. "So what you do?"

"I killed him."

Quita's eyes flapped wildly. "What are you saying? Do you mean that in the literal sense?"

"I mean that in every sense you can think of." She paused. "I'm saying that I put a knife through his heart, turned it, and watched him die. I'm saying that as I'm speaking to you now, the blood is draining from his body, and dampening my feet. I'm saying that this nigga got exactly what he deserved."

"Kimi, you're playing right?"

"I wouldn't play like this with you." She continued. "I'm as serious as you were, when you told me your mother died."

Quita sat as still as a statue in her seat, and didn't make a sound. "I have to go, Kimi," she paused, "I can't do this right now. This shit is too heavy for me."

"But I'm not finished. You told me if I ever did something bad, you would always be my friend. So I have to tell you..."

Quita hung up on her, and took a deep breath. If she lived after tonight, she would try to help Kimi figure out her situation later. But right now, she had to pull herself together and see about Cordon and Flex. Otherwise she was certain that he'd hurt someone else she cared about next.

<--->

AT VALENCIA'S HOUSE
(THREE HOURS LATER)

The cops just pulled off, after speaking to Quita about Demetrius' murder. When Quita walked back into the house after from talking to them out on the lawn, she was even more confused. Someone came over his house, shot him in the head, and left the window open so that if he wasn't found, the funk of his body would alert someone familiar with the smell of death in the air. She couldn't understand how he was over her house one minute and dead in his own bedroom the next.

The cops assured her that although they were leaving now, that he'd be back in the future to ask her more questions. Although they would be back, she felt relieved that they were gone. She knew they would not be able to help her with her situation, because Flex had enough clout to reach her in jail. She needed to remain where she was, and deal with whatever came her way.

Quita walked up to Valencia who was still there, sitting on the couch. One of Flex's goons was guarding her, and she seemed uncomfortable by his presence. Quita threw her purse on the floor, and sat next to her. "I thought you said you were going to take out the trash." She paused. "Before the cops came."

"I lied." She looked at the man, who hadn't said a word since she'd come back. "I went to see my mother, and when I got back, the cops were pulling up, to question me." She looked at her hands. "Flex called me when I was there...so he already knows." She swallowed. "I don't suppose Cordon is back is he?"

She shook her head no. "I'm scared."

"Me too."

"Is your mother...I mean...is she okay?"

Quita silently cried. "No...they actually killed her. They killed my fucking mother! She didn't have anything to do with this shit! Just like me and you!"

They looked at the goon and he stood up. "You got beer here?"

"Yes...it's in the fridge." Valencia said, with a scowl. She looked at the front door and he caught her glance. "Don't think about leaving...I'll fucking kill you!"

Valencia looked at her knees and they quivered. Holding her head down she started crying and whispered, "This is gone too far. They're confusing the situations. One doesn't have anything to do with the other but it looks bad. Real bad." She looked at Quita. "I can't do this no more. I can't go through with this shit. I don't wanna die. I don't want nobody else to die either. Why did I get involved?"

Her words made the hair up on Quita's neck raise in attention. "What you mean you can't do this no more?" She paused. When she didn't answer she said, "Valencia, what do you mean?"

When the goon returned, Valencia didn't respond. Instead the two of them stared at one another, and at that moment, Quita knew she had something to do with everything. Her mother was dead, Cordon was missing and somehow suspected that Demetrius' death was related to this too. If she found out Valencia had any hand in the situation, Quita had plans to kill her herself, with her bare hands.

"You got some weed here?" The goon asked, sipping a beer. "All this shit is making me wanna be high." When neither of them answered he said, "I said you got smoke here?"

"Yeah...it's downstairs, in my bathroom." Valencia finally responded. She looked back at Quita, and begged her with her eyes not to say anything. "You can help yourself. It's under the counter."

"You mind getting it for me? I don't like going through people's houses." Quita thought about how they roamed through the house when they first got there. "Outta respect. Go get the shit."

Valencia looked at Quita, stood up and walked downstairs. She returned a few moments later with a blunt already rolled. He lit it and leaned back into his seat. "Either of you ladies want some?" He asked, removing the blunt from his lips. "I don't mind sharing. It's the least I can do considering your hospitality." He rubbed his stomach. "Beer...now smoke?" He chuckled. "You bitches really know how to treat a nigga around here."

"No thank you." Valencia responded, before focusing on her shoes. She was trying to avoid visual and verbal contact with him.

"I'm good." Quita added. "Not in the mood."

"Suit yourself." He took a few pulls, leaned back again, and blew pillowy clouds of smoke into the air. Now horny, he examined Valencia's thick sexy legs, her pink pouty lips and her fat titties. He groped his dick and said, "Damn, you's a fine ass bitch. If you make it out of here alive, maybe we can get to know each other better later." He paused. "That's if you don't have nothing to do with all this shit."

"That'll be nice," Valencia said, hoping things would end smoothly.

A minute later, Flex entered the house, but he looked different. He was holding a fatigue army duffle bag. However instead of focusing on Quita, his attention, and anger, appeared to be geared toward Valencia. The two goons he had with him earlier were different than the ones who were with him at the moment.

"On my way to drop this bag off, I got a call," He continued, looking into Valencia's eyes. "It was from one of my men. You know what he told me?"

She shook her head and said, "No."

"He told me that I might have to look into the nigga, Tech." Quita looked at Valencia and her heart pounded. After what she said earlier, she believed she was involved too, and now she was about to find out for sure. "They also told me to check out his bitch. That's when I learned the nigga is fucking with you. Is this true?"

"I dealt with Tech in the past if that's what they're saying...but for real he be dealing with Brooke now. I can't even remember the last time I seen him. I think they must be mistaken. Maybe you should check her."

"Brooke who?"

"Brooke from college. She use to live around here, but she ended up going to Florida State. Maybe whoever you were talking to on the phone, was talking about her." She paused, rubbing her sweaty hands on her pants. "Like I said, I haven't dealt with him in a while."

"That's not what I heard." He stepped closer to her.

"What you mean?"

"Did he have something to do with this situation? With my son?" He stood directly over her. "I don't suggest you lie to me now, Valencia. I'm not in the mood."

"I don't know anything about your son. I promise." she shook her head rapidly from right to left. "Like I told you, I haven't spoken to him."

"I was told by the bitch Evanka down the street something different."

"Please, I don't know about nothing he does anymore. I'm serious." The room was silent and it was killing Quita. "Ask Quita." Flex looked at Quita but she looked away.

For the first time since he'd come over originally, he pointed a gun in Valencia's direction. "Where does he live?"

"Can you put that down," she asked, as she jumped on the sofa and placed her hands over her face. As if a bullet wouldn't penetrate her fingers. "You're scaring me! Please don't point that thing at me!"

"Not until you tell me where this nigga lives!"

Before she could answer the question, the phone rang again. "Answer it." Flex told Quita. When she didn't move quickly enough he said, "Hurry the fuck up!"

Feeling the situation escalated, she jumped up and ran toward the phone. Snatching it off the hook she said, "Hello." It was the same caller as before. "He says to put him on the speaker again."

"Do it." Flex said.

She hit the button and said, "You're on speaker."

"Good...where that nigga at?" the abductor said.

"I'm right here, mothafucka." Flex responded in an easy tone.

"Good...because you didn't follow directions. I told you to bring the money and you didn't show up! What the fuck is wrong with you? You think this a joke? You think I'm one of them dumb ass niggas you got beef with in the streets?"

"I didn't bring you the money, because I didn't have it." He lied, as the duffle on the floor proved otherwise. "But I'm working on that now. Although I have to admit, I don't think dropping the dough off in a McDonald's trash can will be the safest route to take. Maybe I can meet you somewhere a little more private, like your house."

Silence.

"You *do* think this is a joke don't you? You think I'm really playing?" He laughed. "You don't know shit about me, if you think that's the case. I don't have no problem popping my gun! And that includes into people you love! You hear what I'm saying?"

"I don't know nothing about you to think you're playing with me! I'm just trying to make the exchange, in the safest way possible."

"Good…then let me worry about all the details. You don't need to be worrying yourself silly, thinking about things that are beyond your control. I handle all the plans in this arrangement and that means I make the calls. I'm the boss now! You understand what I'm saying, boy?"

"I hear you."

"Good! Now bring my mothafuckin' money in two hours, at the same location, or the next call you get will be from me!"

"Saying what?" Flex taunted.

"Telling you where you'll be able to pick his dead body up. Are we clear?"

"Like I said, I see what you saying."

"Good! Now make it happen! My money…get it together…NOW!"

When he hung up Flex looked back at Valencia. "Where does he live?"

"I don't know who he is!" She sobbed, hoping he would not suspect her. "Why are you blaming me for this shit? I'm just as shocked as you are that he's calling here. I wouldn't be involved in no shit like this! You gotta believe me! Please don't hurt…"

"Make the call," Flex told his goon. When his goon dialed a number on a cell phone, he handed it to Valencia. "The phone is for you. Take it."

She took the phone, and it quivered in her hand, before she placed it against her ear. "Hello."

"Hello…what's going on?" The woman cried into the handset.

Valencia's eyes widened. "Mama…is that you?"

"Valencia, baby, what's going on? Are you okay? Are some people hurting you too?" She cried. *Hurting you too*, meant her mother was being harmed.

"Oh my, God! Don't hurt my mother! Please." She sobbed. After Quita's mother was murdered, she knew the men were capable of anything. She had better start helping out, or else she would lose the one person who loved her unconditionally. Shit had gotten serious a long time ago. "I'll do whatever you want...just let her go."

Quita was more nervous because although her mother was dead, she didn't want anybody else getting hurt. And that included Valencia and her mother.

"Baby, talk to me!" Her mother continued to yell. "Who are these men?"

Valencia wept and Flex snatched the phone back. "Now stop fucking around, and tell me where he lives."

←――――――――――――――――――――――――――――――→

TECH'S MOTHER HOUSE

Valencia opened the door to Tech's mother's house, with her key. When she walked inside he said, "Baby, what you doing here? I ain't get the money from the nigga yet. You 'bout to get us late! You can't let them see you come..."

Before he could finish his statement, Flex, his men, and Quita, pushed their way inside. Tech tried to run to the back of the house, but was shot in the leg by one of Flex's men. They picked him up off the floor, and threw him on the sofa, as he screamed at the top of his lungs.

"What's going on? Who the fuck are you?" The pain hurt so badly, it appeared to travel up the side of his leg and to his head. "You gotta get me to a hospital! Please!"

"So now you don't know me?" Flex paused. "After all that shit you was just spitting on the phone a moment ago, now you don't who the fuck I am? Nigga, where the fuck is my son? I'm tired of bullshittin' around with ya'll in this mothafucka! I'm 'bout to start blazing!" His men cocked their weapons and aimed in Tech's direction. "Now where the fuck is my kid!"

Tech leaned in and said, "I swear, I'm not even playing with you." He paused. "But on everything I love, I don't have your son!

And that's being real to you because I'm a man too and wouldn't play them type of games." Flex chuckled, because of his lies. He had his boy and he was sure of it. "And I wouldn't want somebody trying to play me."

Flex looked at the goon closest to Tech and said, "Do it."

One of Flex's men took his index finger, and dug into the bullet wound. He screamed out in pain and fell to the floor, "Ahhhhh! Oh my Gawd! Please don't do that! I didn't do what you think I did! This shit is crazy, I want to clear it up, but I don't want to make things worse!"

Flex looked at his goon, instructing him to stop. "Now…where's my son?"

"I swear…I don't have your son." He sobbed. Spit oozed out of his mouth and onto his chin. "My leg! You hurt my leg. Get me a doctor! Please!"

"So you mean to tell me, that you were shaking me up, when you didn't even have my boy?"

"I swear, I would never have made a move on your kid. I don't know who told you that shit, but they got the information wrong." He looked at Valencia. "Did you lie on me, Bitch? I knew I should've left your bitch ass alone when I had a chance! You know this ain't my idea! This was yours!"

Everyone looked at Valencia and she said, "Tell the truth, Tech! I never told you to kidnap nobody! Don't put me more into this than I already am! These niggas gonna kill me! Please be honest."

"If you don't have my son, why did you lie?" Flex asked. "What was all that shit you were spitting on the phone? Huh?"

"It wasn't about no kid!" he assured him. "Let me show you?" He said, with wide eyes, sweat pouring down his face.

"Show me what?"

"What's going on, downstairs…in my basement"

Flex's goons helped him up off the floor, by way of an ear pull. He looked at his men and said, "Naw…they going with you." They followed him downstairs, and into the basement, before returning with someone Flex wasn't expecting to see.

The man's arms were tied behind his back with rope, and one of Flex's men snatched the tape off of his mouth. "Son…what's going on? Did you bring this boy his money? So he can let me go?" Flex looked at Leroy, his father and fell into the loveseat. He came so far to get his son, only for his search to end in vain. "What's going on, Thomas? Why does he have me?"

"Are you trying to tell me, you don't have my son?" Flex asked. "Were you actually shaking me up for money, because of this mothafucka right here?"

"That's what's I'm saying," Tech continued. "I never said I had your kid. If you remember my conversation you'll know what I'm saying is true. Play the tapes back in your mind." He paused. "I may have been trying to get some money, but it wasn't because I had your lil man."

As Flex looked at the scene, and contemplated who to kill next, Quita said, "I think I know where he is. Give me an hour and I may have an answer for you." Something about what the father said, gave her an idea.

"I thought you weren't involved." Flex frowned, appraising her with his eyes. "You mean to tell me you been fucking with my head all this time too?"

"Look...you have killed my mothafuckin' mother! That woman was everything to me, and now she's never gonna be in my life again. Now I care about Cordon...he's a nice boy, who never did nothing but respect me. But if you gonna keep threatening me, you might as well put a fucking bullet in my head right now, because I don't care no more."

Flex looked at her. "I'm listening."

"Give me an hour, you can even send one of your men to follow me. I just need whoever you send to hang back, so I can make sure first."

"You got the hour...and he's going with you." He pointed to one of his men. "If you don't have my son, and come back at the right time, I'm killing this bitch, and anybody else who may have ever loved you, and that includes the kids at your center."

THE RIGHT FACE

When there was a knock at Cash's front door, Kimi was nervous because she wasn't expecting company. When she opened it up, she was surprised to see Quita standing on the other side of the door. She looked behind Quita to be sure no one was watching, stepped outside and closed the door. Pulling her robe closed because of the breeze she said, "Quita…what you doing here? I didn't even know you knew where Cash lived."

"I know a lot of things you don't know I do, Kimi." She tried to look into the window from where she stood outside of the house. "I gotta talk to you. And it can't wait."

"This really isn't a good time. I really need to be alone, especially after what I told you earlier. I hope you understand." She turned around to walk back inside.

"Kimi, we've been friends for years. You laid a lot on me and I need to talk to you. Just give me a few minutes, and if you want me gone after that, I'll be gone."

"I don't know about this, Quita." She backed up a few feet away from her.

"Can I come in, Kimi? Please?"

"What is the real reason you here? There is nothing you can do to get me to change what has already happened. That mothafucka hurt me and he had to pay the price." She paused. "You can't play the hero nor can you save me. It's too late for me."

"Kimi, that's not why I'm here. You think I care about a man who raped my friend? I remember how sad you were all those days although I never knew why. And if he was the cause of that, in my book he deserved to die." Quita looked into her eyes. "I'm not here with the police, and you already told me about what you did. It's done. All I want to do is talk to you alone. Please."

Kimi looked at her feet, backed up and opened the door so Quita could come inside. "I only have a few minutes."

Once inside, Kimi locked the door and they both walked into the living room. The house looked worn down, like it had scene its share of violence and dismay. The hardwood floors were covered in carpet so thin, it might as well have been paper. It smelled like dirty clothes and old furniture and the aroma made Quita sick. "Who lives here with Cash?"

"Nobody…his mother left him this house." She looked around. "His cousins told him to burn it down, but he didn't take their advice. Now it's the same house he died in."

"Right…it's a mess in here." Quita looked at the ceiling. "Where's he now?"

"Where's who?" Kimi frowned.

"Cash…who did you think I was talking about?"

Kimi shrugged. "I thought you were talking about Cash." She walked into the kitchen. "But I don't know where he is. Maybe heaven…but probably hell." She grinned. "Now can I get you a Coke? Or a beer?"

"A beer if you have one." When she remembered she was in Cash's house she said, "Or if he has one." Quita followed her into the kitchen and looked around. Outside of it being extremely grungy, at first glance, it didn't appear as if anything was out of order or that a murder had taken place. "Where is his body, Kimi?"

"I got rid of it. Earlier tonight." She opened the fridge and handed her the beer. "Why, you gonna tell the cops on me or something?"

"No…why would I?" She paused. "It ain't like I didn't do my dirt in the past. You forgot you're talking to a convicted felon."

"I remember. That's why I wanted to talk to you about what I did to Cash. Only somebody who can pull a gun and use it can understand the concept of death. We are the same." She paused. "The only difference is I used a knife."

"Now where's the other person?" Quita said slowly.

Kimi's eyes met hers and nervousness filled her movements. "I just told you…I got rid of him."

"You know what I mean, and you know what I'm talking about."

"How did you know? You didn't give me a chance to finish telling you when I called earlier about him."

Kimi walked out of the kitchen and sat on the old brown sofa in the living room. Quita sat next to her, and placed her beer on the worn out wooden table. "I met Thomas today. Well, I knew him before, but I knew him as Flex, Charlene's husband. A lot of shit is going on behind this little boy being missing, Kimi. My mother's dead, other people are being held hostage and more might die." She paused, looking over at her. "Before you tell me anything, I want to know how you got him."

"The dude, Demetrius had him in the back of his car. He was trying to kidnap him. I followed him to his house, murdered him and left with Cordon." She smiled and looked out in front of her. "Cordon...I love that name. It was the only good choice he made."

"How do you know Flex? Or...Thomas?"

"It's a long story." She paused, rubbing her arms.

"Please...can you tell me what's going on? I won't interrupt you this time, Kimi." Quita picked up her beer. "I promise."

Kimi looked at her and smiled awkwardly. "I love it when I have your undivided attention. You know...when you care more about me, than you do about Valencia it makes me feel loved."

"I always cared about you," she paused. "I just figured you were stronger than Valencia. That's why I took up for her more. You always seemed like you had your shit together, and Valencia...well, she's like me. Confused, needy and wanting to be loved."

"For the first time ever, I understand the bond and the reason you were so close to her. Before now, I thought it was all about me and that you didn't think I was cool enough." She exhaled. "It sounds stupid now. So thank you for clearing that up." She paused and looked out in front of her again.

"When I came to Valencia's house, the day you were in the living room with Vonzella, I almost died. I remember being forced into a panic attack, and not being able to breathe. So I called my mother, and asked her to tell me if she could hear my voice. I wanted to make sure I was alive and actually looking at my own child. That's when you came downstairs and saw me holding my phone."

"I remember."

"You gotta understand, I thought he was dead, but I guess it's true, a mother always knows her child."

"I knew something was up with you when I came downstairs, after speaking to Vonzella."

"I couldn't believe it at first, until I looked into his eyes. I thought God was fucking with my head, and trying to make me feel bad for everything I did in my life. But then, when he looked at me too, and smiled, it was like there was some sort of recognition on both of our parts." Tears rolled down her cheeks and she brushed them away with her hands. "He was my son, Quita. He was my boy and it took everything in me, not to run out of there with him. But I knew I would be back. That's why I told you I would never be able to come inside again, after what I planned to do."

Silence.

"Please continue, Kimi."

"So I thought about everything, like what he was doing at the center and who took care of him. I could tell he was being loved because he was happy, clean and healthy. The only thing that hurt was that it was without me. That made me sad. My mind was moving fast, real fast, and then I remembered you said Flex was his father. I never put one and one together when I heard that name before. His father called him Flex because he could get out of tight situations. Flex and Thomas was one in the same. I did some more research and found out Charlene was told she could not have babies, even though she eventually did get pregnant by her father in law. So it made sense, Flex made me have the baby, so they could raise him as their own."

"What are you saying?"

"I'm saying Cordon is my son. Are you not listening to me?"

"Yes," she frowned. "It's just so confusing."

"It made so much sense to me once I really thought about it. When I was with Flex, he seemed to be more focused on getting me pregnant than being with me. He kept pressing the issue of having raw sex, and how bad he wanted to be a father. But when I told him I was finally pregnant, he claimed he wasn't ready for any kids of his own. I remembered being devastated and confused! What was weird now that I look at it, was that he didn't tell me until it was too late for me to get an abortion. It was like he wanted me to have it, but he didn't want me to keep it."

She pulled out a newspaper article from her pocket. "I just read this the day I left Valencia's house." Kimi continued. "It's a newspaper article about a missing baby he gave me. I could never read this when it happened but pulled it out to finally read. Kimi handed the article to Quita, and she skimmed through it. "This baby was a week older than my baby, but Flex gave this to me, so that I would believe my baby was dead. It turns out Flex was married, and wanted me to have the baby for his wife. He wanted to raise the baby as their own, without me."

"But Charlene wasn't that type of person! She would never have done something like that to anybody."

"But she did it to me," she placed her hand over her heart. "I'm living proof that Charlene had more shit with her than you realize."

"It's not true!"

"Even now you can't believe me!" She snatched the article out of her hand and stuffed it in her pocket. "You've always taken up for everybody else but me! Valencia, your kids, your men...everybody but me! Even now."

Quita thought about the kind of person Charlene was. She was kind, loving and always seemed to give her all. And then she thought about the day Flex visited her, and asked her to take care of Cordon. He said that Charlene wanted Cordon to be around her and she never understood the reason, until now. Charlene knew Kimi was her son's real mother, and she wanted them to have an opportunity to meet and get to know one another. However, Quita was sure that she didn't want it to go down like this,

"Where's Cordon?"

Kimi shook her head. "What does that mean?"

Quita yelled. "Where is he?!"

"I can't tell you." She paused. "I really am sorry."

"Did you hurt him, Kimi?" Quita asked. "Did you hurt Cordon?"

"If I can't have him, nobody will."

The beer Quita was holding fell out of her hand, and rolled to the floor. The suds scattered along the dirty carpet, before the can landed against a wall. "Please tell me that you didn't hurt him. You can't say you love him and put him in harm's way."

Kimi stood up. "I'm not well, Quita. I'm very sick. Mentally ill. You know what I'm saying?" She said in a monotone voice.

"But I want to be there for you! Like I never was before. I said I would always be your friend, no matter what you do, and I want to prove that to you now. But some very bad people are looking for that little boy, and you have to come clean."

"I don't want to hurt you...but I will...so you have to leave now." She opened the door and when she did, Flex and his men were standing outside. They heard the entire conversation.

A HOTEL ROOM

Pooh sat in a chair, in a run down hotel room in Virginia, waiting on her cousin Kimi to call her back. Although she agreed to watch the kids for money, she was hoping that she wouldn't be out too late. Her boyfriend wanted to take her to the movies, and with the money Kimi was giving her later, she was going to buy a fifty bag of weed.

From the bed Miranda asked, "Can I get something else to drink?" She paused, looking at Pooh. "I'm kind of thirsty.

"You got money for another drink?" Pooh retaliated, as she busied herself with her cell phone. "That makes your third drink!"

"She ain't got no money but I do." Cordon smiled.

Pooh could never get mad with him because he was such a cool kid.

"Aight...let me finish this text and I'll get it for you in a second."

When Pooh looked at Cordon and Miranda, she wondered why all the secrecy. She hated lying to Vonzella, when she picked up Miranda. She told her that she was taking Cordon to the movies and asked if Miranda could go. The only reason she did it was because Kimi told her how important it was that Cordon enjoyed himself.

When Cordon smiled, Pooh's heart fluttered. She finally understood where she'd seen the child before. Although she had not seen him in a certain place, outside of the daycare center, his eyes belonged to her cousin Kimi. At first she wondered why she was so hush-hush about bringing him there, and now she understood why. She was kid-napping her own child.

DAY QUITA'S SCARE CENTER 2

COMING SOON

CARTEL PUBLICATIONS
PRESENTS

The Cartel Collection
Established in January 2008
We're growing stronger by the month!!!
www.thecartelpublications.com

Cartel Publications Order Form
Inmates ONLY get novels for $10.00 per book!

Titles	_Fee_
Shyt List	$15.00
Shyt List 2	$15.00
Pitbulls In A Skirt	$15.00
Pitbulls In A Skirt 2	$15.00
Pitbulls In A Skirt 3	$15.00
Victoria's Secret	$15.00
Poison	$15.00
Poison 2	$15.00
Hell Razor Honeys	$15.00
Hell Razor Honeys 2	$15.00
A Hustler's Son 2	$15.00
Black And Ugly As Ever	$15.00
Year of The Crack Mom	$15.00
The Face That Launched a Thousand Bullets	$15.00
The Unusual Suspects	$15.00
Miss Wayne & The Queens of DC	$15.00
Year of The Crack Mom	$15.00
Familia Divided	$15.00
Shyt List III	$15.00
Raunchy	$15.00
Raunchy 2	$15.00
Reversed	$15.00
Quita's Dayscare Center	$15.00

Please add $4.00 per book for shipping and handling.
The Cartel Publications * P.O. Box 486 * Owings Mills * MD * 21117

Name: _____

Address: _____

City/State: _____

Contact # & Email: _____

Please allow 5-7 business days for delivery. The Cartel is not
responsible for prison orders rejected.

CARTEL URBAN CINEMA

WWW.CARTELURBANCINEMA.COM

CPSIA information can be obtained at www.ICGtesting.com
Printed in the USA
LVOW111617240412

278949LV00003B/1/P

9 780984 303014